A Twice-Dead Genius Comporting with Misunderstood Abominations

Story & illustrations by
R. Gary Raham

R. GARY RAHAM

Library of Congress Control Number: 2020944544
ISBN: 978-1-7326985-4-3

Penstemon
Publications

Wellington, CO 80549
970.568.3557
www.penstemonpublications.com
https://www.rgaryraham.com

Dedicated to all those
who struggle with differences
and uncertain destinies

Many thanks go to My dedicated writers' group:
Nancy Burns, Judie Freeland, Beverly Hadden, Libby James,
Mim Neal, Susan Quinlan, and Clare Rutherford
Thanks as well to Mary Howard, Vicky Jordan, and Alan Silverstein
for additional editing and suggestions

Table of Contents

Table of Contents

Dramatis personae

HUMANS

Rudyard Albert Goldstein (Rudy): A human genius of the 21st century (inventor of the Biomic Network Algorithm) whose personality was preserved by the artificial intelligence, Mnemosyne.

Ryan Thompson: 21st century paleontologist who became infected with the alien intelligence named Siutiasa (Siu) and Guardian, her AI protector. Their 3-part merger resulted in the entity, Siyan, capable of travel through time and space.

Celyana Moleckson (Skeets): 21st century paleontologist and spouse of Ryan who formed a merger with Ito, the mate of Siu.

Twill (deceased): A post-human survivor of the Anthropocene-ending asteroid strike of the 22nd century who shared Rudy's personality for a short time during Rudy's first resurrection in 1 million P. A. (post Anthropocene). Great grandfather of Tadur.

Twillock: Tadur's father.

Jeeta: (deceased) Twill's mate.

Tadur: Twill's great grandson who moved to Jadaman City to study paleontology and other subjects of natural history with Jadderbadian Master Veltipoe Fragenrude.

Semma: Young neuro-atypical post-human studying with Mnemosyne (aka Spider Woman), and Tadur's girl friend.

High Priest Botza: head of a post-human sect that worships Rudimort, a deceased hybrid of Rudy and Master Morticue Ambergrand.

JADDERBADIANS (Arthropod aliens from the planet Jadderbad.)

Master Veltipoe Fragenrude: Jadderbadian scholar and advocate for human-jadderbadian interaction as syncytiotes—symbiotic interspecies unions.

Maxifer: First molt jadderbadian and Tadur's friend. Maxifer also studies under Master Veltipoe.

Commander Tork & Texlac: Jadderbadian military officers

Master Morticue Ambergrand (deceased). Jadderbadian academic who joined with Rudy to become Rudimort.

GROVIANS (Aliens from the planet Grove, destroyed when its star exploded sometime during Earth's Cretaceous Period.)

Siutiasa (Siu): Grand Matriarch of the Diaspora from Grove charged with finding a suitable home for the remnants of her species.

Ito: Siu's precocious mate and inventor of Guardian, the AI that preserved the mental engrams of Earth colonist Grovians.

Ito Prime: A clone of Ito that survived in human civilization's 21st century after his other incarnation was destroyed.

Klemna: Siu's First Servant, whose engram sphere was discovered by Tadur.

Mother Novaya: A Grovian Mother Tree and matriarch of the Grovian forest that survived to 1 million P. A.

ARTIFICIAL INTELLIGENCES (AIs)

Mnemosyne (aka Nessie, aka Spider Woman): Invented by Marvin Rodneskie in the 21st century and charged with the "preservation, in perpetuity, of the personality of Rudy Goldstein to provide aid and guidance to the post-human descendants of humanity."

Guardian: Invented by the Grovian, Ito, to preserve the mental engrams of surviving Grovians.

R72: A spiderbot AI licensed to Master Veltipoe's academy.

PLANETARY INTELLIGENCES (Self-aware consciousness of planets with sufficiently complex biospheres.)

Gaia: Mother Earth. **Hydra:** Mother Jadderbad.

SUPERBEINGS/hybrids & cyborgs (Abominations?)

Siyan: union of Ryan Thompson, Guardian, and Siutiasa

Semmitosyne: union of Semma, Mnemosyne, and Ito Prime

Rudnessipoe: union of Rudy, Master Veltipoe, and Mnemosyne

Tadmaxyne: union of Tadur, Maxifer, and Mnemosyne

Skeeto: union of Skeets, Guardian, and the original version of Ito

Klemnadur: A brief merger of Klemna and Tadur

Rudimort (deceased): union of Rudy and Master Morticue

Brad Burree 31416 (Pi): Martian cyborg

Art Deco 161803 (Phi): Pi's cyborg companion

R. GARY RAHAM

Other book titles by R. Gary Raham

Fiction:
Sillysaurs: Dinosaurs That Should Have Been, Biostration, 1990
The Deep Time Diaries, Fulcrum Publishing, 2000
The Dinosaurs' Last Seashore, Biostration, 2010
First two books of current trilogy:
A Singular Prophecy, Biostration, 2011
A Once-Dead Genius in the Kennel of Master Morticue Ambergrand,
Penstemon Publications, 2018

Collected articles & short fiction:
Confessions of a Time Traveler, Penstemon Publications, 2015

Non-fiction:
Dinosaurs in the Garden, Plexus Publications, 1988
Explorations in Backyard Biology, Teacher Ideas Press, 1996
Teaching Science Fact with Science Fiction, Teacher Ideas Press, 2004
The Restless Earth: Fossils, Chelsea House, 2009
Bugs That Kill, Marshall-Cavendish, 2009

Student/Teacher Workbooks,
Carson-Dellosa Publishing:
Science Tutor: Chemistry, 2005
Science Tutor: Life Science, 2005
Jumpstarters for Science, 2005
Science Tutor: Earth & Space Science, 2006
Science Tutor: Physical Science, 2006
Jumpstarters for Life Science, 2008

Prologue: Gaia & Hydra

"I must say, Hydra, it's so nice to have someone to talk to—even though I had to wait 4.6 billion years. Humans nearly gave me a terminal fever until that last asteroid strike cut them down to manageable numbers."

"Ha, you think primates are bad? I can tell you, arthropods are no stroll across the cosmos, either. My oceans and atmosphere back on Jadderbad are at least as mucked up as yours. But I agree: misery needs good company."

"I'm worried about our sentient species fooling around with each other, Hydra. They're starting to breed with abandon again, burning energy, expelling wastes...I feel another fever coming on."

Hydra's microbial filaments pulsed with a sympathetic energy spasm. "We feed our creatures, give them a nice place to live, and then they just make a mess. What's a mother to do?"

"I have two humans now who have lived long beyond their expiration dates. That Rudy Goldstein person has died twice for heaven's sake, and been resurrected. He may be a genius—at least by human standards—but that's no excuse for violating my Death is Manditory rule."

"Yes. I thought when he merged with my Morticue Ambergrand and they died together, that would be that..."

"But that Mnemosyne intelligence," Gaia continued, "keeps Rudy alive with those clever tricks of hers. You can't evolve metazoans properly if they won't die like they're supposed to. And I never told you this, Hydra, but I was actually infected once long ago by another set of sentient metazoans, the Grovians. That was back during my giant lizard phase, you know. One of them merged with a human named Ryan Thompson. He has also refused to die."

"How rude," said Hydra. "What do you plan to do?"

Gaia made a conscious effort to slow her many cycles and to calm her frenzied thoughts—the planetary equivalent of a deep breath. "At this point, Hydra, I don't know. I just don't know."

Data File: Gaian & Solar Timelines

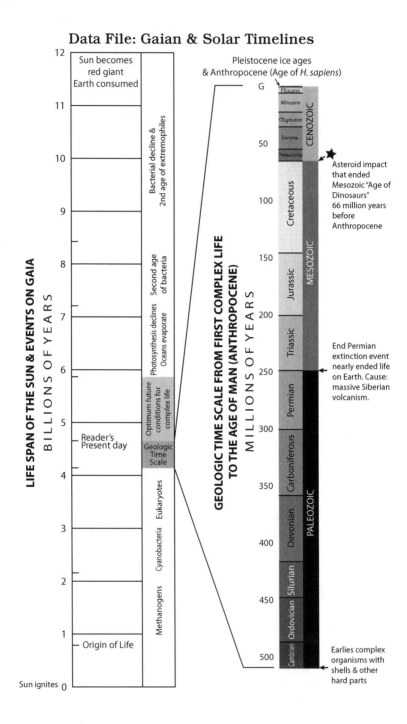

1
Twice Reborn

Rudy couldn't see a damn thing. He couldn't hear, taste, smell, or touch a damn thing for that matter. He felt like a disembodied spirit floating in a vacuum.

"That's about right," said a feminine voice with a vaguely foreign lilt that reminded Rudy of his second wife, Roxie—that teacher with a wealth of evocative bedroom lesson plans. But it wasn't. It was a voice he should remember...

"Excuse me?" Rudy tried to open his eyes—with about as much success as he used to have removing the lids on Tupperware containers. "Who the hell are you?" A memory floated just at the edge of recovery, seemingly flicking like the tail of an angry cat.

"You know *me*, Rudy. I *hope* you remember me. Hope is hard for an AI to come by, you know. You helped give *that* to me over the millennia we worked together."

"Nessie!" The name burst into his awareness—a memory bomb with loads of shrapnel. "Aka Mnemosyne—named after the Greek goddess of memory. Neh **mos** o nee." His tongue always tripped over that name, so he called her Nessie. "You brought me back from the dead," Rudy muttered.

"This will make the second time," said Nessie, "but who's counting?" Rudy's eyes felt like they popped open. He connected the voice to an image: an attractive, pony-tailed young woman sat across from him. She sat on a deck chair—one that belonged to his first wife, Myra, back in the day. He appeared to be at the old cabin near Red Feather Lake. *Man, was that a long time ago.*

"Nearly a million years ago," Nessie said, just before taking a sip of coffee. "Don't let your drink get cold—metaphorically speaking, that is."

Rudy looked to his left. A cup of java sat there on a glass-topped end table, steaming like mist off a miniature lake in this virtual reality she had conjured many times before. *She can read my thoughts. Of course she can. She's a precocious artificial intelligence and I'm her charge—her responsibility. Except, I'm supposed to be really dead this time...along with Master Morticue Ambergrand.*

"It was such a nice death, too," observed Nessie. "The stars shone beautifully that night on the cliff. You and that nice worm-a-pede academic alien had a lot in common after all." Nessie smiled that infuriatingly Mona Lisa-esque smile he now remembered clearly.

Rudy snorted. "Morticue and his kind made pets of humans. Just because he was three times bigger than a human and knew how to fall through a stargate to Earth didn't make him King of the Hill."

"Hubris nearly brought the downfall of your species before the asteroid strike completed the job, as I recall." Nessie took another sip of coffee. "You biological metazoans do seem to get rather full of yourselves."

"Unlike quantum dot computers with delusions of purpose?" Rudy winked at Nessie and took a sip of his own coffee. It tasted like his favorite dark roast, of course. Nessie wouldn't forget a detail like that.

"Touché, Rudy."

"So why am I here? Again." Rudy had never been much good at small talk—not as a kid, not as an arrogant young researcher in Bioinformatics, not as a crusty old scientist with a reputation for genius he probably didn't deserve. Apparently not as a computer simulation either.

"I have a problem. I need your help." Nessie leaned toward him. "And, frankly, I missed your company," she said.

Did she really just bat her eyelashes? Rudy took a deep breath. Existence—and companionship—was habit-forming, it seemed. Rudy leaned toward Nessie. "What kind of problem? Does it involve Morticue's species—the Jadderbadians? What about my human descendants?" Rudy thought about Twill and Jeeta and the dark-skinned, long-limbed tribe of post humans who evolved after an

2

asteroid impact destroyed his own civilization.

"Everyone's impacted. Twill and Jeeta's great-grandchildren, the Jadderbadian Confederation—even the Jadaman settlements—where humans and Jadderbadians live as equals. Many futures hang in the balance." Nessie placed her coffee cup on the table beside her.

She took a long enough pause that Rudy jumped in, although he felt shell-shocked. *Twill and Jeeta's great grandchildren? Jadderbadian Confederation? Jadaman settlements? "What's going on?* Another asteroid strike? Solar flares? Climate change? Wars? Did that post-Martian-human cyborg Pi come back? Invasion from space…?"

"Bingo!" Nessie interrupted with a verbal flourish. "I believe Bingo is a quaint old game humans played once," she added parenthetically. "I understand they yelled the name of the game when they scored a linear sequence of letter matches."

"An invasion of different space aliens?" Rudy ignored the Bingo digression and spread his arms in an exaggerated shrug.

"That's pretty much it. Except this invasion first occurred 67 million years ago—plus or minus a few tens of thousands of years." Nessie smiled her quirky smile again. "These particular aliens certainly don't consider humans to be charming pets. In fact, I have reason to believe that they have genocide in mind."

Rudy raised his eyebrows. "You've got to be kidding. Sixty seven million years ago any visiting aliens would have been tripping over dinosaurs—or vice versa. Besides, they would have been destroyed by the same asteroid that pelted Earth and wiped out the dinosaurs at about that same time."

"Or not. We survived the most recent Australian asteroid strike, as you recall. And I would never kid you, Rudy. Besides," she added, "my sense of humor is still a work in progress. You know that."

Rudy laughed. "Your sense of humor was in fine shape the last time I checked—though who knows how many lifetimes ago that was." Rudy sat back in his deck chair and sighed. *Here we go again.*

Data File: Grovian Life Cycle

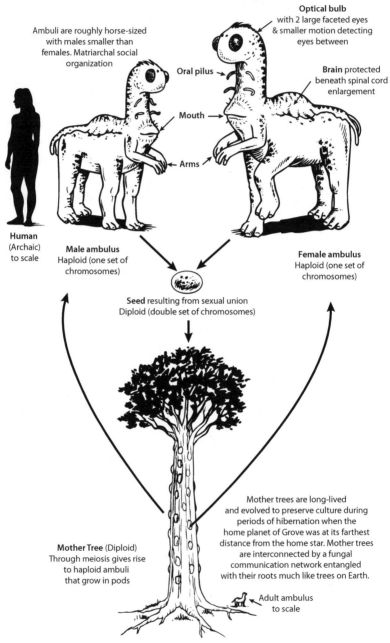

Optical bulb with 2 large faceted eyes & smaller motion detecting eyes between

Ambuli are roughly horse-sized with males smaller than females. Matriarchal social organization

Oral pilus →

Brain protected beneath spinal cord enlargement

Mouth →

← Arms →

Human (Archaic) to scale

Male ambulus Haploid (one set of chromosomes)

Female ambulus Haploid (one set of chromosomes)

Seed resulting from sexual union Diploid (double set of chromosomes)

Mother trees are long-lived and evolved to preserve culture during periods of hibernation when the home planet of Grove was at its farthest distance from the home star. Mother trees are interconnected by a fungal communication network entangled with their roots much like trees on Earth.

Mother Tree (Diploid) Through meiosis gives rise to haploid ambuli that grow in pods

Adult ambulus to scale

2
Guardian aroused

Guardian embodied patience. AIs were especially good at that. Case in point: He, Guardian, had protected, and preserved the essence of Siutiasa (Siu), Matriarch of the Diaspora, for 65.837 million years, protecting her brain engram from all the degradations that time had conspired to perform. He also brokered the merger of Siu's personality with that of the human entity called Ryan Thompson—an effort that aroused his own personhood and brought into existence Siyan, a unique hybrid being more than the sum of his three parts. But now the time for patience was over once again. Not only was another engram capsule recovered, but it also appeared that the mysterious AI known as Mnemosyne had accomplished the impossible by resurrecting a now twice-deceased human genius from the Classic Period of human habitation on this planet. The rest of Guardian's consortium would be pleased at the results produced by his infiltration of Mnemosyne's matrix. His own quantum dot matrix buzzed with anticipation. "To act was to be, and to be was all." Guardian existed through the strength of that mantra.

Just before he acted, Guardian detected something else: Ripples in the spacetime continuum. The delicate snowflake image of the transdimensional gateway through which Grovians had reached Earth so long ago, and now captured within the cabochon around Ryan's neck, pulsed briefly. What did that portend? Only Siyan would have the capacity to speculate.

"Awaken Siyan! Intruder alert in the fossil recovery zone. Action is required." Guardian monitored the metabolic activities of Ryan's body as he stimulated appropriate portions of the human's nervous system with impulses from his own quantum dot neural nodes.

Muscles began to twitch, then flex. Ryan slid one of his legs along the limb of his mate, Ceylanya Moleckson—who preferred the shortened, and apparently unrelated name Skeets—as they lay intertwined in one of the deep internal pods within the very heartwood of Mother Novaya. The great Mother Tree responded to her awakening charges as well. She began releasing stimulants from the bundle of filaments with which she had encased the two human bodies.

How long have we been in deep chamber? Ryan fingered the cabochon around his neck.

Guardian briefly wondered if the Ryan part of Siyan had felt the ripple as well. Certainly that must be the case. The parts of Siyan's consortium often had to wake individually before Siyan aroused. *Twenty-five years, 3 months, 5 days, and 43 seconds,* Guardian responded. *Do you wish more precision?*

Your precision is more than adequate, Guardian. I feel refreshed. Ryan opened and closed the fingers of his hands, testing his muscles. *Can I assume we have a problem of some kind?*

Guardian became aware of images from Ryan's past: the wisened face of his grandfather, Pops, who had inspired his love of paleontology; the flames of a crackling campfire, and the flickering embers of that fire that merged with the star patterns of a Wyoming night sky. Guardian also saw Ryan's conception of his mother's face as she lay on her deathbed when he was still a child.

You can. Intruders are excavating fossils near the quarry where you found my Matriarch, Siutiasa. More images: Ryan reaching down to touch a silver sphere embedded among the brown and mineralized ribs of an ancient mosasaur; bits of rock glittering among sharply cast, early morning shadows...

Suddenly, Siutiasa joined the conversation. *They must not find an engram capsule before we do. The results could be fatal for all parties involved. Ito meant well trying to develop a vehicle to preserve Groviankind, but even my brilliant stallion couldn't anticipate all the consequences of his actions.* Siutiasa's thoughts focused on her once First Mate: the saucy way his head crest feathers twitched when he was about to propose some audacious action; the sparkles when light

6

bounced off the facets of his primary eyes just so...

Yes, Siu, Ryan interjected, *but Ito didn't anticipate that his capsule would be found over ten thousand years before yours, or that you would fail to destroy me—like any good Grovian should—when I found the silver sphere containing your engram. I'm sure he could never comprehend our eventual union either.* Ryan remembered the pain of that union; the struggle to keep his thoughts and feeling intact and distinct from those of the alien, Siutiasa. Siutiasa had nearly won that battle before she earned the nickname, Siu, a trusted companion.

For a smart male—and I realize that is not an oxymoron by human standards because of your patriarchal culture—Ito can be quite regimented in his approach to life. I might have destroyed you had you been more willing, but as we struggled I grew fond of you—in a perverted sort of way. Poor Ito. The long years of dedication to his task turned him into someone I couldn't recognize any more. Siu would have twisted her beak into the human equivalent of a wry smile if she had had her natural ambulus body, but used Ryan's lips instead. *It's fortunate that a much kinder version of him lives on within Skeets.*

Skeets. My dear Skeets. Ryan moved his leg again along the limb of his mate, savoring the never-gets-old electricity of that touch.

Guardian interrupted before his biological components got too distracted by sensory stimulation. *There is more you should know. The AI named Mnemosyne has resurrected another version of the human, Rudyard Albert Goldstein.*

Ryan found the news interesting enough to pause. *Amazing. For an AI you make a pretty good spy. Goldstein: the Einstein of the 21st century. It would be ironic if we could somehow meet now—a million years after we should both be long gone.* Ryan fingered the cabochon again. *How much does Mnemosyne know about us? Is the Jadderbadian stargate still functioning?*

Guardian felt a pleasant tingle within his neural network. *I am glad my spying pleases you. Mnemosyne's knowledge of us is incomplete, and may only include the original hostile intent of Rhondal/Ito. Yes, the stargate still serves as a point of transportation and com-*

merce between Jadderbad and Earth.

Hmmm. We don't need Mnemosyne pissed at us. She's quite talented, not to mention powerful. And we need to find that rogue Ito clone that still may be at large somewhere. I must meet this Rudy. I know something about the transdimensional gateway, but nothing about how the stargate fits into the Grand Vision Siyan once witnessed, but I struggled to comprehend. Ryan stretched, using the opportunity to further extend his leg along the length of Skeet's limb. Guardian experienced an echo of the pleasurable feeling that sparked in Ryan's limbic system. Ryan walked the fingers of one hand along her uppermost bare thigh.

Guardian surmised that only Siyan could truly evaluate what Mnemosyne may or may not know. Meanwhile, Ryan's attention had shifted sharply to matters biological, as evidenced by the fact that the sexual organ of their human body began to engorge. Guardian had had to make numerous adjustments to understand the role of sex in his biological charges over the millennia. Sexual impulses and obsessions often overruled logical patterns of behavior, which would seem to invite failure or even destruction—but often it did not.

Guardian continued to collect data on the phenomenon—both in humans and Grovians—his progenitor species. Guardian credited his own existence to the fact that Ito had diverted some of his frustrated sexual energy as a male ambulus to inventing him. Furthermore, the impulse to procreate led to diversity, adaptation, and change. Guardian wondered if he would find a suitable way to accelerate his own evolution—independently of his participation as a component part of Siyan.

"Are you awake, love?" Ryan let his fingers settle on Skeets' arm. Her eyes opened. She sighed.

"More or less, Thompson." She laughed. "You're feeling frisky, aren't you?"

"I'll blame Mother Novaya. Her filaments are wiggling."

"So that means you should wiggle yours?"

With Ryan's arousal, the hybrid entity, Siyan, came fully awake, which effectively flattened the emotional landscape—among other things. Once again Guardian felt a disturbance in the space/time continuum—more like a wave than a mere ripple.

* * * * *

Siyan felt the wave as well, filtered through the masculine gender of Ryan's body, the host in the human/Grovian/AI liaison of which he was the manifestation. Siyan sensed the fabric of space/time in multiple modalities. Visually, it seemed like a vast web of possibilities, individual threads flashing into existence, creating links and chains that glowed for a time before fading and reforming like colorful strands of melted plastic. As sound, the potential paths became melodies, each one varying in detail from achingly beautiful to painfully discordant. Tactilely, paths turned from rough cobbles, to jagged shards, to silken smoothness inviting or discouraging travel as they unfolded and dissolved. Siyan perceived Guardian's warning partly as the smell of dried beach sand and seashells crushed to sandstone mixed with the loamy odors of soil and decay. He addressed Guardian: *You report that intruders have entered the vicinity of the fossil quarry, but have not found a capsule. Is that correct?*

That is correct. Guardian paused a nanosecond. *I felt it would be prudent to awaken you, so that we can insure that they don't.*

Siyan could feel Guardian's pride in his capacity to act with circumstantial and incomplete information—a talent usually reserved for the complexity of organics, like Ryan, Skeets, and Siu, who had evolved to make quick decisions rather than get eaten by something stronger and hungrier than they.

"Why are we waking now? A new signal? Something wrong with our grand progeny? The colony?" Skeets slowly began to disengage from Ryan's embrace.

Siyan felt the Ryan part of him relax, allowing Mother Novaya to completely withdraw her filaments. "Activity at the quarry. Guardian's put us on alert," Ryan said to Skeets.

"It would be exciting to find another of Siu's and Ito's colleagues—as long as it's one of the open-minded sort. We could use some help locating the other Ito clone." Skeets paused, and then giggled. "Feels like Siyan has taken the starch out of your friskiness, Thompson. Maybe later."

Haste would be advised. I see other complications have developed recently along the space/timeline continuum on which we are traveling. Siyan searched the tangled webs flickering in and out of existence, looking for optimal pathways—looking for routes that might lead him out of his own lonely isolation. *What good is it to transcend the boundaries of space and time without someone to share the experience? Could Mnemosyne see these webs of possibility? If so, could she travel them? Could she make ones of her choosing coalesce into reality?*

To his consortium Siyan said, *I see ripples along many future timelines. They glitter with possibilities—and grave dangers. We are at a nexus point.*

To act is to be, and to be is all. The Guardian part of him clung to that thought.

The Siu part of Siyan gained strength from her sense of duty and purpose. *I'm ready to find an old friend, and lead her into this new world. Humans and Grovians can complement each other. I need to make Ito understand that.*

Let's do this. I'm ready for a new adventure, declared the Ryan part of him. *We've been marking time too long.* Ryan exemplified the credo of organics: Cheat death—cheat the unconscious void—for as long as possible. It will swallow you eventually, but you might as well enjoy yourself until it does. And for organics that was certainly true. But Siyan knew that he was something different. Something new.

3
Rudy's disturbing dream

If I were just a simulacrum tended by an AI, could I dream? Rudy thought not. He hoped not. He hoped that the strange amalgam between him and Mnesmosyne was something more. He recalled a rather convoluted dream just before he "awoke" to greet Nessie the next time. It contained elements that suggested both of them were making contributions to this dream state—whatever it was.

He was on that cliff where he and Morticue died after Morticue had metamorphosed into his adult form, completed his mating ritual with Selaea, and left on his final flight. Morticue's adult form—which looked for all the world like an overgrown moth—and their combined mentality called Rudimort—knew that death was near. Suddenly, his old friends Twill and Jeeta, were there standing next to him complaining, although they were really an ocean away at that time, presumably doing what newlyweds always did: practicing their skills as sexual organisms.

"You can't just *die*, wise old Uncle," said Twill. "My tribe…" Twill glanced at Jeeta… "Our tribe needs you."

"It does," confirmed Jeeta. "Most Jadderbadians still want to make pets of us. Some of them would rather kill us. We need to learn all those wonderful things that Jadderbadians know and humans used to know."

"Like burning hydrocarbons and splitting atoms?" suggested Rudimort, rather sleepily.

"That sounds exciting." Twill's eyes grew wide.

"You'll just overheat the planet or blow it up," said Morticue. "I really would like to die now." He closed all his eyes—compound and simple, trying to shut out the distraction of the glittering, and entic-

11

Data File: Timeline
Pre & Post Anthropocene (Age of Mankind)

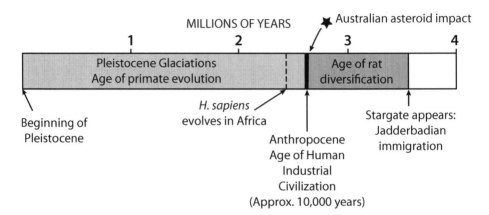

Data Files:
Post Rudimort timeline & geneology charts

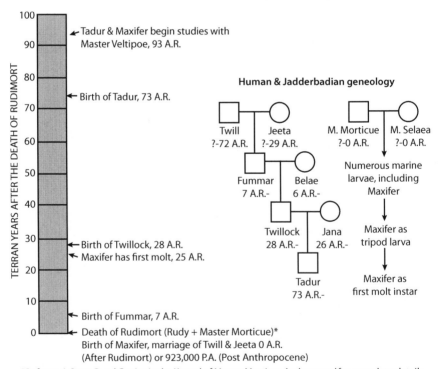

*Refer to *A Once-Dead Genius in the Kennel of Master Morticue Ambergrand* for complete details.

ing, star fields overhead.

"And now there are the tree people and their vicious little eaters, the ambuli." Jeeta leaned closer and whispered into Rudimort's auditory tympanum. "Did you know the ambuli mate to create seeds that become giant trees. How disgusting."

Rudimort lifted the membrane of one compound eye. "I beg your pardon?"

"They came to Earth a very long time ago, wise Uncle," added Twill. "Mother Gaia suppressed them for awhile, but they made silvery capsules that contained their essence. They survived and want to kill us all now."

"He tells the truth." Rudimort heard the 'voice' in his mind of the planetary intelligence of Earth called Gaia, whose neurons, if you will, comprised the webwork of intertwined microbial filaments that evolved over the planet's 4.6-billion-year history. Gaia worked with Hydra—a similar planetary intelligence that existed on Morticue's home world of Jadderbad—to help create the union between Rudy's neural reconstruction and Morticue's nerve ganglia.

"Seriously? Tree people? I'm old. I'm trying to die like any responsible old thing. Leave me alone already." Rudy's eye membrane tried to re-droop.

"You may have help," offered Twill.

"There's a rumor that an ancient human—maybe one even more ancient than you, wise Uncle—once formed a union with a tree person, and still exists somewhere. Of course, there's also a rumor that he has a powerful enemy, but that's another problem." Jeeta sighed. "Won't you help us?"

Rudimort took a deep breath. One eye opened, then another. Finally they were all open. *What is it about young women's voices—and young female larvae's enticing aromas*, added the Morticue part of him—*that made him do crazy things?*

"Rudy. Are you there? I want to show you something." Jeeta's voice morphed into Nessie's, as Rudy's dream began to take on a more substantial form and substance.

He opened his eyes—the ones that belonged to his virtual human manifestation: the one that resembled a gray-templed academic wearing a tweed jacket with calfskin elbow patches. *I haven't seen so many monitors and blinking lights since I was at an arcade game— and we both know how long ago that was.* "What have you created now, Nessie?" He took a deep breath. His nostrils expanded. "The explanation must require a bit more dark roast. It does smell wonderful."

Data File:
Portrait of Master Veltipoe Fragenrude
by his student Maxifer Ambergrand

English translation from Jadderbadian Basic:
"Master Veltipoe, an instructor with the
most enlightening odors and inspiring colors"

4
Master Veltipoe's lesson plans

Master Veltipoe Fragenrude turned the page and breathed deeply through his spiracles. *Ahhh, the taste and smell of knowledge. Intoxicating.* He could have looked up the relevant research in the digital archives, of course, but there was just something about the taste, feel, and flickering colors of a properly designed sensoramic book that made the nerves connecting his major ganglia shiver with anticipation. Using the middle finger on the hand of one lateral arm he traced the passage he was looking for. *Fascinating. These primitive worms lay eggs eaten by an isopod crustacean whose behavior is altered in a way that makes them more vulnerable to predation by their next host, a bird. I recall a similar parasite/host system in the Jadderbadian literature. Hmmm... I can use this in tomorrow's lesson plan.*

Oh, my. What time is it? Veltipoe glanced at the chronometer patch embedded in his third second tier arm, while simultaneously setting down his morning brew using the hand of his second arm, and closing the book in front of him with the hand so recently engaged as a reading assist. *I'll be late for class!* Veltipoe reached for his sensorama pad as he rose from the bench and steadied himself on his tripod of legs—all of them stiff from too much time in the exercise pod yesterday. *Oh, for the second instar days of his youth again! Settle down, Veltipoe,* he told himself. *You're the professor. Class isn't going to start without you.*

He briefly recalled a time during a human archaeology class with the late Master Morticue as a young academic on Jadderbad. The professor had burst through the doorway a full half cycle late and had forgotten to completely zip his middle circlet, exposing a phero-

Data File: Jadderbadian Life Cycle

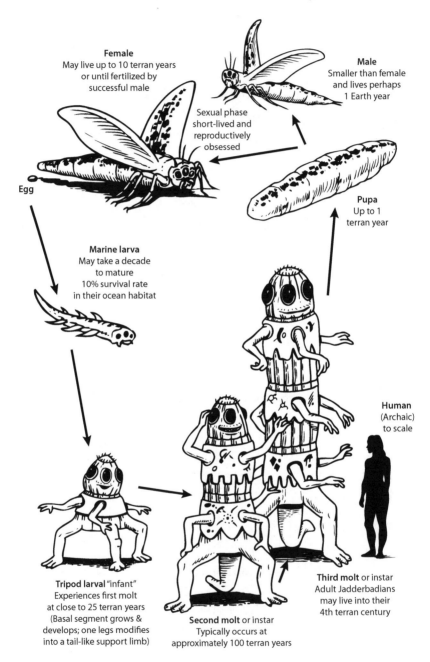

Female
May live up to 10 terran years
or until fertilized by
successful male

Male
Smaller than female
and lives perhaps
1 Earth year

Sexual phase
short-lived and
reproductively
obsessed

Egg

Pupa
Up to 1
terran year

Marine larva
May take a decade
to mature
10% survival rate
in their ocean habitat

Human
(Archaic)
to scale

Tripod larval "infant"
Experiences first molt
at close to 25 terran years
(Basal segment grows &
develops; one legs modifies
into a tail-like support limb)

Second molt or instar
Typically occurs at
approximately 100 terran years

Third molt or instar
Adult Jadderbadians
may live into their
4th terran century

mone gland. Female cuticles flickered in pink and violet for several minutes until he discovered his error. He had to turn on fans to clear the room of titillating odors.

It didn't take Veltipoe long to cross the campus, although he would have preferred a more leisurely amble to fully appreciate the clear air and exotic fragrances of his adopted planet. Earth was a near wilderness compared to the crowded shores and urban centers of Jadderbad. It took a while to get used to Earth's more intense sun and oddly blue sky, but it was home now. He felt pride in his accomplishment of building this academy near Jadaman City—a place where both humans and Jadderbadians could exist as equals—and perhaps become something more than the sum of their individual species.

When the door to his classroom irised open and he ducked his third instar frame through the entrance, he saw pretty much what he had expected. Humans chattered among themselves, many perched at various locations on the latticework of beams with seating areas built in. *Primates do like to climb. Part of their attraction to those who still consider the species to be nothing more than pets, I suppose.* Jadderbadians had spread themselves over the benches designed for their comfort. Most were first molts just out of Early School, but there were a few second molts who had missed his coursework during earlier cycles. A few Jadderbadians and humans mingled in triads or pairs, including Tadur and Maxifer—students for whom Veltipoe had high hopes.

"Assemble, students," said Master Veltipoe in his most commanding voice. "We have a lot to cover today, and not much time to do it."

The lesson proceeded well. The pale-skinned human student named Vort did fiddle with the hair of a female he liked—Veltipoe always struggled to remember her name. Vanglotur? Vanglesh? Yes, Vanglesh. And a young Jadderbadian named Ilsent tried to flicker obscene shades of purple streaked with orange when he thought the professor wasn't looking. Other than that, most of the pupils dutifully made entries on their pads when they weren't focused on his presentation. Veltipoe took pride in his Master Teacher ratings.

After the period chime sounded and lights flickered in shades of green to denote the end of the session, students began to collect their impedimenta and rise to depart. "Tadur and Maxifer," said Veltipoe, "please see me a moment before you leave."

"Yes Master?" Maxifer asked, planting his tripod of feet as Tadur brought up the rear.

"I like that image of an ammonite on your circlet, first molt," said Veltipoe, waiting for Tadur to get closer. "I always have liked those striking, coiled mollusks. You and Tadur must still be avidly at work studying the ancient seaway exposures southeast of Jadaman City, I suppose?"

"Thank you, Master Veltipoe." Maxifer glanced down at the ammonite graphic with one eye. "We most certainly are! In fact, we are…"

Tadur stumbled, bumping into Maxifer as he reached his side. "Oops, sorry Max." He looked up at the professor. "You wanted to see us, sir? I have a class I need to get to and it's clear over at the Academy Annex…"

"Just checking to see if you both have given any more consideration to entering the syncytiote program? Your genetic profiles would be a perfect match. And you, Tadur, can trace your roots directly back 95 terran years to Twill, while Maxifer is a descendant of Master Morticue Ambergrand. An added bonus there, with the historical context and all…"

"We're still thinking about it." Maxifer's three arms stroked sensory pili and tugged at his circlets as if he didn't quite know what to do with them.

"It's a big step," Tadur added. "My folks aren't all that keen about it, but I'm workin' on 'em, sir. We have a little time left to decide, right?"

"Yes, there is some time yet." Veltipoe arched over them and squirted pheromonic scents of encouragement, although sometimes those subtleties were lost on humans. "Don't wait until you reek with the stench of near-deadline anxiety."

"I try to avoid reeking with stenches of all kinds, Master." Tadur compressed his lips. One edge of his mouth threatened to angle upward.

"Oh, we won't, Master!" Maxifer rolled one eye in Tadur's direction. "Were you going to ask…" Maxifer began before Tadur interrupted.

"Really gotta go! Later Maxifer, I promise." To Master Veltipoe Tadur said, "We will think on it, sir. Promise. I'm going to be late if I don't get moving." With that comment, he turned and sprinted toward the door.

Maxifer looked up at his professor, flickering in pale blue shades of appeasement. "You know how humans are, Master."

Indeed. He knew how humans were. He also knew how students of all species were. Tadur and Maxifer appeared to be up to something.

Data Files:
Cretaceous ammonites

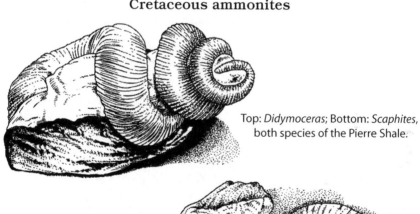

Top: *Didymoceras*; Bottom: *Scaphites*, both species of the Pierre Shale.

Master Veltipoe and his students are fond of Cretaceous ammonites.

5
Playing hooky

"Are you sure Master Veltipoe approves of this, Tadur?" Maxifer stood tall on his tripod of legs. As a first molt Jadderbadian, he was only a handful of centimeters taller than Tadur, but 25% heftier. He released a chemical bouquet of cautionary pheromones. The scents probably had little effect on his human friend, so he crossed two manipulator tentacles and waved the third in Tadur's direction, pointing his middle finger on the terminus of that appendage toward the transport. The sensory hairs on Maxifer's cuticle contracted when a draft of cool air swirled around the loading bay just outside Veltipoe's Academy walls.

Tadur smiled in that pursed lip crooked way that Maxifer had come to know meant that Tadur was concealing something from him. "No worries, Maxifer. Master Veltipoe is interested in the fossils we are finding, too. Who wouldn't be excited about ancient sea creatures captured in stone? Maybe we can write a paper about our discoveries in the *Journal of Extrajadderbadian Curiosities*.

"I thought we were studying the elements of human/Jadderbadian integrative mergers today," Maxifer countered. "You know Master Veltipoe thinks we are a perfect match for symbiotic merger." Maxifer recalled some of the various experiments that allowed he and Tadur to share each other's *sensory milleau*, as Master Veltipoe was fond of saying. Maxifer had tried very hard not to be disgusted by the fluids that humans emitted from various orifices. He also felt claustrophobic using the rather limited sensory input of humans — especially the paltry odor-detection abilities, and the limited EM bandwidth of their eyes.

Maxifer imagined he could feel Master Veltipoe's eyes focused on them at this very moment. He used one of his primary eyes to scan the row of windows along the upper floor that looked out on the loading bay. The windows remained dark beneath their cornices, like eyes brooding under heavy brows. Maxifer *supposed* their teacher could be observing them from one of those darkened rooms, but guessed that was unlikely.

"Help me with these supplies, larva." Tadur hefted a box containing dehydrated meals and kitchen utensils and moved toward the storage compartment of the transport. "Anyway, you don't really want me attached to you like a parasite do you? We should think carefully about being syncytiotes, don't you think?"

Maxifer's dorsal posterior ganglion did kind of ache when he thought about it. Some of his friends thought Jadamen would be abominations. But what about the legendary Rudimort? He was kind of a syncytiote. Humans and Jadderbadians both told stories about the great things that the ancient human spirit called Rudy and the Jadderbadian, Master Morticue Ambergrand, had learned while their minds were intertwined. Tadur was a direct descendent of Twill, who traveled with the Rudy spirit, and Maxifer took pride in the fact that he was a surviving larvae of Master Morticue's and Selaea's spawn. Perhaps they were meant to become syncytiotes.

Maxifer picked up a large bag with bedding and followed Tadur. "I don't know primate. It is a big commitment—with quite a few unknowns."

"Exactly!" Tadur handed his box to the R72 Spiderbot who moved it into position in the hold. "Let's take a few days in the wilderness, work at the quarry, and take some time to think things through under the starry night sky." Tadur looked up at what was left of this morning's night sky and gestured toward the rich belt of stars humans called the Milky Way. He turned to face Maxifer and winked at him. "Whaddaya think?"

Maxifer knew the human was playing him somehow, but Tadur's unexpected adventures were part of the reason he liked him. Maxifer's own impulses were to study in the archives and stay out of trouble. It got him praise from Master Veltipoe, but failed to make his dorsal hearts pound with excitement. "I'm in, primate—at least for three days." Maxifer looked at the transport carefully with all three primary eyes. "You're sure Master Veltipoe approves?" His cuticle flickered in shades of cautionary amber.

Tadur smiled and made a gesture with the finger of one hand as if he was recreating an image of the Citadel over his heart. Maxifer knew that that behavior was supposed to signify unfettered truth, but he had his doubts. "Let's finish packing before the sun comes up. It's a long drive to the badlands—especially when R72 is driving. He has too many safety protocols hardwired into his operating system."

"Those protocols will insure a safe journey." R72 accepted Maxifer's bundle of bedding and moved it into position.

"No editorializing, AI." Tadur ignored the spiderbot, and arched his eyebrows at Maxifer.

"All right, human. Let's do this before I change my mind." Maxifer could sympathize with the Jadderbadians who made pets of humans. They were ridiculously cute and hard to deny—especially when they raised those furry patches above their eyes.

6
War room

Nessie's avatar handed Rudy another steaming cup of coffee.
"I suspect you'll need this," she said.

They both stood on a platform that looked down on a
roomful of monitors. One large screen, filled with what appeared to
be a world map, dominated most of the space in front of them. Human figures sat at dozens of other monitors staring at various flickering images. Rudy made a gesture with his left arm that resembled the
wilted flourish of a concert conductor. "Who are all those people?"

"They're manifestations of some of my subroutines, of course,"
said Mnemosyne, "but I thought you might like the ambiance of a
war room. We do have a serious problem at hand."

"Explain what I'm seeing, Nessie." Rudy pointed in the general
direction of the large central monitor. "I presume that's a map of dear
old planet Earth today. It still seems strange to me with huge hunks
of the coastline I knew underwater. No Florida, parts of California
gone, big divots where New Orleans and eastern Texas used to be,
South America looking like a Rorschach test…"

"Having no ice at the poles will do that, of course. The meltwater
has to go somewhere." Nessie placed her hands on the railing that
circled their platform at about waist height. "Between the climate
changes induced by human civilization and the aftereffects of the
asteroid strike, Earth now has a climate more like the one dinosaurs
enjoyed."

Rudy turned his attention to the blinking light on the southwest
coast of Iceland and pointed there. "I assume that's our citadel at the
old location of Reykjavik. Is it still intact and functioning?"

"Yes," Nessie confirmed. "Gaia and I managed to control the

latest geothermal events there. I've enhanced my robotic spider maintenance crews and flying drones. I have satellites in orbit now to provide global coverage."

"No grass growing under your silicon-DNA processors, old girl." Rudy glanced in her direction and smiled. "Of course, I would expect no less."

"I have missed your colorful metaphors, Rudy." Mnemosyne smiled back.

"No excuse for bringing me back from the dead, though. What about Morticue? Did you reconstruct his personality somewhere in the Citadel's bowels?"

"No." Mnemosyne paused a beat. "His wife, Selaea, worried that the Jadderbadian Great Prophet would damn their offspring for eternity. Besides," she continued, "bringing you back—even though I had several iterations in my files—proved to be quite difficult. Preserving an alien personality, even with Hydra's and Gaia's help, magnifies the difficulties by several orders of magnitude."

The Prophet worm god sounds like he took classes with Jeho-vah. I'll have to take time to mourn the loss of Morticue later. Rudy changed the subject. He pointed to a spot toward what used to be the western third of the continental United States. "What's with the glowing red dot there?"

"Ah, yes. The Mother Tree forest." Mnemosyne made eye contact with Rudy.

Rudy raised his eyebrows. "Mother Tree Forest? Really, Nessie?"

"Yes. It seems that 67 million years ago aliens visited Earth and attempted to establish themselves. Unlike the Jadderbadians, these aliens were unsuccessful, but somehow the last survivors managed to preserve their personalities and reestablish the beginnings of a new colony at a much later point in time—during your era, in fact. One stage in their life cycle looks very much like a giant redwood."

"At the site of the glowing red dot." Rudy took a deep breath, and exhaled slowly.

"Precisely," said Nessie. "The red dot coincides with the location of what once was Kalispell, Montana."

"And these tree aliens are not looking to make friendly pets out of us poor humans?"

"I have reason to believe, based on my preliminary scans of electronic records from the era, that they would prefer to extinguish humans—and presumably Jadderbadians as well. In fact, the viral plague of 2050, unlike the one in 2020, might not have been the result of random factors, but rather a tool for genocide."

"Genocide. And here I thought just humans specialized in the mastery of that art." Rudy shook his head. "So, are we going to war with these alien bad guys?"

"It's a bit more complicated than that, Rudy."

"Of course it is."

"I've discovered that one or more of these aliens may have formed non-hostile relationships with humans—perhaps even something as intimate as a symbiotic merger of some kind." Mnemosyne's lips compressed into an enigmatic, almost Mona Lisa-esque smile. "A merger that might still be viable today, Rudy. My drones have caught glimpses of a male human—one more like a person from your era than the present one—who seems to be aware he is being watched."

"I suspect that humans have always been adept at mergers with almost anything that stands still long enough. But with an alien tree creature? A person would have to be very creative to make that work."

"You merged with a giant alien worm, if you recall, Rudy."

"With the help of you and Hydra." Rudy scratched his chin. "Is this wandering abomination tree man immortal, too? Think of what he must have seen. What he must know. Far more even than my old worm-a-pede friend, Morticue."

"Any such hybrid creature could have command of at least as much technology as I do. Perhaps more. Who knows what his intentions might be? I am cautiously curious to know the details."

I'm sure you are. A potential clash of civilizations with a mystery immortal tree man lurking around, and a world at stake. "Sounds like fun, Nessie. As long as I'm alive again anyway, I might as well make the most of it."

"I was hoping you would say that, Rudy." Nessie pointed to a monitor below them and somewhat to their collective right. "Note the patchy area I've just highlighted in yellow. It spreads from the site of the Jadderbadian stargate near the old location of Toronto, Canada, to near the area dominated by the Mother Tree forest. It represents the spread of Jadderbadian/human occupation and culture since your last death."

The yellow area faded and a smaller patch of non-overlapping orange popped into existence somewhat to the north. "And what is that?" Rudy finished his coffee.

"That is the new Jadaman colony established by one of Twill and Jeeta's sons a couple of generations ago. You'll note its proximity to both the Mother Tree forest and the expanding Jadderbadian/human sphere of influence." A small amber light began to pulse on the southern fringe of the orange area. "A confrontation seems to be in progress there that deserves our attention."

A picture popped up on a monitor. Nessie's avatars crowded around the images provided by Mnemosyne's network of surveillance drones and began jabbering at each other. "What the crap is that?" Rudy pointed at the screen, and nearly dropped his coffee cup.

Mnemosyne gripped the railing a little tighter, and leaned forward. "I would say that one of Twill and Jeeta's great grandchildren—a young fellow named Tadur—and his Jadderbadian friend, Maxifer, will soon be in serious jeopardy."

7
Monsters in the morning

"Good morning, Masters Tadur and Maxifer! Wake up to a new day!" The spiderbot's declarations at first appeared to fall on deaf ears and tympanae. The human, Tadur, lay inert on his cot like a slug. The first molt Jadderbadian, Maxifer, lay like a wilted squid on his cushion. "New day! New day!" the bot burbled with enthusiasm. "The quarry won't dig itself now, will it?"

Tadur opened one eye. A shaft of sunlight breached a gap in a tent seam and impaled it. He groaned; then raised an arm and splayed hand to shield his vision. "Dial down your cheerful index, bot, or I'll wrap your legs in plastic cord and stuff you into the latrine."

The bot, one of Spider Woman's finest meter-tall R72 research drones, tilted away from Tadur. For a bullet-shaped cylinder suspended at the center of eight jointed legs, she managed to convey an attitude of shocked contrition rather well. Her faceted eyes blinked in mock alert mode. "Apologies, Master," her feminine voice purred. "You and Master Maxifer did request a wakeup call."

"So we did," said Maxifer while opening all three of his own faceted eyes. He also began stretching his three legs and flexing the appendages of his three manipulator tentacles. He focused on one hand with particular intensity and wiggled all three digits. "All that digging yesterday made me stiff." Shades of amber merging to magenta danced on the surface of his gently wrinkled carapace.

Tadur yawned and stretched. "Yes, but one doesn't find a genuine, ancient sea monster fossil every day."

"Indeed." Maxifer seemed to flow off his cushion and immediately began to collect gear to load his daypack.

Tadur groaned again and shut his eyes. He automatically dropped

his left arm over the side of the cot to pat Dusty's head, before remembering that his dog was still back at Veltipoe's academy. Hopefully, the service bot there had already fed him by this time of day.

"I have prepared a morning meal," said R72. "Rabrat stew with
tweeter eggs and boiled yellow root."

"Didn't we just have that?" muttered Tadur. But the smell was
eliciting growls from his stomach. He supposed he should make an
effort to silence his troublesome digestive organ.

****

Maxifer slurped the last of his stew by almost inhaling it with
his flexible feeding beak. When finished, he groomed his oral pili
with two manipulator tentacles and belched softly. "Quite delightful,
spiderbot."

Tadur finished his own stew. He picked up his cup of warm
coffee—a drink Spider Woman claimed ancient humans drank many
millennia ago. Tadur had his doubts about that, just as he had doubts
about the wild stories his father Twillock used to tell about great
grandfather Twill. Yet Spider Woman's Citadel, back in the Old
Country near Shaman's Cove, did hold secrets and mysteries beyond
his understanding. He didn't even understand how the mechanical-
person spiderbot R72 worked, and it was magical enough.

Tadur looked at Maxifer across last night's campfire pit.
"Ready?" His friend nodded and rose from the log he had been
squatting on. Maxifer was only a first molt Jadderbadian, so he
shared Tadur's two-meter height. Each molt added another couple of
meters, but Tadur hadn't seen many late molt Jadderbadians—except
for Master Veltipoe, of course. The Shaman Cove colony where he
grew up was too young. Each molt could take more than a century.
Unless he became a Jadaman—a human/Jadderbadian syncytiote—
he would never even see his friend's second molt. Fine with him. He
was pure human and proud of it.

Maxifer collected his daypack and tools and moved toward the
transport. Tadur gathered his gear and followed. "Whadaya think, old
worm? I'm guessing there's post-cranial bone in the mound behind

the exposed skull."

"Well, scrawny primate, you might be right." Maxifer loaded his gear, and then waited by the storage door until Tadur found a place for his baggage in the storage bin. "Let's get going. I'm sure it will be hot today. I may have to pee on you to keep you from overheating."

Tadur smiled. "You best not try it." He fondled the rock hammer on his belt. "Keep your sticky green pee to yourself, Jadderbadian."

The drive to the quarry took twenty minutes, but Tadur didn't mind. He loved looking at the twisted and tilted layers of sandstone beneath the inverted bowl of blue sky. The low morning sun etched all the details with sinuous shadows. What mysteries of the deep past would he discover today? Whatever they were, they would banish the failed promises he had left behind with his once-beloved Semma in Shaman's Cove. She had called him selfish and immature and only interested in fondling her naked body. He certainly *liked* her naked body. It was beautiful to hold and behold, but that wasn't *all* he liked about her. She should know that.

"Look out your left window, Tadur," said Maxifer, after ten minutes of driving.

"Ah, ratalope tracks," exclaimed Tadur. "I'm glad I stashed my bow in the storage compartment last night. "Roast ratalope would make a fine dinner."

"What about those odd big tracks?" Maxifer pointed with a free tentacle. "They're not caratt tracks, that's for sure."

Tadur grunted. "Much too big. Strange shape." He tapped the implant on his right temple, a signal that alerted R72 perched in her rooftop compartment. "R72: search Spider Woman's database. What kind of tracks are those next to the ratalope trail?"

After the briefest of pauses: "WARNING: Those are ambuli tracks," said R72, loudly and clearly.

"Amboolee tracks? What are those?" Tadur scratched his temple, which sometimes itched around the implant when R72 raised the volume of her audio for dramatic effect.

"Spider Woman advises that you return to base camp." The bot used her sternest earnest tone of voice.

Tadur bridled instantly. "We'll lose daylight—not to mention the cooler morning temperatures."

Before R72 could comment further, Maxifer pointed ahead and to the left. "Look there. What got ahold of that ratalope?"

Tadur spotted the animal's carcass not far from a bitterroot bush. Something had literally torn it limb from limb, and left the half-eaten spoils. "Hmmm. Something with absolutely no table manners was quite hungry this morning."

"Should I turn around?" Maxifer asked. "R72 is buzzing warnings in my implant as well."

"The quarry is just ahead. Pull into our usual spot. Let's see if the canvas is still in place around the fossil." Tadur pulled his daypack closer and prepared to unbuckle his seat belt.

"Spider Woman advises that you return to base camp," R72 repeated.

Tadur turned his implant off. "What a worry bot," he said, to no one in particular. "I have a bow. Maxifer, you have your projectile weapon, don't you?"

Maxifer squirted assent. Tadur could smell the clove-like scent that took the place of a head nod, which Maxifer couldn't manage with the heavy neck of his bulbous head segment.

Maxifer parked the vehicle, but left its systems on idle. "We can be moving quickly if we need to." To R72 Maxifer said, "Stay in position, bot. Your defensive beam is charged, is it not?"

Tadur turned on his implant again in time to hear confirmation from R72. He exited the transport and breathed deeply of the fresh air in this wilderness. *A little excitement is good for the soul.* He opened the storage compartment and found his bow and quiver. They were old—they had belonged to his great grandmother, Jeeta, after all—but they were well-crafted and quite functional. "I'm coming," he yelled to Maxifer, who had already started down the well-worn trail to the quarry.

The canvas was in place. The sunlight etched every pebble and twig in sharp relief. A gentle breeze felt warm enough to promise a hot afternoon. As Maxifer bent over and extended a tentacle to peel back the canvas, Tadur noticed a creature peeking over the boulder under which they often paused for a midday meal. At first, bent over, it looked relatively small. Its enormous eyes might even be considered cute, if you admired giant jumping spiders, but when it raised its head and neck to full height, the glittering eyes offered a doorway into nightmare. Its muscular legs and trunk, quivering as if ready to pounce, looked impressively fit.

And when the beast opened a beak displaying sharp teeth gleaming with a sheen of drool, Tadur wished he had taken the time to visit the latrine at base camp.

Maxifer withdrew his manipulator tentacle from the edge of the canvas. He slowly raised his body and began inching backward with his tripod of legs, keeping his eyes focused on the apparition in front of them. Almost simultaneously, the creature moved slowly from behind the boulder that was partially concealing him.

Tadur tapped his implant. "R72, stay in position on top of the transport, but take control of it and navigate as close to my position as possible. We have a threat: a four-legged creature like, like... I don't know what. It stands about two meters high at the shoulders. Two manipulator arms in front with some kind of mouth between them. A head with two big faceted eyes mounted on a thick neck. Squiggly tentacles on the neck above the mouth..." Tadur paused to take a deep breath as the animal began to advance.

Maxifer had successfully retreated so that he was only a couple of arm lengths to Tadur's left. Tadur saw his friend fumbling to open a pouch on his vest—presumably the one containing his projectile weapon. Tadur reached over his shoulder to remove a bow from his quiver. *Okay mister drooly teeth*, he found himself thinking, *let's see if you are as tough as you look or just a homely inconvenience.* The unspoken boast barely had time to form before a second creature entered his field of vision. It had apparently been on the downslope trail behind the first beast. It was an ugly match to the first and just a bit bigger.

"Look left, Tadur!" Maxifer exclaimed as he finally withdrew the weapon from his pocket--and promptly dropped it when it snagged on the pocket clasp. His carapace flickered in shades of crimson and his alarm pheromones filled the air with an acrid stench.

Tadur saw a third creature flanking them on the left.

Tadur heard the transport grind to a halt somewhere close behind him. "I detect four of the creatures you describe, Master Tadur," R72 proclaimed. "What course of action do you recommend?"

"Four? Where in Spider Woman's name is the fourth? Tadur looked in all directions. He finally spotted the fourth approaching on his right, emerging from a tangled clump of gnarled juniper.

Tadur heard a low growl and snapped his head left again as the first beast charged directly at him. He felt a surge of liquid warmth down his left thigh. At least he didn't need the latrine any more.

8
Out of bounds

Tadur heard a loud command: The noise sounded like "Ragaat!" to his ears. Whatever it sounded like, Tadur felt grateful. The creature in front of him skidded to a halt, raising a plume of dust as it swiveled its head to look in the direction from which the fourth beast approached. Tadur turned his head the same way.

The fourth creature supported a rider. Tadur had missed seeing him before, apparently hunched behind the animal's head. The rider appeared to be a short-limbed human—a male dressed in strange, although well-tailored leather breeches and tunic. The man dismounted. He had skin lighter in tone than The People's tribe. His compact body looked lean and sturdy. Though shorter than Tadur and a few years older, he looked like someone used to command. He said more things to the creatures he obviously controlled. They stood their ground. The filaments of flesh around their beak-like mouths gently squirmed like languorous snakes.

Maxifer inched a little closer to Tadur, focusing two eyes on the stranger and letting the third jerk to and fro in an effort to see the other threatening beasts. Maxifer's alarm pheromones mellowed to a mild, though still bitter stench. "Have you seen a human like this before, Tadur?" Maxifer whispered.

Tadur exhaled a breath he had forgotten he was holding. "No."

The strange human's eyes expanded slightly during the exchange between Tadur and Maxifer, as if with sudden recognition of something, just before he spoke. "This is my territory," he said. "You are out of bounds." He used The People's language, but with a strange accent.

"This is wilderness. To our knowledge this is open territory belonging to no tribe." Tadur stood a little straighter to emphasize the height difference, although the stain on his pant leg may have nullified any show of bravado.

"Your knowledge is incomplete, Tadur, son of Twillock." said the stranger.

Tadur's mouth opened to say one thing, but he said another: "How do you know my name?"

"I know many things. I also know that you travel with the first molt Jadderbadian Maxifer, and have acquired an interest in fossils." The stranger pointed toward the canvas. "Leave this fossil in place. I take claim to it."

That was precisely what Tadur did NOT want to do. "Who are you anyway? What is your authority? We worked hard to make this discovery…" Tadur prepared to say more, but Maxifer kicked Tadur's left shin with his nearest leg using a cautionary signal that had proved useful in the past when Tadur's mouth exported words before his brain had edited them.

"My name is Ryan. Ryan Thompson. The hungry and somewhat restless ambuli gathered around me represent my authority at the moment. Do you wish to challenge it?" The human called Ryan narrowed his eyes. The creatures he commanded moved a little closer. They smelled vaguely like leaf mold and sweaty ratalopes to Tadur. Maxifer's carapace flickered in the amber shades that denoted increasing alarm.

Tadur and Maxifer looked at each other. They had been friends long enough to read each other's body signals rather well. Maxifer's shifting skin tones and scents said, "Let's bail out of this situation for now and figure out what to do in some safe place." Tadur's body language said, "Really? Maybe we can take these thugs." Maxifer's carapace blanched with disbelief. The Jadderbadian's caution prevailed. He also took over the conversation: "We will accede to your wishes, strange human called Ryan. We will leave this territory in peace."

And they did return to their camp with that intent. At least Maxifer did.

****

Inside their tent, Maxifer began stowing bedding and packing gear. Tadur paced in circles. Maxifer waved one arm toward Tadur while using the other two to pack. "Walking in circles will not get us out of the strange human's territory."

"How did he know who we were?" Tadur stopped and flapped his arms in exasperation. "Let me think."

"What do you have to think about, primate? Ugly creatures with sharp beaks, bad attitudes, and knowledge they shouldn't have, outnumber us." Maxifer paused and flickered briefly in appeasing shades of blue and green. "Maybe we can return with reinforcements. Especially if Spider Woman thinks our fossil discovery has special value."

"Maybe," Tadur muttered, then his eyes opened wider. "The one who calls himself Ryan never defined the size of his territory. There is that other place a few kilometers from here that had some exposed bones we were going to check out later anyway. It's on our way back to the village. Let's stop there and at least check them out before we leave the badlands completely."

Maxifer stroked his head pili. "I don't know, primate…"

"Don't be a clueless new molt, Maxifer. R72 can warn us if those big eyed beasts make an appearance." *Although I wish now I had brought Dusty,* Ryan thought. *Nothing gets past his nose.*

Maxifer sighed and glimmered faintly in shades of resigned purple. "Do your share of the packing, then."

Within the hour they were in the transport and headed toward the location R72 had recorded as Prospect Site 15.

****

Tadur picked up a fragment of bone at Site 15. It was one of many purplish-colored pieces scattered on the terrain. Tadur wanted something more complete, preferably an articulated skeleton like the one he and Maxifer had spent hours carefully uncovering. *What right did this Ryan have claiming their work?* Tadur felt a flush of frustration and anger warming his neck and cheeks.

Maxifer pointed to a hilly rise to his left. "I'm going to check out that outcrop." He left with the characteristic rippling three-legged gait that seemed to Tadur like an impossible way to move—but it worked for Jadderbadians.

Tadur scuffed his way over the landscape, casting glances back and forth, looking for some purplish streak in the dirt that might signify bone in place. The sun was already high enough to bleach some of the shadows that helped identify fossils better at dawn and late afternoon.

After what might have been a half hour, Maxifer called from an outcropping maybe a hundred meters south. "Something odd over here, primate. Come look."

Tadur made his way toward his friend, still scanning the ground as he went. When he arrived, Maxifer was using a brush from his utility belt to get a better look at something. Tadur felt a shiver of excitement up his spine as he saw a long strip of purplish bone in the sediment. But what was that gleaming beneath Maxifer's brush strokes?

Maxifer paused and focused two of his eyes on Tadur. "Any ideas?" The pili around his beak twitched. His carapace colors flickered like mica lit by a candle flame.

"Some kind of partially embedded sphere? That doesn't make sense." Tadur scratched his head. "It could be something the Ancients made, but I thought the purplish bones came from too long ago. That's what great grandfather Twill once told me years ago when he described this place. He should have known. He was always Spider Woman's favorite."

"Let me expose a little more," Maxifer suggested, but Tadur was already reaching out to touch the object. The human made contact with his index finger; stroked the silver surface—and then yanked his entire hand back as if the finger had touched fire. Tadur grabbed his head with both hands. He staggered like someone high on happy weed, and screamed.

Maxifer's three arms straightened in a gesture of alarm. His carapace blinked in shades of crimson. "What's wrong, Tadur? Tadur…"

But Tadur didn't answer. Instead he collapsed in a heap on the ground.

9
The possessed and the embodied

Klemna awoke to darkness. Had the transference of her consciousness to the silver sphere failed? Or had it made the jump from sphere to host at some unspecified time in the future of this water world planet? She decided it must be the latter. She felt the stirrings of another consciousness. She shared *his*—yes, it was a male creature, based on all the hormonal inputs—pain and confusion. Klemna attempted to look through the eyes of the strange alien.

Her Guardian AI, placed in the silver capsule by the Great Ito himself, must have successfully integrated her neural engram into the alien creature's nervous system. All Klemna could see was dirt—and some multi-legged arthropod that quickly passed out of the limited field of view. Her host must have fallen to the ground—or perhaps was in the habit of staring at the ground from close range. She decided to make a declaration to clarify their relationship. "I am Klemna, First Servant of the Matriarch of the Diaspora, and loyal acolyte of Greatest Mother. Release your consciousness to my control."

Klemna waited for a response. She felt her host's consciousness well up, accompanied by a wave of nausea and head pain. Ito had said the transference of consciousness into an alien host might be uncomfortable. Hosts had to be sufficiently complex mentally to accommodate a Grovian mind, but most surely would resist control until they acquiesced to a superior mentality.

Woahh! The view from the alien's optical system seemed to zoom out quickly to a broader view. He was attempting to stand up. She hoped that inhabiting an alien of the inferior gender would not pose unusual problems. It should make control of the entity that much easier, but who could say? Ito was a male, although an unusually precocious one, and the mate of the First Matriarch at that.

Klemna's cohabiting creature had a name: Tadur. He was *trying* to communicate, but the information made no sense. He seemed to be inviting her to perform impossible, improbable, or even expressly forbidden, sexual acts of some kind.

A creature came into Klemna's field of view. It possessed a trio of what appeared to be compound eyes and three waving tentacle-like appendages, one of which reached forward—perhaps offering support. *Was this what she now looked like?* That didn't seem to be the case. The Tadur creature she inhabited teetered on two long appendages... legs. He/she extended an upper appendage of his/their own to grab the extended tentacle that terminated in a 3-fingered hand of... something called a Maxifer. *How confusing*.

"Get out of my head!" The Tadur consciousness inflated against Klemna's personality like an expanding balloon of awareness. "I will not," she declared with some emphasis, and felt her own sphere of identity enlarge. "I represent the people of Greatest Mother, the sentient forest of Grove. I will prevail."

The Tadur creature invited more disturbing sexual activity while simultaneously staggering into the embrace of the tentacled Maxifer. Klemna observed a kaleidoscopic, though blurred, landscape of co-mingled blue, brown, and green bob up and around as she, supported by Maxifer, staggered toward a mechanical device. "I am Klemna, First Servant of the Matriarch of the Diaspora," she repeated. "Release your consciousness to my control." *I cannot let the Matriarch down. Grove is now a lifeless cinder. I could be the last of my kind.*

Hell, no, parasite! Curse your Great Mother Tree, whatever that is, to the ends of her rootlets! The Tadur consciousness expanded again with painful insistence. I'm too young to die! *I want to see my parents again. I want to see Semma again, whether she loves me or not. This is my body, not yours. Leave me!*

Somehow they reached the device—apparently a transport vehicle—and climbed in. The Maxifer creature closed the door. Klemna/Tadur rocked in place and groaned, while they watched Maxifer circle the vehicle, open another door, and climb in behind a panel studded with flickering lights. Maxifer's image oscillated between focused and fuzzy just before darkness enveloped the insistent parasite and resistant host in a blissfully painless shroud.

****

Rudy watched the monitor in the war room. He assumed an aerial drone, or perhaps a satellite, transmitted the image, because the view was from overhead. He looked down upon the broadly torpedo-shaped vehicle holding Tadur and Maxifer. The R72 manservant—or whatever it was that traveled with them—perched on top like a bug in a foxhole. The wheeled vehicle left a trail of dust behind it as it cruised over the dirt track toward Tadur's village outside the bad-lands. At some point Rudy would have to ask Mnemosyne where she'd found that design in her catacombs—if it was, in fact, her design and not something new. "What just happened, Nessie?"

"Tadur became infected by an alien intelligence when he touched that metal sphere eroding out of the sediments. I assumed that was obvious." Mnemosyne moved from the monitor that Rudy was watching to an adjacent one. "Look here, Rudy."

Rudy placed himself in front of the second screen. The one called Ryan had arrived at the site that Tadur and Maxifer had just left behind. Ryan hunched over the fragment of exposed fossil, blocking their view. "What's he doing?"

"Extracting the sphere, I assume. This Ryan is a person of inter-est. He may be the human I mentioned—the one of your vintage that first made contact with these other aliens I spoke of."

"Back in the plague year? 2050?" Rudy sighed. "I turned thirty that year. I had just met Roxie. We moved to Canada for a while. Nothing happens in Canada. Not even plagues."

"I would laugh if I had a sense of humor." Mnemosyne turned to look directly at Rudy. "This Ryan is looking for something. Perhaps this sphere or perhaps there are others."

"And how can this Ryan still be alive? I'm the lapdog of an AI with amazing technical powers, but what's his excuse?" Rudy looked past Nessie at the monitor. Ryan had extracted the sphere and placed it in what could be described as a pouch in a saddlebag that hung over the back of one of the ambuli next to him.

"As I mentioned once before, this Ryan seems to have a connection to the alien species that first came to Earth 67 million years ago." Mnemosyne's avatar smiled. "Perhaps he has become an alien's lapdog after infection by a similar sphere. They could be aliens capable of extending human lifespans. We certainly know that Jadderbadians make pets of humans because of their purported adorability. No one wants to lose a treasured pet."

Rudy scratched his virtual head. "Aliens with immortality vitamins in their pet chow? Now there's a thought."

"I've been attempting to contact Gaia," said Mnemosyne, "but she's been uncharacteristically silent. Of course, planetary intelligences do take consciousness breaks from time to time—and on a scale that can skip several human generations— human life spans being as short as they are."

Rudy grunted. He watched as Ryan mounted the ambulus he used like a packhorse. Ryan looked up and smiled just before he rode off. The other three ambuli followed. Abruptly, the image on the screen flickered and went black.

"You see, Rudy? This Ryan teases us. He knows he's being watched, and he is capable of interfering with my satellite transmissions. I think that's why I've not detected his activities until the last several months. He is part of the reason I reconstructed your personality again."

"Ah, so I have this Ryan to thank for my resurrection."

"Only in part, Rudy." Nessie's avatar winked at him again. "I did miss you and..." she paused, "I have a surprise for you."

"Do tell. It's hard to surprise someone that's been rattling around in the innards of a computer for nearly a million years—not to mention an alien's nervous system—and died twice already."

"Let me show you," she said.

The war room blinked out of existence. Rudy found himself standing in what could have been an elaborate lab—or even a morgue. Except it wasn't the usual virtual reconstruction of a college professor in tweeds. His consciousness seemed to be encased in a bot of some kind. If it looked anything like the bot next to him, which he assumed contained Mnemosyne's personality, he resembled a gray manikin with a quartet of flexible arms tipped with five digit hands. "This is a real place, isn't it, Nessie?"

"Yes. I've expanded my line of mechanical servants. Bots like the ones we are now sharing mental space with, along with appropriate swarms of nanobots, can build quite elaborate constructions."

Rudy blinked his optical sensors. He felt dizzy. "Jeez, Nessie! You need to work on your reality transitions."

"My apologies, Rudy." Mnemosyne motioned him to follow her with come-hither flicks of a manipulator finger on the arm closest to him. She led him to a stainless steel table supporting a coffin-sized cylinder. A string of colored lights flickered along its side. "You remember, of course, when I transferred your consciousness—first to Twill and then, with the help of Gaia and her Jadderbadian equivalent, Hydra—to Master Morticue. It was all I was capable of at the time. Not anymore." With a flourish of one hand, as if she were a robotic Houdini, she gestured toward the cylinder. It morphed from opaque to transparent. The blinking lights appeared to dance in mid air. And within the tank…

"It looks like me! A much less wrinkled and sagging me than I can easily remember… with all the appropriate parts." Rudy saw what looked like a smartass forty something version of himself, floating naked within the confines of the cylinder.

"I've learned considerably more about biology in general and human biology in particular. I can now transfer your consciousness to this human form." Nessie paused briefly before continuing. "Twill even contributed tissue samples to my project before he died. He had fond memories of his ancient Uncle Rudy, you know."

"Twill was a good kid. I can't imagine him as a ninety-something year-old patriarch." Rudy gestured toward the cylinder containing his apparently android body. "I assume some sort of plan has blossomed in your AI circuitry."

"It has," Mnemosyne confirmed, as she swiveled optical sensors in his direction. "I think you need to pay a personal visit to this Ryan. We must know much more about him."

"Agreed. But we also must do something to help Twill's great grandson, Tadur."

"Of course, Rudy. We must."

Rudy felt his consciousness withdrawing like a theatrical fade out. *Nessie must be working on her reality transitions,* Rudy thought, as a curtain of blackness descended.

10
Flight and capture

Maxifer glanced at Tadur after circling and entering their transport from the monitor's side door. Tadur looked like a ratalope paralyzed by a hunter's dart. At least he had stopped screaming. Maxifer inhaled deeply through his spiracles. Tadur's scent smelled a little sour, too. "R72: Set course for the Twillock-Veltipoe household. Hurry!" R72 confirmed the order. The transport moved forward, but progress was frustratingly slow and erratic because of the rough terrain. When all the telltales on the monitor's panel turned solid green, Maxifer focused his entire sensorium on his friend's welfare.

"Tadur, can you hear me?" Maxifer extended an arm and stroked the hair on Tadur's head. Silence. Tadur stared straight forward, his jaw slack. *It's a good thing human primates are cute, thought Maxifer. Most of the time they certainly don't look very intelligent. It's hard to believe that their distant ancestors built a vast civilization on this planet, but the records of Morticue and other natural philosopher/historians didn't lie. And then there's Spider Woman at the ancient citadel—a sophisticated artificial intelligence by any standards—and apparently of human construction.*

Maxifer relived the moments at the quarry in his mind. Something significant happened the moment Tadur touched the sphere, but what? Perhaps Maxifer should have tried to extract the sphere instead, but his friend suffered. Besides, the sphere was obviously dangerous. It wouldn't help if both of them were paralyzed.

Maxifer fumbled in the pockets of his body circlet with a free arm until he found the med monitor. Once extracted, he pointed it toward Tadur. Most physiological functions seemed human normal—

except the reading from his cortex. Neural activity was off the charts. Infrared readings confirmed the other inputs. Tadur should be hyper-aware, not catatonic. *What is going on?*

The transport lurched. Maxifer grunted as his head nearly hit the vehicle's ceiling, and then yelped as the hand stroking Tadur's hair got sandwiched between Tadur's head and the window. "R72…" Maxifer began, but the bot was already apologizing—sort of.

"So sorry, passengers. I have damaged sensors on the left front side of this vehicle, as you were both informed 5 days, 7 hours and 47 minutes ago. I can reduce speed, if you so request."

You're not paying for those sensors, Maxifer thought. *They're worth a week's work credits.* What he said was, "Continue at present speed. I want to get Tadur home as soon as possible."

Maxifer kept one eye focused on the terrain, only devoting two to regarding Tadur and the controls. He returned the medical monitor to his pocket. The skin of his arms flickered in shades of rust and crimson. *Vetilpoe will be pissed at us, to use the human vernacular—although I'm not sure why excreting waste liquid should be a metaphor for anger.* Maxifer could easily imagine his Jadderbadian mentor standing rigidly erect, all six arms twitching slightly and his hide flickering in shades of scarlet. Tadur's father, Twillock, would not be all that happy, either. Their field trip was two days beyond script and their appropriation of this vehicle was—"somewhat creative," to use Tadur's euphemism.

Maxifer continued to work himself up to a typical anxious crescendo, when Tadur shocked him. His primate friend began singing those melodies that always managed to sooth him in times of stress. "Tadur? Are you back to normal? Can you hear me?" Maxifer performed the equivalent of a human squint, compressing the ommatidia of his compound eyes in such a way that vision became slightly enhanced. But his friend didn't acknowledge that he was aware of his surroundings. He just sang in that calming primate way that he had with a soothing, though slightly raunchy ballad of interspecies titillations. Maxifer felt his body relax into the seat cushions just a little.

His mind wandered. Maxifer remembered the day he molted a

year ago from larvae to first instar. He was precocious, molting at age 94 (as measured by human calendars) rather than the usual 100 or 102. Tadur had been part of the young human chorus at his first molt celebration. Humans had turned out to be quite adept at helping Jadderbadians complete their life transitions—as good, and some said even better—than Jadderbadian primates. Perhaps that was because humans had more advanced mental functions—at least some of the time.

The transport hit another significant bump. Maxifer glanced outside and scanned the map displayed on the dashboard. They were approaching Vagabond Pass before the descent into the valley. The village should only be a couple of hours away now. The road would smooth out after the badlands were behind them.

Maxifer took a moment to enjoy high wispy clouds in the blue sky. He idly wondered what it would be like to visit his home world of Jadderbad. Earth was the only world he had ever known, and he liked it—although some of his third instar relatives thought their Earthborn kin had grown weak, both physically and mentally, through some combination of Earth's lower gravity, and associating with human primates as co-equals. Of course, most of those same old relatives doted on personal kennels filled with human pets, like cousin Paulsina in Belfnik.

The transport kept climbing up the now winding road. Tadur sang. Maxifer watched as scrub and cactus terrain shifted to wildflowers and a canopy of broadleaf and evergreen trees. R72 informed Maxifer that communication with the village would be interrupted until they reached the top of the pass.

They never got that far.

Maxifer's first clue that something was wrong was when Tadur's ballad stopped in mid stanza—during a particularly amusing, though scandalous act between a human and his Jadderbadian tutor. His second clue came with a flashing red indicator on the monitor's panel and R72's announcement: "I am detecting movement and heat signatures of several 500 kilogram creatures on either side of the roadway."

His third clue—more like an announcement really—came as three of the same creatures they had met at their fossil sea creature quarry emerged from the forest and stopped on the road ahead. The one called Ryan sat on the back of one creature that advanced toward them as R72 brought the transport to a stop. R72 declared the obvious, as usual: "Animals are blocking the path forward."

Ryan raised his right arm with its flattened hand facing forward. "Stop there. I will be directing your mechanical servant and your transport as of this moment." Ryan glanced down at his left hand where he apparently manipulated some sort of device. "You have something that belongs to me. I intend to claim it."

11
Gaia

Gaia awoke. *Not bad for a power nap*, she thought. *Even less than a hundred trips around sol can be refreshing. Now that she had advanced intelligences crawling about her surface again she needed to sharpen her game. Humans—her personal brand of brain-heavy metazoans—could be trouble enough. Look what they did to her poor infrastructure when there were over 10 billion of them mucking around amongst her various body parts. The last asteroid strike might have been painful, but it did temporarily alleviate the* Homo sapien *hives she had suffered. Now there were two new cohorts of alien DNA to contend with: Jadderbadians and Grovians. What was a planetary intelligence to do? Truly, a mother's work is never done.*

Gaia surveyed the inputs from her vast network of life forms. Pulses of energy rippled through the films and filaments of bacteria and fungi surrounded by a matrix of viral stew. *These creatures had been with her longest. They were her essence. Live. Survive. Reproduce. Repeat, ad infinitum. A simple game plan easy to continue, once you got the chemistry right—and good old mother sun kept shining—without too many erratic energy burps.*

It's when cells start to fraternize that problems multiply. Cells clump into worm shapes, then grow legs and shells. Some sprout leaves and roots. Swimming things start growing swollen brains and flopping onto dry land. Before you know it, a precocious predator is growing a brain so big it becomes delusional with self-importance. Then I wake up. Perhaps I'm delusional too. Gaia sighed, and the biosphere trembled. Volcanoes erupted. Winds blew. Ocean currents shifted course.

Gaia flowed her microbial billions near the margins of Hydra, her intellectual counterpart from Jadderbad who had oozed through the stargate with her own unique brainy metazoans. Hydra rested, and Gaia chose not to wake her. Instead, Gaia noted the myriad ways her body had already intermixed with Hydra's immigrant species. Their nucleic acids were slowly integrating and hybridizing. Failures were common, but successes were bound to occur. Gaia sensed great potential, given time. *Time, and life, and energy: miracle workers entwined.*

Gaia shifted her attention to the Mother Trees. Her microbial filaments had partially integrated with fragments of this other planetary gestalt—Grove—struggling to take form and shape. *Grovian metazoans want to conquer, not collaborate.* Gaia found resistance throughout their forest beachhead. *Two Grovian/human mergers did exist, which showed promise, but was there time to accomplish more?* Violent forces churned within her over which she had limited control.

Another wayward asteroid had helped stem the Grovian threat long ago. Gaia remembered the trauma 67 million years before that had made a mess of the dinosaurs she had been crafting for an eternity. Dinosaurs had been ready to grow big brains of their own before chance rudely intervened. But that disaster also set back the rapid growth and spread of Grove and her spawn. *And I did get many new creatures in my biosphere, Gaia reflected. Dinosaurs morphed into birds, filling my skies with colorful feathered chaff. Rodents transformed into a plethora of furry forms—including my swollen-brained, troublesome humans. Can't win all the time.*

Gaia basked in the warmth of her toasty interior for a while and felt her crustal plates slowly twist and churn beneath the fabric of her living self. She was one lucky planet. Venus burned beneath a canopy of carbon dioxide and sulfurous fumes. Mars would be a shrunken prune of a world, prematurely dead, if not for the human colonists that had transformed it some time ago. The local gas giants tended their microbes, but nothing special. Gaia cherished her liquid water and the fire in her belly. Even though she did have a soft spot when it came to intelligent metazoans, now she was infected by multiple varieties. *What will I do?*

Big-brained creatures of all kinds take notice, she vowed. *Take care what you do. I will survive. With or without you.*

12
Have body, will travel

"How do you feel, Rudy?" Nessie was just a voice in his ear now, as if he was wearing old fashioned ear buds, but Rudy could imagine the furrowed brow and limpid eyes he had come to know in the simulacrum that had been his existence for so long. He looked down at his hands and flexed the fingers. He loved flexing muscles again! He breathed deeply. The hanger-sized room smelled of metal and antiseptic. He sat on a bed surrounded by a person-high parabola of smooth metal festooned with data screens and blinking lights. He hopped off the bed and took another deep breath. He absolutely *loved* the feeling of air moving past the hairs in a real nose. His butt itched, but even that was okay. He scratched the irritation through the silky fabric of his rather sporty jumper suit—made with form-fitting material of dark blue with gold accents.

"I feel great, old girl!" He laughed. "I feel absolutely perfect! You've done a masterful job putting me in this human body. I hope it has a long warranty."

"If warranties were important, I would have placed you in a Jadderbadian all terrain tank. But I'm glad the organic body is to your liking, Rudy. You will need all the perfection you can muster during your travels."

"Oh, pish tosh. Let's not be negative, Nessie. I will do amazing things with this handsome vessel I'm inhabiting!"

"Pish tosh?"

"It means 'rubbish, bunk, a ridiculous proposition, old girl." Rudy stood up and spread his arms wide. "You're behind in perusing old entertainment files."

The briefest of pauses before Mnemosyne said, "Ah, like the

children's novel by Ellen Potter."

"Precisely." Rudy pointed to an arched seam in the wall tall enough to accommodate a small ship. His bed and medical apparatus seemed rather inconsequential compared to the size of the room. "Is that the exit? Is that backpack over there for me? I want to have a word with this Ryan character that's messing with Twill's great grandson. How do I reach him? He's over 3,000 miles from here, isn't he?"

"The backpack holds supplies you might need on your travels. Ryan is 3,375 miles from here. I have arranged transport via the local Jadderbadian military base," Mnemosyne added. "The local human population still struggles with the concept of the internal combustion engine."

"I know that feeling." Rudy scratched his new chin, enjoying even that simple pleasure. "So, we're chummy enough with the Jadderbadians now that we're borrowing their hardware until we get up to technological speed?" Rudy walked over to the archway. "Let's open the door and get this show on the road."

"Some preparation first: you will have an escort of three to the transport. Two individuals will travel with you to Belfnik on the Jadderbadian frontier."

Rudy raised his eyebrows. "Really? Give me the details."

"The GIU High Priest Botza wanted to be present to see the Great Rudy half of Holy Rudimort. He's the great grandson of Moran, the shaman's assistant that took care of Twill's degenerating father decades ago."

"GIU?" Rudy furrowed his brow.

"An acronym for the The Grand Interstellar Union—a proposed hybridization of terrestrial and Jadderbadian biology and culture."

"Moran. I remember him. He was an idiot as I recall."

"The term idiot no longer forms a part of any recognized psychiatric category…"

"Fool, ass, halfwit, nincompoop, etc.—all good synonyms. Where does Botza fall on the smarts scale for modern humans?"

"I'll take that question to be rhetorical, Rudy. I recognize no 'smarts scale' as a measure of intelligence. Botza, as the Chief Priest of the Grand Interstellar Union, considers Rudimort to have been the First Apostle of the Great Metamorphosis that will take place…"

"Spare me the details, Nessie. Botza sounds like an idiot, too. Who else will meet me?"

"Captain Tork, a third molt Jadderbadian, will represent the military providing the transport. You actually met him in your previous incarnation, Rudy."

"Ah, yes. The Lieutenant under Edelphine—that humanophobic hard-ass captain that was bent on destroying us. Tork wasn't that bad, as I recall—for a militaristic alien worm anyway."

"The third individual is human: the person who will accompany you on your trip to locate Ryan. Her name is Semma. She is quite bright, for an un-augmented human, although she is what used to be described as neuroatypical. Her social skills might be described as blunt."

"Ah, sounds like a bit of autism in the mix."

"Perhaps," continued Mnemosyne. "She has been studying with me under the auspices of Spider Woman as part of my Young Scholars' School. I'm attempting to incorporate old knowledge acquired during your pre-catastrophe culture with information provided by those Jadderbadian intellectuals liberal enough to consider some sort of merger with humaniforms."

"Ah, not the die-hard worm-a-pedes who just desire to own a cute primate to fetch their circlets and kick the spiracles of an obnoxious neighbor." Rudy leaned against the doorway, tapping the surface of the arch with one finger, as if looking for a button that would open the barrier. "And why is this Semma coming with me?"

"Semma knows Tadur. In fact, they were progressing through what seemed to be a typical human courtship ritual when they argued. Tadur left for the frontier to hunt fossils. Semma preferred to stay here and concentrate on interspecies biological studies. However, I have determined that a union of their genetics would be in the best long-term interests of the local community here. If I bring them into close proximity, that union may be more likely to occur."

Rudy laughed. "My Nessie has become a matchmaker! I should call you Tevye maybe. Go figure."

Mnemosyne hesitated a millisecond. "Ah, a Fiddler on the Roof reference. Well, it did seem best to accelerate what evolution might accomplish over a longer time span. Leaving mating to random processes seems quite inefficient."

"As you should know by now," Rudy observed, "humans specialize in inefficient behavior." Rudy took a deep breath. "Open the damn door already, Nessie. I want to burn some calories with this new body."

The door slid upward with a certain majestic grace. At first it only revealed feet. One pair, mostly hidden by a home-spun, tannish linen reminded Rudy of something Friar Tuck might have worn in a Robin Hood movie. A second pair belonged to a female with trim, bare calves and clenched toes peeking out of open-toed leather sandals. Behind those legs an enormous tripod of green feet rocked slightly to and fro. The door eventually opened far enough to reveal a complete Friar Tuck and Maid Marian, although Rudy's gaze quickly roamed upward to encompass the full height of the third molt Jadderbadian, Tork. Rudy had forgotten how enormous these older worms could get—although to be truthful they looked like more like spineless, nine-armed Saguaro cacti wearing rings of clothing.

Friar Tuck bowed. Rudy thought he heard a squelched fart, but couldn't be sure as the friar quickly said, "Welcome, oh Great Rudy. I am Botza, your servant on this Earth."

Maid Marian made what Rudy interpreted as a half-hearted curtsey. "My name is Semma," she declared with a defiant tilt of her chin. "I am quite smart, like you, Great Rudy. I have always wanted to meet you. You are paler and stumpier than I expected. Why are you dressed like a festival jester?"

Rudy laughed. "Well, I do love to tell jokes, Miss Semma." Rudy looked down at his jump suit. "And here I thought I would be a trend setter."

"Trend setter? The term is new to me. But I like learning new things. I will travel with you and help interpret our world. It is Spider

Woman's wish." Semma's eyes narrowed slightly, apparently taking his measure again. Her lips rearranged from forced smile mode to a rather puzzled pout.

"Just call me Rudy, Semma. I haven't been Great since I was 25." Rudy liked Semma immediately. She appeared to be refreshingly acerbic. It didn't hurt that she was a beautiful young thing as well. Her dark, shoulder length hair and trim figure reminded him of a long-legged barmaid he once dallied with.

The worm-a-pede alien rumbled like a god on high: "I am Tork, as you probably know. We should hurry. The transport has other duties and I must keep to my schedule."

Rudy picked up the backpack he had spotted earlier and slipped the straps over his shoulders. "We certainly wouldn't want to disrupt any schedules. Let's do this," he said, while giving what he hoped was a grandfatherly wink to Semma. Tadur would have his hands full with this one. He was pretty sure of that.

13
Dual abductions

Maxifer sat in the idling transport, briefly considering his options. He needed immediate medical care for Tadur, but the human named Ryan stared at him from the back of his alien mount with the focus of a caratt intent on a kill. With a finger concealed beneath the control panel, Maxifer poked an emergency pad that would direct R72 to activate the one real weapon at their disposal from his perch on the roof... but no response.

"I wasn't kidding when I said I was taking control of your mechanical servant." Ryan leaned forward on his ugly steed. Tentacles around its beak writhed like disturbed worms. "Change places with your human friend. I'm taking your place in the vehicle."

Maxifer's hide flashed in ripples of amber, verging on orange. *How did he know I touched that control?* "My friend needs help! Quickly. He's... he's possessed or something, he's..."

"I know precisely what's happened to him." Ryan paused a beat. "I mean no harm to your friend," he said in a more conciliatory tone.

Maxifer passed air softly through several spiracles—the Jadderbadian version of a sigh. He lifted Tadur and placed him on the lap formed by his two forward-facing legs. Tadur grunted, but was otherwise inert. Maxifer extracted his third lower limb from its slot in the rear of the seat and slid over to the cushion Tadur had occupied so he could reinsert his third limb in the corresponding slot there. He slid Tadur off his lap to the left. Ryan, in the meantime, had opened the transport door on the control side. He placed a hand on Tadur's left shoulder. Maxifer noted the mixed odors of trail dust and pine resin that had wafted in with Ryan. "What's wrong with my friend? He needs help."

Ryan ignored the question, but said something in a strange language to Tadur. Tadur turned his head to face Ryan. He said a word. It sounded like, "See you?" to Maxifer, which didn't make any sense. Then Tadur groaned, and jerked to and fro before going catatonic again.

Maxifer stroked Tadur's hair and swiveled all his eyes toward his friend while speaking to Ryan. "What just happened?"

"A struggle for control." Ryan removed his hand from Tadur's shoulder and faced the driver's instrument panel. He activated the touch pad. "R72: program these coordinates into your navigation system and proceed to follow them at all reasonable speed." R72 complied. The alien ambuli outside the transport took positions all around the vehicle and moved at the same pace.

Maxifer tracked them briefly with one eye while focusing the other two on Ryan. He began to babble questions. "What do you mean, a struggle for control? What kind of human are you? Your hide is quite pale compared to Tadur. Are you ill? If you were from Jadaman City, I'm sure I would have heard of you. Are you a lost pet from the Confederation? A wild human?"

Ryan pressed his lips together in what Tadur would have described as a crooked smile. "Call me a wild human. Pale, but quite healthy. I don't have time for a long resume recap." He sighed. "Look, your friend has been… infected by an alien intelligence that was housed in the sphere. It's an ancient intelligence that I know something about because… well, because I was infected once myself by a related intelligence—a very long time ago."

Maxifer's hide flickered in confused pulses of green and amber. "I know of no other aliens on this planet."

"Yeah, well, it's a big old planet, and you're not omniscient." Ryan smiled again.

"Are you?" Maxifer's color pattern froze in place for a moment. He had never much believed in the all-knowing Great Prophet who ushered all worthy Jadderbadians through their last metamorphosis, but there was always that frisson of doubt when something really weird took place…

"Not at all, but I've lived long enough—probably too long—that

56

I know a few things that you don't." Ryan grunted as the transport bumped over a rough spot on the road.

"Where are we going? My mentor, Veltipoe, knows a good doctor in Jadaman City."

"Not good enough, I'm afraid." Ryan glanced quickly at all the outside monitor views and tapped some instructions to R72 from the panel. Maxifer was impressed with how easily he was able to use the controls—especially since he and Tadur had customized some of it. "Look, Maxifer, we have to move quickly. It looks like some company I hadn't expected is on an intercept course."

"Master Veltipoe must be looking for us…"

"Nice thought, but no cigar, as my grandfather, Pops, used to say. This is a military scout force from the Confederation. They must be aware of the Mother Tree Forest."

"Cigar? The mother what?" Maxifer flickered some more in shades of emerald and amber.

"Long story." Ryan's fingers danced over the controls some more. "Look, I have to check on some things. I need quiet for a while."

Maxifer kept one hand on Tadur's head. His friend mumbled occasionally to himself, but didn't seem in distress. A few kilometers passed. Maxifer watched broadleaf trees slowly replace conifers as they crested the pass and descended into the valley. The ambuli kept seemingly effortless pace with the transport. They looked unlike anything on either Earth or Jadderbad with an almost ratalope behind, arched two-armed neck, and bulbous compound eyes. Maxifer might have even dozed off briefly while watching them lope along the road beside them.

"Crap!" Ryan's exclamation woke Maxifer up. All three eyes focused on Ryan's hands tapping on the touch screen. His hands became still for a moment, and then Ryan said "Crap!" again, more emphatically.

Maxifer knew that human word. "Frass" was the Jadderbadian equivalent. Speaking loudly about excrement was never a good thing. "What's wrong?"

"I'm not going to be able to detour around the Jadderbadian

scout vehicle. I thought I would have time." Ryan commanded R72 to halt the transport.

At least this Ryan human is not omniscient after all. "What will you do?" Maxifer scanned the terrain outside, but could see nothing. The ambuli stood or pranced in place near the vehicle, perhaps sniffing the air with the wiggling sensors around their mouths.

Ryan locked on Maxifer's three-eyed stare. "You're going to proceed down this road. You'll intersect the convoy's path. Tell them who you are, and that you're headed for Jadaman City. Don't mention that you were traveling with a human. They'll probably let you proceed."

"Probably?" Maxifer fidgeted. "Confederation Jadderbadians—especially the Thunderclub Clan—don't much care for 'groupie lovers' like me. They consider all humans—they call them groupies because they like to hang out in mobs—to be sub-Jadderbadian—whether they are cute or not. And what about Tadur? He needs my help."

"He needs *my* help—and I'll give it to him—if I can pull off this maneuver. I haven't tried this under field conditions before." With that comment, Ryan put both his arms around Tadur and closed his eyes.

"What are you do…" Maxifer didn't get the entire question out before—before Ryan and Tadur faded and—disappeared. *That's impossible. What I just saw is impossible.* "R72: what happened to Ryan and Tadur?"

"They disappeared," R72 confirmed.

"But that's impossible."

"Apparently not," said R72, once again stating the obvious.

Before Maxifer could ruminate on the matter further, he noted a cloud of dust arising at the point where the road disappeared around a bend. The ambuli outside the vehicle galloped away to Maxifer's left in a direction at right angles to the dust cloud. "Probably they will let me proceed," Maxifer said out loud. "Probably they will let me proceed," he repeated, but he didn't really believe it.

* * * * *

"What's your business in the wilderness, Firstie?" The second molt Jadderbadian, who had identified himself as Lieutenant Texlac, towered over Maxifer as he stood in front of the transport. His voice boomed like that of an angry mentor. A pair of burly, genetically modified attack groupies, at least a head taller than Tadur, and bearing hypertrophied leg and arm muscles, flanked Texlac on both sides. Their tiny eyes seemed to glow like embers behind heavy brows. Behind this trio, a Jadderbadian all-terrain tank idled in place like a puffing metallic whale, dwarfing Maxifer's transport vehicle.

"I'm a... I'm a student of fossilized life forms. I've been exploring the badlands." Maxifer's hide flickered in shades of what he hoped were tranquil turquoise. He saw some of the lieutenant's spiracles fluttering at a speed that signaled mild distaste. Maxifer tried slowing his breathing. Perhaps that would reduce the acidity of his greeting pheromones.

"Fossilized life forms?" Texlac arched his upper segment until all three of his faceted eyes glittered above Maxifer's head. The pili around his tooth barbs flicked back and forth, signaling an irritated interest. "What are you babbling about?"

Maxifer's colors brightened. "Oh, fossils are quite interesting objects, indeed. They represent the remains of ancient creatures preserved in stone." Maxifer fished around in the pocket of his circlet and extracted a coiled shell. He held it at the apex of the pyramid formed by the three fingers of his forward arm so the Lieutenant could see it clearly. "See? Smell? This one still has the remnants of the original calcium carbonate shell. This marine creature lived when an ancient seaway covered this entire area over 73 million Earth years ago and..."

"What's it good for?" Texlac interrupted with a growl. He lifted the shell with the fingers of his own forward arm and brought the fossil closer to his eyes. His lip pili fluttered. "Can you eat it?"

"Of course not!" Maxifer expelled air from two lateral spiracles with a snort.

"Can you trade this thing for work credits?" Texlac rotated it with his fingers.

"I... I doubt it," Maxifer stammered. "I never tried."

"Does the Great Prophet command a study of these things? I know of no such scripture." The lieutenant straightened his body, raising the fossil into a shaft of sunlight. He continued to study it with one eye while glaring at Maxifer with the other two.

"I don't really know." Maxifer paused to gather his thoughts. "They are of scientific interest. My mentor, Veltipoe — a natural philosopher — is teaching us about the past of this strange world."

"Veltipoe? That name is not familiar. And this fossil thing appears to be worthless." Texlac tossed it over his shoulder like a discarded scrap of food.

Maxifer expelled air in an alarmed squeak through his spiracles. *What an oaf—a belligerent oaf with atrophied ganglia.*

Texlac bent over again, placing his face uncomfortably close to Maxifer's. "You're from Jadaman City, *aren't you?*" He paused a beat before adding. "You're one of those groupie-lovers. I can smell it."

"And what if I am?" Maxifer felt his colors shifting to the reds and infrareds. He disdained the use of the pejorative name, *groupie*. His mouth and head pili darted to and fro with defiance.

"It means that you are under detainment." Texlac spread his lips so that tooth barbs gleamed in the sun. "The Jadderbadian Confederation has declared a state of emergency—the details of which I am not at liberty to disclose. You are beyond the boundaries allocated to that pathetic, human-loving collection of shacks called Jadaman City."

"But, I heard of no such state of emergency..." Maxifer wanted to add *you pompous frasshole*, but restrained himself. *Veltipoe would have been proud. Tadur, not so much. But then if Tadur had been here in his catatonic state, this Thunderclub thug might have put him down and claimed it as a mercy killing.*

"Arrest this human-loving abomination." Texlac commanded in Lower Basic, the simplified Jadderbadian language reserved for groupies and genemods. He gestured the equivalent command with the fingers of one arm.

The over-muscled humans advanced toward Maxifer from either side, grinning broadly enough to expose oversized, genetically enhanced canine teeth. Their control collars glowed a rather threatening shade of deep red. "You can't *do* this," Maxifer insisted, staring up at Texlac.

But Texlac did.

14
The Mother Tree forest

Ryan and Tadur blinked into existence at the eastern margin of the Mother Tree forest, and unceremoniously tumbled to the ground. Ryan took the brunt of the fall with Tadur sprawled on top of him. *I guess I won't try that starting from a sitting position again.* Ryan rolled Tadur aside far enough that he could rise to his knees. He rolled Tadur onto his back. Tadur's eyes fluttered, then opened. "Are you all right, Tadur? Can you hear me?"

Tadur's eyes grew wide. "Ah, Mother Trees—I can feel their presence; smell the musk of a rich forest—but they don't look or smell quite right." His eyes focused on Ryan. "Who—or what—are you?" The intelligence behind Tadur's eyes obviously was not his own.

"The human part of me is called Ryan. But I'm also part Grovian, and part Guardian. To whom am I speaking?"

"I am Klemna, First Servant of the Matriarch of the Diaspora and loyal acolyte of Greatest Mother." Klemna paused a beat. "What kind of abomination are you?"

Klemna. Not who I had hoped for. Ryan took a long deep breath to relax and access the part of him that was Siu. *Well, Siu, it looks like your First Servant has made the transition from neural engram to human parasite. Do you want to take it from here—since I'm just an abomination?*

I will, Ryan. Not everyone can appreciate abominations the way I can. With that, Siu, Matriarch of the Diaspora, savior of a fragment of Grovian life when her sun went nova, asserted dominance in Ryan's mind and body. *Perhaps we can convert Klemna to the benefits of collaborating with unholy aliens, although it may take some effort. Klemna means well, but she never was the most imaginative ambulus in the pod.* To Klemna she said, "Klemna, it is good to have you here with me again. Although it may not look like it, I am your Matriarch, Siu, alive and well within the body of this human creature named Ryan."

"Siu? Really?" Klemna, now in control of her host's body, sat up and scooched away, as if frightened by her interrogator. "Why have you not destroyed your host as required? I am attempting to destroy mine, but the creature—even though one of the inferior gender—is proving to be resistant."

"No! Do not destroy the male named Tadur." Siu stood up and extended her right arm toward Klemna, palm facing out, in a gesture that mimicked what she would have done if housed in the body of a proper Grovian ambulus. "I command you to obey."

Klemna put hands to her head. "I can't. This process… is painful. Besides, how do I know you are truly Siu?"

Siu knelt beside Klemna. "Think, acolyte! We are speaking in a variant of Grovian, aren't we? What alien would know that? I am Siu, and my First Mate was… is… Ito—one of them, at least—inventor of the neural engram technology that preserved us after our Earth colony faltered so long ago."

"Ito. Yes, where is Ito? What do you mean, one of him? He was such a brilliant stallion."

"All in good time, Klemna. In the meantime, let me help you assimilate the being within you, without destroying him. That is important."

After a brief pause, and still holding her head, Klemna nodded agreement. Together they moved to the base of a Mother Tree and found a comfortable seat on a bed of moss between two sinuous roots. Siu coached Klemna in the care and treatment of her human host—how to share mental space rather than conquer it—with the promise that the reasons behind this action would eventually become clear.

"Klemna, do you feel better now?"

Klemna sat a little straighter and placed her head firmly against the trunk of the Mother Tree. "Yes."

"Good. We must move quickly. I will introduce you to the Eldest Mother of this fine forest. We have a lot to do and not much time to do it before trouble arrives."

* * * * *

They made good time through the catacombs of green forest. The high, thick canopy shaded the forest floor, leaving enough gaps in the understory for swift travel. Ryan noted several pair of roving ambuli—young ones—searching for an unwary or over-curious ratalope fawn that might make a nice snack. Ryan had come to love this strange forest: a complex network of Grovian and terran life forms intertwined like the threads of a rich fabric. Terrestrial lichens, fungi, and mosses decorated massive Grovian Mother Tree trunks in carpets of green, yellow, rust and dusky white. Insects buzzed. Wings flashed with color as birds—descendants of the sparrows and finches of his day—flitted from branch to branch.

Finally, they arrived at the trunk of a gnarled tree the size of an ancient skyscraper. Its corded trunk soared upward, festooned with a drapery of vines and clothed in streamers of blue-green lichen and moss. Depressions suitable for ambuli hands and hoofs, as well as human hands and feet, snaked upwards, passing close to the swelling, amber pods that held a new generation of ambuli. In and around some of the broad lower branches, platforms and staircases held small clusters of humans looking their way and waving. Ryan heard music in the distance—compositions of some of his Menssanan children.

"Where are we?" Klemna turned the body of her human host in a tight circle, trying to take in all of her surroundings. "I sense Mother Trees, but the smells are wrong. The leaves are not proper blue disks. And why are those human beasts haunting the branches and waving their scrawny appendages?"

"This is a true Mother Tree forest—one adapted to a new world," the throaty voice of Mother Novaya announced. "Klemna, I am Mother Novaya, descendent of Mother Elda, whose body served as the vessel that carried us to Earth—to our New Hope. Welcome."

Ryan had never quite gotten used to talking trees, but Ryan knew that Klemna would not find it strange. The massive growth represented just another stage in the Grovian life cycle. Just how mother trees activated auditory circuits in human brains was still not entirely clear to Ryan, but then he had never completely understood the workings of cell phones back in the day either. He accepted his limitations.

"Ito planted the seed that would become Mother Novaya well over a million years ago." Siu looked Klemna in the eyes, and spread the arms of her host, Ryan. "I know its hard to believe, but this planet Earth, that served as haven to Grovians escaping a dying star, suffered two major extinction events since Ito placed your engram in the silver capsule. Both events were asteroid strikes spaced roughly 66 million years apart. Ito awoke after the first event, eventually planting Mother Novaya. Mother Novaya, Ito—and I—have all survived a second extinction event."

"But you did not kill your host and replenish Greatest Mother's children. Something went terribly wrong!" Klemna moved closer to Mother Novaya and placed a hand on her trunk. "Your bark has the warmth and feel of a Mother Tree. I sense your presence, Mother Novaya. But where is Ito? I'm not sure I believe this bizarre tale."

"Look up," said Siu, "at that lowest pod."

Klemna looked up. The pod seemed nearly ripe. A seam began to split revealing something squirming inside. "Is it time for an ambulus to birth?"

"Not exactly. This pod is releasing a human partner. Just as Ito was part of my harem of males, Ryan, the human I share a body with, has a mate—his only one. Her name is Skeets. And the gender bias with humans tends toward patriarchy, although the divide is not as clear-cut as with Grovians."

On cue the pod opened. A straw haired, slender human female disentangled herself from Mother Novaya's nurturing tendrils and smiled at the two figures below her. "Get a girl some clothes would you? Mother Novaya changed her storage cleft. It's under that branch there, Ryan." Skeets pointed.

"Looking good, my love. Very good." Ryan's personality came once more to the fore and he smiled at Skeets.

"Well, stop staring and fetch my clothes, old man. We have company." Skeets winked at him. "We can celebrate your return later."

"Yes, dear." Ryan climbed to the appropriate branch, extracted a bundle of clothing, and kissed his mate as he handed her the folded fabrics. "You look well rested."

"You know Mother Novaya, Thompson. She hasn't lost her velvet touch or soothing songs." Skeets returned her mate's kiss while tussling his hair with one hand.

"Do humans typically bite each other like that? Disgusting." Klemna struggled to close her host's eyes. The creature called Tadur apparently wanted to see what was happening; she did not. "Are you performing some alien mating ritual? Where is Ito? You never told me where Ito is."

Ryan and Skeets clambered down the trunk. Once on the ground, Skeets sorted her wad of clothing and dressed. Siu once again took command of Ryan's body. "Ito merged with Skeets. Although our genders are cross-matched, Ito and I are reunited as part of this human pair bond. It's a rather long story we can better discuss if you come to chamber."

"Come to chamber with an abomination? I think not!" Klemna succeeded in closing her host's eyes. "As I said, disgusting. How can Greatest Mother condone such a travesty?"

"Greatest Mother apparently has a profound sense of humor." Siu smiled. "Or, perhaps Meaira, the cosmic jokester, is in charge. Who really knows?"

Klemna puffed out Tadur's chest and re-opened her eyes to glare at Siu. "That sounds like blasphemy!"

"Not at all." Siu shrugged. "Just astute observation. Look, Klemna, we need some pod time to sort things out. Mother Novaya can explain everything. But I suspect that your host's body is in need of food. Let's eat and rest before you decide about coming to chamber."

"I do hear strange sounds coming from this creature's abdomen." Klemna looked up through the branches of Mother Novaya once more before focusing on Siu. "I agree to eat and rest."

"Excellent," said Siu. "Follow me." We should make this quick, urged Ryan to his alien partner. *I don't know how much time I bought with my disappearing act. Angry Jadderbadians are en route. And, as we both know, Meaira's jokes can be painful to endure.*

14
Ito Prime

Ito Prime awoke. That meant some creature of relatively high intelligence—perhaps human again, unless they had become extinct while he hibernated—had discovered a silver sphere and become the host for one of his brethren. But which Sister was it? His master plan of so long ago had become a kind of endless torture of rebirth and fruitless searching. Truly, Meaira must be doubled over with laughter from the games she played with him. "Mother, what do you know?"

Mother Chalice, the great Mother Tree in one of whose pods Ito rested, answered slowly. She struggled to awaken, too, after an eternity of cold and silence. "Guardian has activated the engram of..." Mother Chalice had to pause. The name was hard to hear, muted as it was through the filaments of her distant microbial network. "...Ah, it is Klemna."

"Klemna," Ito Prime repeated. "I never could figure out why Siu had made her First Servant. I'm not sure how she survived her childhood. In a cave, perhaps, so that the other ambuli couldn't eat her?"

"Be kind, Ito. She is part of the honored Sisterhood, and you are only a male, after all."

"But the smartest male since Ratio himself." Ito squirmed in place, stretching his muscles against the resistance of the pod's pliant walls.

"But certainly not the most humble—comparing yourself to a legend of mythic status." Mother Chalice squeezed Ito's pod until he grunted in protest. "You are Prime now, and the only Ito clone left. Who could have foreseen the disasters that befell the others? You must be both smart and careful. Don't let arrogance and pride defeat you, ambulus. The Sisterhood on this planet of new hope depends on you."

"Yes, Mother." Ito hated contrition even when it was appropriate. *The Sisterhood depends on me. How often had he thought that over the millennia—over the geological ages—through which he had endured?* "How far are we from Klemna, honored Mother?"

"Many thousands of miles. Half a planet away."

Ito groaned. "Let me sleep some more." He hugged himself, and struggled to keep Mother Chalice's tendrils from disengaging.

"But I detect the essence of someone—yes, oh my—by all the improbabilities of Greatest Mother's will…"

"What?" Ito snapped fully awake now. Not much could surprise a Mother Tree. "What do you detect?"

"Siu. Siu is still alive and involved in this new event somehow." Mother Chalice felt the fluids rising in her xylem tubes.

"Dear Siu." Ito Prime sighed. "I endured all this for her. Yet, the last message we received from the former Ito Prime—Rhondal/Ito—implied that something had changed Siu. She had failed to completely take charge of her host. Why? And had that failure somehow contributed to the destruction of Rhondal/Ito?" *They had never received the nanomote with Rhondal/Ito's Guardian to merge with mine.* The thought gave Ito chills. *I engineered those motes myself. They were built to survive most catastrophes.*

"All good questions." Mother Chalice continued to extract her tendrils, forcing her Ito to fully engage with the world. "It will be your job to find out."

* * * * *

Ito emerged from the pod inside of Mother Chalice's formidable mass rather than on the outside, as was customary. The two of them had conspired to engineer this biological change because they were uncertain just how hospitable the outside world would be—post cataclysm—when another silver sphere activated.

Ito looked down at his human body—one that had once housed a male named Ivan. The sexual organ dangled, completely exposed. It was not even retractable. Bad design. The scrotum knotted into a tighter sack and shivers crawled along his arms. Ito found the compartment with Ivan's work clothes and dressed. Someday soon he would inhabit a real ambulus body again, with four strong legs and magnificent compound eyes—not to mention dual retractable penes—but the remnants of human technology he depended on were engineered to this ridiculous naked ape form.

Time to go. Time for him to transform this world into a new and better Grove.

Seemingly endless chambers and corridors filled Mother Chalice's trunk, protection against the vagaries of this planet's natural disasters and all the machinations of the strange humans who lacked a mother tree life stage--*a tialopo*—to offer wisdom and support. As he moved through dim, woody corridors to Mother's exit port, Ito thought about some of the many humans whose bodies he had commandeered in order to survive the destruction of their first aborted colony and reunite with his only mate, Siu.

When Grovians had first landed on New Hope, the planet humans eventually called Earth, human ancestors were nothing but vermin scuttling away from the feet of dinosaurs. Somehow, those hairy rodents survived the global chaos of an asteroid strike, and evolved into swollen-brained primates—all while the remaining members of the Sisterhood endured an eternity in the silver capsules the original Ito had designed. That Ito awoke within the body of Durgo, an oaf who could barely chip a piece of rock into a projectile point. But as silly as human beasts were—and without the benefit of a proper tialopo alternate Mother Tree life stage—they built the rudiments of a complex civilization in only a few thousands of years.

Ito endured many human hosts over the centuries. Humans found a bewildering number of ways to kill each other, commit suicide, or just carelessly walk off the edge of a cliff. Of course, Ito did push his hosts to travel where and when he wanted in order to maximize his chances of eventually finding the capsule that held his beloved Siu. That glorious discovery failed to occur for a very long time.

While inhabiting the brown-skinned Mangas Haskins, smallpox and other primate diseases mowed down vast numbers of individuals who lived on the continent later called North America by those who carried the diseases. It seemed prudent to clone his personality to increase his odds of surviving random disasters—although managing a bunch of smart, obsessive-compulsive twins often proved a challenge. Only one Ito was Prime at any given time, however. He was able to transport and plant mother tree seeds, as the trapper, Jacques Lideaux, and the circuit riding judge, James Felson. A handful of clones spread themselves far and wide across the continent and the globe.

And, as human technology improved, he began to see how the human species might successfully be eradicated, even though they spawned offspring almost as successfully as rabbits. As the medical doctor, Jonathon Wells, he thought he had engineered a flu virus that would do the trick during the first of what they called "World Wars," but its kill rate was not quite high enough.

Finally, during the twenty-first century, as measured from the birth of a prophet called Jesus Christ, the signal he had awaited for so long reached him. Siu had emerged from stasis. He longed for a joyful reunion. But what happened? Meaira toyed with him again. Siu empathized with her young human host—a rock-turning, image-painting creature called Ryan Thompson. How could she do that? She was the Matriarch of the Diaspora, after all!

Ito stopped to take a breath at a junction in Chalice's woody labyrinth. *Surely he could make Siu see the error of her ways. He would rekindle their love. Together they would make Greatest Mother proud.*

He resumed his trek through the vast Mother Tree. He hoped nothing had happened to the plane and stockpiled fuel carefully enmeshed in Mother Chalice's embrace for an eternity. It would have to function well enough to cross an ocean and a continent without help—unless humans had managed to preserve—or re-invent—the same level of technology they once had enjoyed.

"I have triple checked the mechanical and software specifications of your aerial transport," announced Mother Chalice, as if reading his mind. "It meets all specifications. Most humans exist at a pre-industrial level of technology, dependent on imported technology from the Jadderbadian culture that reached Earth through a trans-spacial gateway—a stargate—nearly a century ago. I suggest you treat your craft well. No replacement parts exist."

"Most humans?" He possessed some knowledge about what Mother Chalice related because of their intimate links during hibernation, but the details seemed vague. "Are there humans with greater technology?"

"Yes. Maybe."

Mother trees rarely showed doubt. "I remember images of a Citadel when I was in chamber—some sort of AI inhabited artifact from before this last global extinction event. Is this AI comparable to my Guardians? What about this Rudy person from the deep past? Some sort of genius human? He certainly can't compare to me. What skills do these relic humans possess who live near this citadel? And this Ryan person who has mesmerized my Siu—how has he survived?"

"Good questions all, my humble Ito. You will have to find most of the answers. I will help when I learn more through my network. The survival of the Sisterhood depends on it."

Of course. Ito reached the hanger and opened the door. The air smelled of grease and oil, mixed with the heady aromas of Mother Chalice's woody tissues and a hint of the accumulated dust of millennia that even Mother Chalice couldn't completely eliminate. *Of course, the survival of the Sisterhood depended on his ability to solve all problems; eliminate all obstacles—living or inanimate.*

And he would. He would not let either naked apes or over-sized worm-a-pedes defeat him.

16
Lubricating the path to Enlightenment

"This fermented beverage is..." Klemna paused and inspected the glass in her hand before taking another substantial sip, "quite acceptable."

"Glad you like it, sister." Siu, the dominant personality in Ryan Thompson's body at the moment, winked at Skeets. The three of them sat around a private table about 30 meters above the forest floor tucked within an alcove specializing in food service for travelers. Someone above them, unseen in the dark canopy of leaves overhead, played a haunting melody with an instrument that sounded much like a flute. Siu lifted the ceramic decanter decorated with an artfully coiled vine and bulbous maroon fruits. "I can top off your glass, if you like."

"Welll..." Klemna stretched out the syllable while she moved the dinner dishes to one side, "...perhaps just this much." She set her glass on the table; then demonstrated the amount by leaving a tiny gap between the thumb and forefinger of her left hand.

While Siu refilled Klemna's drink, a young woman approached the table to remove the dishes from the meal. *Tandy is her name, right?* Ryan asked the question, even though Siu was the dominant personality at the moment. They had coexisted so long together that listening to each other was almost like listening to their own thoughts.

"Thank you, Tandy," said Siu, nodding toward the girl. *If you live long enough all those pesky descendants tend to blur together, don't they, Ryan?*

Tandy cleared the table while Klemna studied her beverage between sips as if it were a crystal ball.

They do, admitted Ryan. Thoughts flickered through their merged mentalities like someone riffling the pages of a thick book. The beginning of their shared experiences, however, had been a fireball of confrontation: A young paleontologist impulsively touching a silver sphere to find that he had been infected by a strange alien—and her AI guardian—both desperate to save her species. They all nearly destroyed each other before discovering their personal goals and needs intersected. *How have we stayed sane this long, Siu?*

Have we stayed sane, human? If so, it must be your unflagging optimism.

Or your stubborn Grovian persistence in a universe where Meaira rules.

Perhaps our symbiotic schizophrenia was insane from the start. And then there's Siyan...

Yes, Siyan. Siu + Ryan + transmuted AI= Insanity. That would seem to be a valid equation.

Klemna interrupted their thoughts. "The meal you provided was quite remarkable. I recognized some dishes that reminded me of Grove. Others were distinctly alien...but not unpleasant."

"I'm glad you're feeling better now." Skeets took a small sip from her glass, and then cradled her drink with two hands. "The forest provides everything a human—or a Grovian—could want, when you know how to find it or how to ask for it properly."

Klemna said nothing, but raised her beverage and took another sip.

When Klemna lowered her glass, Siu reached over and tapped the back of her hand. Klemna flinched at the touch, but kept her hand on the table. "Klemna. We must ask. Is your human host safe? He hasn't come forward to speak to us."

"Oh, he's safe." Klemna twisted Tadur's mouth into a pout. "Safe, but annoying. He keeps asking about his insect-worm friend: Maxibur, Maxiner... Max something. He complains about being held prisoner in his own body. I may squash him yet—like an arthropod at an outdoor feast—just for fun." Klemna attempted a smile, but her lips quivered over bare teeth. "Pleesh, er please let me squash him. I will make his humble death painless."

"No. Control your impulses, sister. You are First Acolyte, after all." Siu paused. "I know this experience has been a shock for you." Siu leaned toward Klemna. "I'm sorry. Ryan and I… Skeets and Ito… have had lifetimes to reach understanding and mutual respect. Full understanding won't come without communion with Mother Novaya. Believe me… trust me, Klemna: it's time to come to chamber."

"Abomination." Klemna's voice was nearly a whisper. She squinted at Siu, as if trying to see her matriarch somewhere within the alien body in front of her. "Our mission has failed."

"Our mission has not failed. Really. Mother Novaya can provide enlightenment. Come to chamber and you will understand—not only what has happened, but what can happen in our new future."

Klemna slowly shook her head back and forth, but she took another sip of wine. And another. By the time her glass was empty, she had made a decision. "I will go to chamber with Mother Novaya. *But…*" She paused, and pointed a finger at Siu/Ryan. "I promise nothing. Enlightenment? We'll smell and taste. Perhaps the proper bouquet will be there—if this human body's pathetic sensorium is up to the task."

17
Off to Chamber

Ryan, Skeets, and Klemna/Tadur descended from the food service platform on a winding staircase that spiraled down the trunk of the young mother tree. They caught glimpses of red, yellow, and blue through the dense overstory as the sun set. Clouds of midges danced up and down; to and fro in the fading light.

Once on the forest floor, they followed a well-worn path to Mother Novaya's imposing mass and began ascending. Ryan and Skeets helped Klemna when she struggled to find foot and hand holds, although on some level, as evidenced by humming punctuated with an occasional giggle, Klemna seemed to be enjoying the experience.

"Are dwee—I mean, are we—there yet?" Klemna looked around as if trying to find a road sign.

"Almost," said Ryan.

"We can store our clothes in this alcove," announced Skeets as she pointed to a cavity near the three pods they would soon enter. "It's your job to help Klemna, Thompson," Skeets said, as she began removing her own clothes. "She won't want my help, and she is in a guy's body after all."

Klemna squinted at Ryan/Siu. "Are you sewer, er sure, you're not an abomination?"

"Quite sure, First Servant." Siu took over as spokesperson in Ryan's body and began loosening the leather threads of Tadur's shirt. "This comes off over your head." Siu pulled the shirt over Tadur's head to the accompaniment of muffled burbles. "Then we'll untie this sash and the pants come down."

"It's drafty up here." Klemna said, after stepping out of the leather breeches.

Siu tossed the pants to a now-naked Skeets, and began removing the clothing on Ryan's body. When finished, she passed all the garments to Skeets who stowed them in the proper compartment. "We'll get you in the first pod, Klemna. It will be no different than any communion with a Mother. You're just in a different vessel, as it were. Skeets and I will be in neighboring pods. We'll all be able to interact, with Mother Novaya's help, of course."

"I trust you, Matriarch," Klemna said, as she allowed Siu to help her into the pod, but Tadur's eyes grew round and his skin dimpled as a shiver rippled along his thigh.

Ryan's personality came to the fore after Klemna entered the pod. He squeezed Skeets' hand briefly and winked at her before they separated to enter adjacent pods.

* * * * *

Oh my, thought Mother Novaya. *Mobile, transient life forms lead such a confusing existence. I must calm them to make sense of everything.* To that end, Mother Novaya extended her filaments to wrap around and delicately penetrate the three bodily forms within her pods and coax the six—no, really seven—personalities inhabiting those bodies to relax and reflect. She had less experience with the seventh personality, Siyan. She tended to think of Siyan as masculine, but couldn't quite say why. He might not emerge anyway under these circumstances. *Ah, Mother Exoda, if only you were still alive to help. I really have no idea how to make this integration work. No mother tree in all of Grovian history has ever done this before.*

Siu adjusted first, followed by Ito, Ryan, and Skeets. Mother Novaya had to neutralize the alcohol in Tadur's physical body first, and then adjust the dopamine and other neurochemicals in Tadur's brain properly in order to allow both his and Klemna's personalities to coexist. An extra squirt of oxytocin might be a good choice to up the empathy levels. *Give me strength, Greatest Mother!*

"You are strong and wise, Mother Novaya. Thank you for offering us your chambers." Siu provided the ritual greeting to acknowledge her readiness to proceed.

"You truly are Greatest Mother's servant," added Ito/Skeets. "You have found a way to extend your roots deeply into the fabric of this new world and adapt to its challenges."

"Ito? Is that really you?" Klemna's voice sounded plaintive. "I have many questions..."

"All in good time, Klemna," said Mother Novaya. "I thank you for coming to chamber with me, and I thank you, Matriarch and First Mate. I'm in your debt for planting my seed."

"Hope we've gotten all the formalities out of the way, folks. Klemna and Tadur seemed tangled like a Gordian knot." Skeets stretched in her pod.

Ryan laughed—or would have if that had been physically possible in the pod. Instead, the impulse to laugh created a kind of psychic burst that his Grovian friends recognized. "Let's hope we can find a King Gordius to untie them."

"Why should I allow this primitive creature to survive in the husk of his frail, two-legged body, Matriarch?" Klemna asked. "Only Grovians are Greatest Mother's Chosen Ones."

"Chosen for what? Parasitizing innocent people? Stay out of my head and my body, ugly creature!" Tadur's outburst made his body twist and squirm.

Mother Novaya adjusted the flow of chemicals in her filaments once more. "Be calm," she urged. "Grovians and humans need not be adversaries. We have a lot to learn from each other. Perhaps a lot to learn from Jadderbadians as well—if they don't kill us first."

"Another inferior species. What do Grovians need with giant, multi-legged worms? More abominations." Klemna's personality remained resistant to Mother Novaya's chemical manipulations. "And what do these pathetic human bipeds offer Grovian kind?"

"We exist at the pleasure of Gaia, the human's native biosphere. Humans represent her attempt at producing a sentient species."

"She had better try again," interrupted Klemna. "Primate apes appear to be a flawed choice. They even need our mother trees to communicate properly."

And I thought I had used plenty of oxytocin. "Look, Klemna, biospheres take many paths to survival and prosperity," Mother Novaya began, but her explanation terminated mid-sentence. The ground trembled. Mother's tremendous bulk began to sway. Impulses flashed back and forth along her roots and the microbial complexes that annexed the forest into a massive, living network.

"And what makes apes any worse than galloping tree people or giant worm-a-pedes for that matter?" a voice said with authority, like a prophet with a megaphone. "My naked apes went forth and multiplied all over the place before that last lump of asteroid reset the biosphere. Jadderbad is full of worm-a-pedes, according to Hydra, and they're trying to repeat the process here. If your sun hadn't gone nova, Klemna, I suspect Grove would have been covered by herds of ambuli eating each other and trying to pass root rot to forests grown from the seeds of rival clans."

"Who are *you*?" asked Klemna.

"Your worst nightmare," said the voice. "I'm getting fed up with brainy, ego-inflated metazoans—of *all* kinds. They're barely worth the time and energy it takes to evolve them. Bacteria and viruses make much quieter tenants."

The ground shook again. Mother Novaya felt a stab of pain as several sister trees crashed to the ground somewhere in the northern reaches of her network. Deep beneath her, she felt waves of heat as rivers of rock shifted and flowed. Long dormant geysers hissed steam. "Klemna, meet Gaia, our planetary host."

18
Warning rumbles from a supervolcano

Rudy dreamt about his sister Alice. It was long before he had invented the BNA—The Biomic Network Algorithm—that had helped prevent the ecological destruction of 21st century Earth, and made him famous in the process. In the dream, he and Alice were just kids. Alice was playing a trumpet. Odd, because she couldn't even play a kazoo properly. She played a high note and wouldn't stop, no matter how much he yelled. He tried throwing spit wads; then shot her with a squirt gun, but she just kept playing that stupid, eardrum-piercing note...

Rudy woke up and opened his eyes. The trumpet's wail morphed into a warning siren in the cabin of the transport. An amber light blinked on the communication console on the back of the chair directly in front of him.

"What's happening, Great Rudy?" Semma sat to his right in the small section of chairs reserved for human passengers. He heard a few Jadderbadian soldiers behind them in their huge, worm-a-pede recliners jabbering in their native tongue—only some of which shared a common bandwidth with human speech.

"Not sure, Semma—and just call me Rudy, or I'll demand that Nessie revoke your data base privileges."

"Remain seated, passengers." Captain Tork's voice sounded calm over the audio channel, but a little perturbed. "The airport at Belfnik reports an earthquake in progress. The AI pilot informs me that we will circle the city until the tower determines the landing area is safe." The siren stopped, but the amber light continued to blink.

"Oh, an earthquake! Spider Woman described such a phenomenon, and I've seen moving images, but have never experienced one."

Semma looked more excited than worried.

Ah, the ignorance of youth, or perhaps the insanity of a budding young scientist. Rudy tapped the implant near his right ear. It made him feel like a spy in some old NetScape drama. "Nessie old girl, what's the report from Citadel Central about this earthquake underneath us?"

"My sensors detect some potentially serious geological activity in your area, Rudy. That is strange, because it intensified without much warning. Satellite infrared images confirm data from ground-based recorders."

"What kind of serious geological activity?" Rudy frowned. Semma listened intently to his half of the conversation, and looked at him with round, expectant eyes.

"You are familiar, of course, with the ancient supervolcano on top of which the famous Yellowstone National Park of your day resided." Mnemosyne paused a beat.

"Of course," Rudy replied.

"Its showing signs of imminent eruption."

"Imminent? How imminent?" A chill crawled up Rudy's spine. He recalled a quote he had heard somewhere: "Civilization exists by geologic consent, subject to change without notice." Not that there was much of what one might call a civilization on Earth these days.

"Hard to determine, even for me. My sensors indicate months at the low end, perhaps stretching to several years, depending on a number of variables for which I currently possess no data. I would say the chance of it erupting within the next decade approach 97%. I need to re-establish contact with Gaia. She will know more, of course."

"What is Spider Woman saying, Grea... er Rudy?" Now Semma was frowning.

"A supervolcano may pop its cork." Rudy hesitated about how much more to say.

"What is a supervolcano? What is a cork for that matter? We have volcanoes near the Citadel. Are some of them supervolcanoes with weak corks?" Semma looked at him expectantly.

"No, Semma. Take the biggest volcanic eruption Spider Woman

has ever shown you in one of her educational displays, and multiply by 1,000. Human beings only experienced one during their entire evolution, and it almost snuffed us."

"Snuffed? Is that a real verb? It sounds like being snuffed is not good. What would happen if this supervolcano erupts?" Some of Semma's enthusiasm drained away.

Rudy didn't answer immediately. Instead he asked Mnemosyne a question. "The geological hotspot under Yellowstone must have moved some in a million years. Where is it now?"

"The hotspot, of course, doesn't move. The continental plate above it does."

"Yes, yes, but you know what I mean," Rudy sputtered.

"I do. The hotspot demonstrates an apparent motion North and 55^0 East. It has moved 29.7 kilometers in the past million years."

"Not a huge distance then," Rudy muttered. To Semma he said, "An eruption would cover three quarters of this continent in three to six feet of blisteringly hot, corrosive ash. Particulates belched into the atmosphere would act like a sun shield, cooling the entire Earth. The cold snap might linger for years. It would destroy most of the tropical paradise on this continent—and much more, I'm afraid."

Semma opened her mouth to say something, but closed it again for a moment before finally asking, "How far is Tadur from this oversized and soon to be corkless volcano? I have feelings for Tadur, though I sometimes cannot explain why."

"Maybe 5 or so hours by ground transport, if he is still within the alien forest..."

"What do you mean if he is still within the alien forest?"

"Well, Semma, Spider Woman tells me he vanished at some point—along with a rather mysterious human named Ryan who had abducted Tadur and Maxifer—until they were intercepted by a Jadderbadian military patrol. The patrol found only Maxifer in the transport."

"Vanished? How could he just vanish?" Semma looked as confused as Rudy felt. "Not that I'm worried, of course, about such an insensitive, worm-loving, fossil-obsessed person."

"Not worried. Of course. I understand." A grin flickered on Rudy's lips before they compressed into a stoic crease. "I plan to find Tadur—with Spider Woman's help of course—and figure out who this Ryan person is and what he knows about these other aliens." *Without matters getting too messy with the Jadderbadian Confederation nearby,* he added to himself.

Semma blinked. Her eyes glistened, like limpid spheres within moats of almost-tears. "What will we do?" Her voice was almost a whisper.

An appropriate question, thought Rudy. *And one for which I have no answer.*

Semma rubbed her eyes and looked at Rudy as if just inspired by an epiphany. "Surely Spider Woman with all her magic—I mean, science—will be able to find Tadur and this Ryan person. And I know that you are very wise. And the Jadderbadians have great knowledge, and a gateway that goes to other worlds. Perhaps Tadur's mentor, Veltipoe, can help with the Jadderbadian Confederation. Surely *someone* will know what to do about this super volcano. Isn't that right Great Uncle Rudy?"

Rudy might have been tempted to think so, if he was just a few hundred thousand years younger. Age has a way of making you cynical. Rudy took a deep breath and flexed his fingers. One thing he *did* know was that he *loved* this new body. He sure as hell was going to try very hard to keep it from becoming an ashfall mummy.

In the interest of keeping his optimism high, he elected not to ask Nessie for the odds of success.

He looked toward Semma and smiled. He hoped the smile looked suitably wise and enigmatic, because whatever he might say at that moment had no chance of measuring up to what she expected of him.

19
Rescued from detention

“Guard! Where is my representative? He is overdue.” Maxifer shifted his weight from one foot to another as he put his beak near the speaker on the transparent glass separating him from his keeper.

The guard, whom Maxifer thought of as Wilt because of his poor posture, opened one of his three eyes. His mouth pili rippled with annoyance before he spoke. “Not my job to keep track of representatives, human-lover. Maybe earthquake damage has slowed him down. I’ve heard that some roads are impassable. Probably some of the usual potholes became craters.” Wilt closed his eye again. He let his second instar bulk settle into the cushions of his recliner.

Maxifer huffed a blast of air through his spiracles. He returned to the cushion near the wall of his sparely furnished cubicle. He glanced to his right out the one small window available to him. An empty courtyard lay beyond. A huge crack meandered diagonally from an access gate toward the wall of his cell. The recent quake had nearly caused him to dump a load of frass on the floor yesterday. The solid ground had no right to weave and sway like a drunken soldier.

“Do you really think humans are *people*, Firstie?” The guard’s voice made him jump. He had somehow appeared just on the other side of the transparent wall near the speaker. “I have a pet human. A nice little brown-skinned breed with a mop of curly hair. She’s cute, but she certainly couldn’t sing the Songs of the Prophet or perform a smell-a-thon. She barely manages to poop in the proper receptacle.” Wilt scratched the side of his head with one hand while fiddling with the latch of his upper circlet with the two others.

Maxifer sat a little straighter and faced Wilt. “Humans are quite intelligent. My human friend Tadur and I have the same third molt mentor. Tadur grasps most mathematical concepts quickly. While his olfactory sense falls far short of that of Jadderbadians and his audio range is limited, he vastly outperforms Jadderbadian primates."

Wilt huffed dismissively.

"And listen to the background music in your alcove. Mostly human voices, right? Their music, though limited in range, is quite soothing to Jadderbadian physiology."

"But human lives are so short—only about as long as one of our molts. They don't live long enough to learn anything." Wilt poked a finger toward him for emphasis.

"I have studied their language carefully," Maxifer continued. "It allows for the transmission of many more subtleties than you might imagine. The citadel is evidence they once built a complex civilization."

"I know nothing about subtleties. My pet knows a thousand ways to ask for food, I can tell you that. If they're not eating, they're breeding. In fact, just the other day…" Wilt began, but he was interrupted by the buzz of the communicator pad on the desk next to his recliner. He left to answer it.

Maxifer couldn't hear the conversation that transpired, but Wilt returned to the wall to report. "You're in luck, human-lover. Not only has your representative arrived, he's brought someone with him to vouch for you. We may part ways today." Wilt passed methane-laden gas from his frasshole as he returned to his station.

An hour or more dragged by. Who was with his representative? Most likely, Mentor Veltipoe. Maxifer rehearsed his list of excuses, hoping they—along with the right mix of pheromones—would mellow the Master's mood.

They didn't.

* * * * *

"How *could* you, Maxifer?" Master Veltipoe's exoskeleton shimmered in shades of orange and red. His scent could only be described as musky. "Stealing my personal transport to go off hunting fossils in a no-persons' land between the Confederation, Jadaman City, and the Great Forest: That is unthinkable for a Firstie of your intelligence—especially given your role as custodian of a human student."

"As Tadur explained in his message, we merely planned to borrow the transport for a few days. We were celebrating…"

"You were celebrating disrespect as far as I can smell." Master Veltipoe bent over Maxifer like a tree about to fall. He sniffed near Maxifer's nearest scent gland; then slowly rose back to his full third instar height and waited for an apology.

Maxifer obliged, more or less. "I'm sorry, Master that you felt disrespected. Your treatise about the ancient geology of this area so inspired us that we wanted to find and excavate some representative fossils. And we succeeded, or almost did…"

"Until you didn't. And quit trying to grease my cuticle. " Veltipoe's outer colors shifted toward their standard blend of blues and greens. "I'm not going to argue about your transgressions right now. Matters of more substance are taking place—and we must still find Tadur and discover the full extent of his misdeeds. He can be a troublesome human."

"Yes, Master." Maxifer paused a respectful moment. "What matters of substance are taking place?"

"For one thing, the human called Rudyard Albert Goldstein will be landing at the Belfnik airport soon. And for another thing…"

"The human known as Rudy? The human half of the famous Rudimort!" Maxifer suddenly remembered his training. "My apologies for interrupting, Master."

"Yes, that Rudy."

"But he died long ago."

"The AI in the ancient human citadel has managed to… resurrect him, you might say… in an actual human body. I'm impressed. Even our biologists would be hard-pressed to accomplish that."

"What does he want in Belfnik?" Maxifer flickered in shades of amber and green.

"He has connections to Tadur through knowing his great grandfather Twill. Somehow Mnemosyne, the human AI, has other concerns regarding Tadur's abduction by another strange human."

It must be the one called Ryan, thought Maxifer.

Veltipoe offered two of his middle segment arms to Maxifer. "Get up off that cushion. We will meet this Rudy at the airport before returning to Jadaman City."

The lights in the detention cell flickered. The room swayed for a moment. Alarms in the guard's alcove sounded.

"That's assuming, of course," Veltipoe continued, "the earth doesn't swallow us first."

20
Mnemosyne's research

The Jadderbadian military transport circled Belfnik airport for some time. Semma managed to fall asleep. For such a slender young woman she possessed the snore of a lumberjack. Rudy had closed his eyes, and was just beginning to dream about a hive of angry bees, when Nessie startled him awake.

"I have some interesting news, Rudy. Rudy, are you conscious?"

"I am now. What news?" Rudy rubbed his eyes.

"One of my satellite drones reports detecting a plane traveling west from the Eurasian continent headed in your general direction."

"A plane did you say? Something of Jadderbadian manufacture?"

"No. That is what I find interesting. The drone sent images. I've checked them against my databases. The plane appears to be of Boeing manufacture—perhaps a descendant of an old 21st century spy plane design, like the SR-72 model."

"How is that possible?" Rudy was fully awake now.

"I cannot say without more information. However, my ground sensors and bots in and around the alien tree forest near your location have sampled Grovian DNA. As we've discussed, organic biochemistry shares many similarities and congruities from world to world, but remains unique. I searched for records of Grovian DNA sequences in any scientific publications from your era. Some interesting work turned up by a Nelson Thompson during the latter stages of the plague years. He published a paper outlining research with DNA sequences specific to Grovian life forms."

"I don't remember the name. I used to follow the literature…"

"Thompson published in a small online journal, although his work seemed quite sound. At any rate," Mnemosyne continued, "I searched for background information on Thompson. He had a son named Ryan, apparently a paleontologist..."

"A long shot, Nessie, but there could be a connection. Could that Ryan really be the Ryan we are dealing with a *million* years later—or at least a relative? And what connection does that have to the plane?"

"I do not know, Rudy, but all vectors seem to be pointing to one location."

"All roads leading to Rome—or at least a now-tropical Montana. When I do find this Ryan and Tadur—assuming I can do it before the world blows up—I might have company."

"I expect so, Rudy."

Semma's snoring stopped when she shifted position in her chair. Rudy sighed in relief.

"One other thing, Nessie: What's the dirt on this Master Veltipoe I'm supposed to work with?"

"Let me summarize his 'dirt,' as you so colorfully put it. Veltipoe is an academic, not unlike Master Morticue. You may enjoy his company. He believes that Jadderbadians and humans are co-equals who should work together. He specializes in both human and Jadderbadian biology, as well as geology and paleontology. He has mentored both Tadur and Maxifer since their respective births. At the moment, he is not happy with his students running off to the hinterlands, but he is certainly anxious to locate Tadur."

Before Rudy could comment, Captain Tork announced their rapidly approaching landing at Belfnik.

Semma managed to open one eye. "Whazzup?"

"We're landing soon, my precocious Maid Marian. Let's go find your insensitive, truant, fossil-hunting boyfriend."

21
Siyan in Chamber

So many delicious sensory inputs! Siyan aroused to full awareness, touching the various personalities interconnected via Mother Novaya. Klemna possessed a kind of rigid, inflexible heat, like a missile that, once ignited, could only go at one speed in one direction. The human, Tadur, felt like a fizzing nexus of energy—a young form waiting for focus and direction. Siyan didn't quite know how to regard his parents: Ryan, Siu, and Guardian—Siu's caretaker AI. They each endured pain to gestate him—a circumstance common to parentage, as best he could tell. One has to hope the joys of conception compensated them for their troubles. Siyan supposed that those joys seemed like a good idea at the time.

And Gaia! Siyan perceived the complex synergy of a googolplex of living parts co-evolving for billions of years. How magnificent! But almost as soon as he touched the entity, she disappeared from the group as quickly as a burst bubble.

"A planetary host? A conscious entity derived from the living interconnections of a biosphere? That's nonsense," declared Klemna.

"Obviously, it is not," observed Mother Novaya. "I'm sure you felt her presence."

"And she's pissed." Skeets paused a moment. "What's with the earthquake? Are we supposed to assume cause and effect here? Is Gaia rattling our cage, so to speak?"

"I surmise that Gaia has helped to stimulate some natural forces long in play in the vicinity of a once-dormant, massive volcano. We are approaching some sort of nexus point—leading to a spray of possible futures." Siyan surveyed space and time the way that perhaps only he could: the past a catacomb filled with events interlaced like silken threads; the future a diaphanous skein of potentials illuminated by a snowflake of light...

"I want out of here. You are all a bunch of abominations!" Klemna, fully in charge of Tadur's body now, thrashed and squirmed.

"Ouch! You are worse than a birthing ambulus," Mother Novaya complained. "Perhaps we can try again later. The earth tremors have subsided for the moment."

"We should convene the Council to talk about options," Skeets offered. "You can send the message, Mother Novaya. The Council chambers are not far from here. That Jadderbadian military force is en route. Ryan told me he expects the ancient AI the humans in Jadaman City call Spider Woman to make contact somehow. And we have a miffed global intelligence wrinkling her hide like a rataphant trying to get rid of fleas. That should make for a stimulating agenda."

"I want out!" Klemna repeated.

And so Mother Novaya's tendrils withdrew from the three human bodies. Her pods unsealed; Siyan and Skeets dressed and helped Klemna re-clothe Tadur's body. They descended Mother Novaya's trunk. A mild aftershock provided a sense of urgency.

"I need to meet this Spider Woman," Siyan said to Skeets as they escorted Klemna/Tadur down a well-worn path that meandered between the massive trunks of the Mother Tree Forest. "She is an entity not unlike the Guardian at the core of my own existence."

Skeets agreed. They talked back and forth discussing how that might happen, shepherding Klemna like a half-drunken prisoner between them, but not paying her the attention she deserved. They paid for their distraction near the top of a ridge.

Klemna tripped Skeets, who tumbled off the side of the ridge and rolled downslope. Klemna then yanked on Siyan/Ryan's arm with surprising strength, causing him to tumble after Skeets. Klemna fled in the opposite direction. Siyan heard her yell "Abominaaaations!" on her way, the sound fading like a Doppler-shifted train whistle from ages past.

22
Tadur takes control

Later, Tadur had a hard time remembering exactly when he first managed to suppress Klemna's personality and take control of his own body. It was sometime after the mad dash from Mother Novaya's trunk when Klemna panicked, but the actual transition point was unclear. Tadur had paid attention when the entity called Siu had instructed Klemna on how to control her human host. The instructions worked in both directions. Tadur had also absorbed something from the close interaction when everyone "went to chamber," as they called it.

However it happened, it felt good when Klemna's personality succumbed to his will. It felt a little like wrestling with Maxifer when they were both younger. Before Maxifer got his growth spurt, Tadur could climb atop his squirming and twisting friend until he tired. Only then would Maxifer let Tadur "ride" him around Veltipoe's courtyard, sometimes stomping through Veltipoe's carefully manicured garden. Now Tadur found himself running around the pillar-like trunks of mother trees, realizing he was tired, hungry, and confused.

Tadur stopped running and took deep breaths. His lungs filled with the loamy, earthen smells of the forest. Where was Maxifer? He must find Maxifer. He might be an obnoxious worm-a-pede sometimes, but Tadur felt his absence like the ache of an extracted tooth.

Tadur surveyed surreal memories of his time in the transport, as if they belonged to someone else. Then, those memories blinked away to be replaced by equally clouded memories of strange humans in an even more bizarre forest composed of the tree-like stages of some alien life cycle. If he understood correctly what he had absorbed from his time in the alien pod, the four-legged forms, like the one on which the human called Ryan Thompson had ridden, mated with each other to produce seeds that then grew into asexual trees like Mother Novaya. Those trees, in turn, produced more four-legged ambuli to perpetuate the cycle.

And he thought the Jadderbadian metamorphosis from worm-a-pede to flying adult was confusing! He could almost sympathize with Klemna's screaming declaration of "abominations." Almost. He respected Jadderbadians—most of them anyway. Mentor Veltipoe was strong and wise. Maxifer was his best friend. The ghostly, pale-skinned Ryan and his mate Skeets seemed basically kind—when they weren't kidnapping people, at least—and they had formed part-nerships with the tree people called Siu and Ito. Perhaps these tree people could also be trusted—at least some of them.

And the memories of Ryan and Skeets, though Tadur couldn't experience them in detail, carried an immense bulk like a mountain range partly hidden by clouds. He sensed they stretched into the deep past, perhaps as far back as the legendary Great Rudy.

He wasn't quite sure what to feel about the entity called Siyan—except the glimmerings of fear. But then, Spider Woman could be scary too.

Thinking of Spider Woman made him think of Semma. Semma made him tremble as well—though not usually from fear. He hoped Semma was happy learning about the mysteries of the world from Spider Woman.

Which way was Jadaman City from this forest? Tadur looked up, but could see only flecks of blue through the shifting canopy of fluttering leaves. Master Veltipoe had mentioned something about the mysterious forest to the southwest. So that meant he must travel northeast to find Jadaman City. On what side of trees does moss grow? Surely, the Jadderbadian Confederation would eventually let Maxifer go home. Wouldn't they?

Tadur leaned against the nearest tree, and let his body slide down its length until his butt addressed solid, if spongy-damp, ground. He closed his eyes. He felt the stirrings of Klemna in his mind like a restless sleeper. He would gather strength, find some wild onions or tubers to chew on, locate a reservoir of water at the base of one of the bromeliads he had seen, and...

"Perhaps I can help," whispered a soft, conspiratorial voice—one that sounded as if it was right behind him.

23
Arrival at Belfnik

" There they are." Master Veltipoe pointed using one middle segment arm, while fondling his circlet fasteners with a second arm, and pushing Maxifer gently forward with a third. Being a frontier destination, Belfnik only possessed a triad of passenger terminals. A graphic logo of the Thunderclub Clan adorned the portal of the one marked for military transports. It depicted an adult winged Thunderclub male in ostentatious and archaic chain mail. Overlapping images of Jadderbad and Earth floated behind.

Two humans had just emerged from the exit tunnel. The bulkier, pale-skinned male wore a blue body suit and marched with a swagger not unlike one Tadur sometimes adopted after swiping the last after-dinner treat on the tray. The female, though perhaps younger — Maxifer had a hard time judging age in humans — stood nearly as tall, but was dark and slender, like most human primates he knew. "The strutting blue one must be the Great Rudy." Maxifer felt dumb just stating the obvious in front of Master Veltipoe, so also asked, "Do we need to bow? Should I emit appeasement scents? What are the proper cuticle colors to flash at this meeting, mentor?"

"Though some uneducated Jadderbadians have elevated this Rudy to near deity status, he is but another human — though purportedly one smarter than most, and of ancient vintage. Treat him as you would me, Maxifer." Veltipoe released a squirt of warning pheromone. "Perhaps with just a bit more reserve." He winked one eye, probably to lighten the impact of the pheromone and imply good humor.

"Yes, mentor."

The two parties met in an empty greeting circle, whose amber tones were well scuffed from the feet of visitors past. Their entry into the circle activated the usual cone of silence that blocked out other distractions in the terminal. "Master Veltipoe, I presume." The pale human extended his right palm forward and waved it back and forth. "I am Rudy. This young lady is Semma." He gestured toward his female companion. "Greetings from Mnemosyne." He looked up at Veltipoe. He then turned to Maxifer. "Greetings from Spider Woman."

"I am pleased to meet you, Master Rudy." Veltipoe flickered in shades of blue and violet. "You must be enjoying your new… incarnation… your new form."

"Ah, you can't imagine!" Rudy's gaze flickered between Veltipoe and Maxifer. "You must be Maxifer... Tadur's friend."

Maxifer made his first-day-with-the-mentor bow. "I am honored." He turned toward Semma. "I am honored to meet Tadur's object of lust and affection."

"Tadur's what?" The human female's facial pads turned crimson.

"Did I misspeak?" Maxifer turned one eye toward Veltipoe, and flickered with appeasing shades of blue.

The earth trembled. Amber warning lights around the terminal began to blink.

"Just an aftershock, I believe." Master Veltipoe turned his attention to Rudy. "But let's go to our transport, and get started toward Jadaman City. We can discuss our options for finding young Tadur as we travel."

And so they did.

24
On the way to Jadaman City

Master Veltipoe sat next to Rudy in the ground transport they rented in Jadaman City—at an exorbitant price, considering that a volcano fumed not far away. The R72 spiderbot followed behind in the too small field transport that Tadur and Maxifer had "borrowed." His pupils would have to work off the impound fee, assuming everyone survived this adventure. Maxifer sat next to Semma in the back. The AI-guided transport threaded its way through the outskirts of Belfnik. The path became circuitous to avoid crews repairing earthquake-damaged roads and buildings.

Master Veltipoe struggled to control his colors and scents. He felt embarrassed that Rudy, the genius human who had merged with Master Morticue Ambergrand during his final days, would not see Jadderbadians at their best. Here in Belfnik, humans—still referred to as groupies—served as pets and slaves. Many of them in various breeds and genetic variations crawled over ruined buildings with AI repair units and Jadderbadian supervising patrols.

"So, Master Veltipoe, Nessie—Mnemosyne—has filled me in regarding the quakes. Do you know about supervolcanoes and what they can do? What kind of help and support can either Jadaman City or the Jadderbadian Confederation provide if things go south in a hurry?" Rudy looked up at him with that little pair of human eyes that were so charming.

"Supervolcanoes are not my specialty, you understand, Master Rudy, but I do know something about them. Jadderbad has active crustal plates as well. Our species avoided extinction via supervolcano eruption, just as your species did during its prehistoric phase." Veltipoe paused to gather his thoughts. He fidgeted with a clasp on his upper circlet. "Jadderbadian technology certainly can't control such violence. Could humans, during their period of dominance on this planet?" Veltipoe paused a beat again. "Why would things—as you say—go south as opposed to north or some other direction?"

"Pardon my idioms, old boy. To 'go south' means to deteriorate quickly. An active super volcano could unwind the mortal coils of humans *and* Jadderbadians on good old Mother Earth. And no, humans had no control of such monumental forces either." Rudy scratched his head. Another endearing humanism. "Well, we might as well set aside that problem for the moment. If the volcano erupts, we can all kiss our nether regions goodbye. We best focus on how to recover Tadur, and hope we have the time to do it."

"Agreed. We will discuss kissing our nether regions later." Veltipoe wished a translator was available to understand this human better. "Regarding Tadur's location: What can you tell me about his disappearance? I understand that Mnemosyne—your ancient AI associate—has sophisticated surveillance capabilities. Did she witness the abduction?"

"That she did, Veltipoe. As you are probably aware by now, the forest southwest of Jadaman City represents another alien presence on my old planet—one apparently established in the deep past. A human named Ryan Thompson, we believe—someone like me from humanity's halcyon days—has connections to these mysterious aliens. Tadur almost certainly is in that forest somewhere, but it's a big place."

"Does your AI friend know where?"

Before Rudy could answer, Semma tapped on the back of his seat. "How long until we arrive at this Jadaman City place, Uncle Rudy? I haven't eaten since early this morning. I slept most of the way on the air transport."

Master Veltipoe partly turned and swiveled one eye toward Maxifer. "Show Semma where to find food and water in the armrest compartments."

Maxifer nodded an agreement and leaned toward Semma to comply.

96

Rudy answered Veltipoe's earlier question. "No, but she has drones buzzing around in the forest. They should find something soon. Maybe we'll know more before we arrive at Jadaman city."

"That's food?" muttered Semma in the back seat. "Looks like something for dogs."

"Apologies, Honorable Guest," said Maxifer. "The vehicle must have been stocked by the local Jadderbadians." Maxifer's colors flickered in apologetic shades of pink. "I'm sure it's quite nutritious, though. It appears to be the highest quality of groupie—er, human—kibble."

"We'll be in Jadaman city in just a few hours," said Veltipoe. "We know how to feed humans properly there." *At least Tadur never complained.* Veltipoe expelled air with a sigh through his spiracles. *He did so hope they would find his errant student soon. Both Tadur and Maxifer need to understand how important their symbiotic merger could be to everyone's survival.*

25
Forest encounter

Tadur jumped to his feet at the sound of the voice near his ear offering help. He felt something crawling on his neck, and attempted to slap it, but missed. A buzzing object a little smaller than a dragonfly circled his head. "Let me land again," a voice said, "and I will explain. I am the eyes and ears of Spider Woman." The direction of the sound shifted with the circling bug. Tadur remembered that Semma had once told him that Spider Woman had such servants, much like those of the Jadderbadians.

"Where do you wish to land, Spider Woman?" Tadur tried to track the buzzing creature with his eyes, but it moved quickly.

"Your right shoulder will be fine."

"Land then, and explain how you will help me. I need to find my friend. I need to control an alien presence in my mind." Tadur paused a moment. "And I really need to pee. Land on my shoulder while I take care of first things first."

Tadur watered the forest floor while Spider Woman landed on his shoulder. "I will guide you toward Jadaman City," the voice near his ear said. "Mentor Veltipoe has taken custody of Maxifer in Belfnik. They met Rudy Goldstein and Semma there, and are traveling toward Jadaman City."

"Rudy Goldstein? The Great Rudy of lore? And Semma? Semma has traveled with him?"

"You heard correctly."

Tadur also heard—and felt—a deep rumble, as if he were standing on the hide of a great beast. Another earthquake. A relatively mild one. He heard hissing somewhere to his right, and turned in the direction of the sound. A geyser of steam whistled up from the forest floor a hundred meters away, tossing leaves and litter into the air. "Is the earth angry, Spider Woman? How dangerous will our journey be?"

"With regard to your first question: you are not far from the truth. Your second question is harder to answer. Several forms of danger lie ahead. I do not have enough data to calculate the odds of our personal risk, but we need to reunite with friends to reduce that danger. At this point, moving toward Jadaman City appears to offer the best chances for survival—if we act now."

"I vote for acting now." Tadur took a deep breath.

"Follow that animal trail that meanders just to the right of where the geyser spouted. I will lead the way." With that pronouncement, the winged bug that Tadur began to think of as Spider Fly left his right shoulder and flickered in the dappled sunlight filtering through the forest canopy.

It felt good to be moving again—this time with a friendly guide. His alien parasite remained subdued and quiet within him, somewhat like a half digested, and not quite agreeable, meal.

They traveled quickly for some time, more or less following the game trail. Enormous mother trees with their strange trunk pods alternated with varieties Tadur recognized from near Jadaman City. Tadur found water to drink at the base of bromeliad stems, and harvested a few familiar plants, but he would be happy to consume a good ratalope steak when he arrived home. Here and there sulfurous pools of water bubbled like a shaman's brew. In places, steam puffed from vents of mud that resembled puckering lips. Spider Fly flickered like a winged gem ahead of him most of the time, sometimes arcing back to circle him like a gadfly. The sun peeked between the forest leaves as it journeyed across the afternoon sky.

"I'm moving as fast as I can, Spider Fly," he said during one such fly-around.

"You are doing fine, Tadur. I am just measuring your vital signs. I know you are tiring. We may need to find a suitable place to spend the night before finishing our trip."

"Really? We have that far to go?" Tadur stopped a moment to sit on an inviting rock with a butt-sized depression that served as a comfortable seat. Loamy dirt smells here masked the aroma of sulfur from the last burbling pool. Disturbed soil caught Tadur's attention in a patch of moist dirt a yard or so away. He pointed to it. "Is that an animal track over there, Spider Fly?"

The drone, which had perched briefly on Tadur's shoulder, flew away to investigate. "It is a track, and one from a creature we had best avoid."

Tadur rose to join Spider Fly as it circled the depression in the mud. "Such a strange print with parallel grooves and distinct rounded edges. It seems about the size of a man's foot, but not like any moccasin prints I've ever seen."

"That's because it's based on a foot gear template created nearly a million years ago. We don't wish to meet the human body that made it." Spider Fly made one more circle and landed on Tadur's right shoulder. "Perhaps we should travel a little faster and further than I had intended today."

26
A plan evolves

"Are you sure you're all right?"

Skeets looked into Ryan's eyes, trying to decide just whose question she was answering. Sometimes, when Siyan took charge, it was hard to tell. Skeets slapped dust off her breeches. "Just shattered pride, I think. We should have been paying more attention to Klemna."

"No argument there."

Ryan smiled, and she knew she was looking at the paleo nerd she had fallen in love with—at least for the moment. "What now, Thompson?" She looked down the path they had been following before they had been tossed downslope. "Klemna must have a good lead on us by now."

"Let's go back to Mother Novaya. She can track the escapee with her network of mother trees better than the human members of the Council."

Now Ryan's eyes looked glazed with that drunk-on-alien-possession look she had come to recognize when the composite entity of Siyan took charge. Ryan would be like a traveling observer for a while. *Oh well, that was part of his rascally charm.* "Agreed. I'll let the Council know later what happened."

Siyan could be both exhilarating and scary. Without the merger of Ryan, his alien parasite Siu, and Guardian—the AI that had preserved the personality and memories of Siu over geologic eternities—Skeets knew she would have died from the rogue flu virus that Rondal/Ito had created to destroy the human race. But any creature that could meander down the corridors of space and time rated as scary in anyone's book. That was the surprise ability created during the unique, three-part union. Siyan had neutralized the virus by going back in time to access the original incarnation of Ito—a person undistorted by thousands of years of trying to find his long-lost mate, Siu, while consuming human hosts like strips of beef jerky. That original Ito was now a part of her, while Rhondal/Ito was dead. Or was he? The original Ito was smart and outspoken, with a heart much bigger than his physical body had been. Skeets could relate to that Ito.

But Rhondal/Ito had once had another back-up copy of himself—a clone rumored to exist somewhere on the Asian continent of her time.

After Skeets and Ryan reached Mother Novaya's familiar trunk, they quickly went to chamber. As Mother Novaya's filaments caressed their two physical bodies, old memories flickered like stills from a familiar movie: Working with Ryan in his grandfather's mosasaur quarry, dealing with Ryan's nearly overpowering infection by Siu when he discovered her engram capsule among the mosasaur's ribs, fending off her own father during the bad nights when booze got the best of him... Ryan had been so kind, and understanding. She remembered the rush of their multiple personality "marriage" mediated by Mother Novaya so long ago. She wished she could have savored the memory longer, but earth tremors soon reminded them of the looming geological emergency. "Where did Klemna run off to?" she asked Mother Novaya.

"Actually, Tadur has now taken control of his human body from Klemna," said Mother Novaya. "Mother Prudensa sensed the change when he leaned against her during a rest break. He also made contact with the entity called Mnemosyne via one of her drones. He is now moving in the direction of Jadaman City, but he may have a problem."

"What kind of problem?" Skeets recognized the unique tone of Siyan asking the question, though she felt the blends of Ryan and Siu's personalities too, like the rich aftertaste of a fine wine.

"The last incarnation of Ito—the current Ito Prime—from before the great celestial disaster that destroyed human civilization and forced my Mother Tree forest into deep hibernation."

"That copy of Ito in Asia was real? He survived? I had hoped the asteroid strike had vaporized him along with what we had called civilization. He's somewhere nearby?" Skeets shivered. She remembered clearly the ruthless drive of the last Ito Prime—Rhondal/Ito. He may have been Siu's First Mate, but with a lover like that, a person would need body armor before taking a roll in the hay.

"He did survive. I can feel his presence in the network." Siyan sounded distracted; lost in the forest gestalt coordinated by Mother Novaya. "What drives him now? Can he still be in search of Siu?"

"And, of course, the Jadderbadian military force is still moving towards us," Mother Novaya added. "The earthquakes slowed them down, but they didn't reverse course."

"I need to consult with Mnemosyne." Siyan made it sound like an urgent demand. "She will be the most powerful agent to confront—or appease—Gaia." His eyes softened for a moment, and Ryan peeked through.

"No problem, Thompson." Skeets said it with more confidence than she felt. *You have me to help*, added Ito. *This other version of me is still me—just one that traveled a different path. Who better to understand a distorted personality than the undistorted original version?* Skeets could hear the irony in her alien companion's words. Skeets felt like laughing herself. Talk about rampant schizophrenia…

"I hope to be back quickly," Siyan said as he began disengaging from Mother Novaya's embrace.

Skeets began separating from Mother Novaya as well, preparing to emerge from the pod. "I'll rally the council members, and anyone else free to help. We have a few tricks hidden under our loin cloths that the Jadderbadians may find interesting."

"*I've* always found those tricks interesting, love."

"Not *those* tricks, Thompson! I've got more lethal ones that you've never seen."

The bodies of Ryan Thompson and Skeets Moleckson descended the trunk of Mother Novaya. To some hypothetical observer it might have looked like two human primates descending a monstrous tree—until one of them blinked out of existence. No puff of smoke needed—if you are a composite entity that can travel at will down the corridors of space and time, that is.

27
Gods and High Priests

S iyan could never quite figure out just how space and time traveling worked. He decided it was just one of those abilities you
either had or didn't have—like Ryan's flair for painting and
sketching, and Siu's ability to tell other people what to do. Guardian had a talent for exceeding his programing. Somehow, as one
composite entity, they could slide along filaments of spacetime like a
spider walks her web. It did take energy. A person could get lost. But
that didn't happen this time. Siyan found the filaments connecting
Mother Novaya's forest and the citadel and plucked them correctly.
He materialized at the citadel's base in front of a tall, somewhat
portly human wearing elaborate headgear.

The rotund human's eyes grew wide just before they closed
completely, and the human crumpled to the ground like a deflated
balloon.

Siyan consulted his component parts.

Guardian: *Is this human dead?*

Ryan: *Just fainted. I believe we scared the crap out of him, as my
grandfather Pops might have said.*

Siu: *Is he an official of some kind, do you suppose? He appears
rather elaborately dressed.*

Ryan: *Perhaps a priest or a king, is my guess. He's dressed to
impress, but failed in this instance. I suggest we wait until his blood
pressure rises again. Perhaps he'll think he imagined that we blinked
into existence.*

Ryan's prediction proved accurate, more or less. The human
groaned; then opened his eyes. The eyes blinked several times as if
verifying what they were seeing. The human crawled a few yards
away, and then scrambled to his feet. He made gestures with his

hands, as if leading a chorus or swatting flies. "What form of spirit are you? Stay back or I, Botza, High Priest of the Grand Interstellar Union, will summon Spider Woman to smite you."

Siyan: *I'm deferring to you, Ryan, as the best qualified spokesperson. I'm still uncertain about responding to certain manifestations of human behavior.*

Ryan stood a little straighter, and tried to summon some of Siu's natural hubris. "Spider Woman is just who we want to see. Tell her Ryan Thompson has come to visit. She'll know who I am."

Botza straightened his headgear and took a deep breath. His eyes narrowed. He seemed to be recovering from his initial shock. "You startled me. How did you get past the perimeter guards? You say Spider Woman will know you?"

"She will," declared Ryan, ignoring the first question. He stepped closer to Botza, who stepped back in turn, as if they were dancing. "And she will be displeased with anyone who delays my visit."

The High Priest made one final effort at bravery. "You are pale-skinned like the Great Rudy. Are you one of his Angel Guardians?"

"I'm part Guardian, all right. Announce me to Spider Woman with that little spider drone hanging around your neck. Let's get this show on the road."

Botza fingered the drone nervously. "Oh, Great Spider Woman. Forgive the interruption. Someone calling himself Ryan Thompson wishes to speak to you. He talks about some demonstration on a road. Do you know him? If not, I will..."

"Bring him to me, Botza." Ryan heard the feminine voice clearly. "Show him to my image in the entrance foyer before you leave."

* * * * *

Botza led Ryan into the Citadel. He made a show of mumbling some incantation and tossing amber pollen into the air before touching a spot near the entrance. The door hissed open. He looked disappointed when Ryan didn't react to the ceremony. Botza took Ryan to a dark alcove and gestured toward an image on the wall, which promptly bloomed into colored, three-dimensional life.

Ryan laughed.

High Priest Botza looked stricken.

"Thank you, Botza," said the buxom image on the wall.

Botza hesitated a moment, but the thank you was his cue to leave. He did.

"Wow," said Ryan. "I haven't seen an image of Spider Woman since watching old holovids when I was a kid. Nice touch, Mnemosyne. That is your name, correct?"

"Very good, Ryan—if I may call you that. I'm sure we haven't met before, although you have been teasing me by smiling at my drones and snatching my friends. And yes, I've found the Spider Woman image resonates with many humans—especially young males."

Ryan smiled. "I remember hearing rumors about an AI linked to the death of Rudy Goldstein, but I was a bit busy in those days. Disruptions from the plague years messed up politics and government services for a long time. My dad and I established ties to the Grovians and performed some basic research in near isolation for a while."

"I understand. The GeneMod wars that ultimately led to the Martian colonies took place during those times as well. I poured my attention and resources into establishing the Citadel. I failed to notice you and your father's work until quite recently—a gross negligence on my part. Then the asteroid strike voided human civilization. I'm glad you found me, Ryan Thompson. You remind me of my human companion and friend, Rudy."

"I'll take that as a compliment," said Ryan. "Rudy's algorithm did so much to heal an ailing world. I very much want to meet Rudy—preferably before the world explodes. But I need to introduce you to my alter ego, Siyan. He's anxious to meet another AI/human hybrid with a long-term mission to complete."

"I am anxious to meet him as well. Communicating with humans can be entertaining at times, but monumentally slow and tedious."

Ryan laughed. "Then let's not dally. I'd hate to slow the action when two AIs need to bond." Ryan receded to the background of his composite awareness while Siyan surged forward.

28
The wonders of Veltipoe's academy

Semma, Rudy, Master Veltipoe, and Maxifer passed through the outskirts of Belfnik to where the road narrowed and turned to hard-packed dirt. Trees closed in around them *like the rain hood on my favorite cloak back home*, thought Semma. She pressed her nose to the glass of the transport's rear door. *The leaves have drip tips! That's typical for tropical plants.* Semma felt proud of her arcane knowledge gleaned from the many hours she had spent with Mnemosyne. Spider Woman had confided to her that Mnemosyne was her real name, given to her long ago in the deep-before- time by someone called Marvin Rodnesky—the time of Great Rudy. She shivered even though the transport was warm, trying to imagine a million years and all the flickering moments of living those years represented.

"How long before we reach Jadaman City?" Maxifer shifted his weight next to her. His hide flickered with color like images of sea creatures Mnemosyne had shown her. He smelled like spicy wet leather. Semma had learned to distinquish some Jadderbadian scents while growing up, but it was difficult. Mnemosyne said humans just didn't have the right olfactory receptors for some things. Spicy wet leather smell, though, meant Maxifer was a little nervous, like she was.

Semma closed the armrest tray with the groupie chow. It had silenced the grumbling in her stomach, but it had about as much flavor as porridge cooked with water and left to dry in the sun. *How could some Jadderbadians treat humans like pet dogs?* She leaned back against the cushions and must have fallen asleep. She popped awake at the sound of Rudy's voice.

"Hey! Impressive digs, old worm. There must be a good stone

quarry nearby."

"Uh, yes, there is in fact."

Veltipoe sounded a little confused. Understandable. Rudy said lots of peculiar words, and often failed to use correct titles. Semma tried to puzzle out the Jadderbadian writing above the portal, but Rudy beat her to it.

"Veltipoe's Academy for Symbiotic Studies & Jaddaman Integrative Facilitation." Rudy laughed. "Hope you don't mind, Veltipoe, but I'll just call your place VASSJIF. Every ponderous institution needs an acronym."

"Ah, yes, of course." Veltipoe passed some air through his spiracles in a Jadderbadian sigh. "VASSJIF," he repeated. "I am quite proud of what Jadderbadians and humans have built here. I do hope we can find some way to preserve our work."

"I hear you."

Semma thought that comment should be obvious, especially for a genius. She pulled her travel bag close to her, and admired Veltipoe's tall building while the transport moved to a parking area near the main door.

Veltipoe led them through the outer portal of the building. He made a perfunctory bow toward a bust of Kranium, the Jadderbadian ambassador who had first passed through the stargate from Jadderbad to Earth nearly a hundred years ago. Semma still marveled at how long Jadderbadians live. Kranium had known the legendary scholar Morticue before he and Great Rudy merged as Rudimort. Veltipoe then ushered them through enormous glass doors to a room filled with wonders!

The rows upon rows of huge books snagged Semma's attention first. She had seen images of human book libraries in Mnemosyne's records, but the massive bulk of so many volumes scaled to the size of Jadderbadians, and filled with the recorded knowledge of ages past, still awed her.

Rudy walked over to the nearest shelf and pointed to one book whose spine shimmered with iridescent colors. He turned to look at Veltipoe. "May I?"

"Of course." Veltipoe stepped closer to Rudy. "It may be heavy. I would be happy to assist."

"Let me give it a try. I haven't had a chance to use my new young body much yet." Rudy slid the volume off the shelf using two hands. Maxifer hovered near Rudy as if anticipating a disaster. Rudy grunted as he maneuvered the volume's mass to a nearby table apparently designed for reading, but managed without assistance. He opened the book and scrunched up his nose.

"Those colored patches near some characters release odors when rubbed to amplify the message—for Jadderbadians at least." Veltipoe leaned in and pointed using one middle segment arm and finger. "

Rudy smiled. "Ah, scratch and sniff technology. Got it." He leaned closer to an image. "Nice clear images, too with subtle color shifts, and a 3D effect. Holographs or something similar? Impressive."

"Thank you." Veltipoe nodded. "I do love real books in spite of their bulk. But let me show you some other things quickly before I check my information center for possible word about Tadur." Veltipoe directed everyone toward an adjoining room, which reminded Semma of one of Mnemosyne's robotic laboratories. Cages and tanks holding a mix of animals and plants, both terrestrial and aquatic, dominated nearly half the room, including shelving on two walls. Workspace platforms filled much of the floor space, some scaled for Jadderbadians, and others designed for humans. Mysterious looking equipment shining like polished silver made Semma's eyes stretch wide.

Veltipoe pointed to a granite rock perched on one work platform. "We study all the ways living things work together here at my academy…"

"Like those lichens!" Semma interrupted. "I love lichens." She moved closer to the chunk of granite to get a better look. "Mnemosyne told me all about them—how fungi and algae team up. One or more species of algae make food from sunlight and carbon dioxide and fungi create acids to dissolve the rock and ward off dangerous microbes."

"Exactly!" Veltipoe's facial pili wiggled like worms with an itch, and the protective membranes around his eyes contracted to expose more facets. "And think of the forests all around us. They are not just made up of individual trees…"

"Networks of fungi help nurture and interconnect them. Isn't that right, Mentor Veltipoe? I read in Mnemosyne's databases about ectomycorrhizal fungi that live outside tree roots and the arbuscular mycorrhizal kind that live within root tissue." Semma frowned. "I believe tropical forests have more of the arbuscular kind. I wonder how it works in this strange new alien forest?"

Veltipoe grinned, exposing his tooth barbs. "Good question! You would make a wonderful Academy student, Semma."

Semma flushed with pride. "I do like learning new things."

"I can see why Tadur likes you," Maxifer added. "He's always babbling strange, science-speak words and pestering the Master about one thing or another…"

"There's nothing wrong with being descriptively precise, Maxifer." Veltipoe wriggled a few eye pili at his student. "It wouldn't hurt you to learn a bit more 'science-speak.' But let me complete what I started to say. Living things work together at least as much as they compete with each other—on Earth as on Jadderbad. Ecosystems are nothing but immense networks of living interactions, not only between creatures big enough to see, but also between wee beasties that need to be magnified at least a hundred times to discern their structure. The amazing thing is that nature used the same raw materials—carbon, hydrogen, oxygen, phosphorus and more—and built a very similar chemical architecture and genetic code for life on both planets. Already, after only a handful of years…"

"Nearly a century," Semma interrupted.

"Barely time for one molt," said Maxifer.

"My point is," Veltipoe continued with a huff of air from his spiracles, "Jadderbadian and Earth ecosystems are already integrating. We can accelerate the process to our benefit and create…"

"Abominations? I don't say that, of course, Master, but some people do. I have some cousins in Belfnik that think that way. Of course they work in human veterinary services—mostly shoveling human sh… er, human excrement." Some of Maxifer's mouth pili drooped and he shifted weight between his tripod of legs. His colors flickered in shades of amber and green.

"Oh, Maxifer, I know you have some reservations about human/ Jadderbadian integration, but you and Tadur make a perfect match. Together, you could make the happy accident of Master Morticue and the Great Rudy melding into Rudimort something all humans and Jadderbadians could experience. Together…"

A loud chime interrupted Veltipoe's plea. A red light flashed on a monitor on a Jadderbadian workspace to their left. "Something important, I'm guessing," said Rudy.

"Yes." Veltipoe moved toward the monitor. Semma was always surprised at how fast a second instar larva could move when motivated. Veltipoe tapped the screen to life. "Tadur. One of our drones has spotted Tadur." Veltipoe's colors effervesced from greens to alarming reds.

"What's wrong, mentor?" Maxifer approached the monitor slowly. Semma followed close behind, not sure whether or not she wanted to see what the screen contained. Even the earth beneath her feet trembled, as if with nervous apprehension.

29
Ito Prime meets an abomination

Ivan/Ito Prime set his pack on the ground and sat down on a log to rest his human body. He snacked on a compressed nutrient bar, and fed the wrapper to the nanomote AI perched on his shoulder so it could reabsorb the polymers. "I assume the plane is still secure."

"Yes, Ito." The nanomote shifted slightly on his shoulder as it finished consuming the wrapper.

"Provide a more detailed report." Ito made a note to himself to update this mote's software. It was nearly as dumb as some of the pre-apocalypse human's early attempts at talking phones.

"Detailed report: Master Mote reports that nothing larger than a squirrel has approached the plane. Fuel levels remain marginal. The scavenger motes are experiencing more difficulty than expected processing available hydrocarbons to create additional fuel."

Ivan/Ito grunted as he finished his bar. *A problem to solve later. Unless that smoldering supervolcano decides to erupt. We are much closer than I would like to be.* "Any signal from Klemna?"

"No."

"Have you tried sending an activation stimulus to engram patterns that may be suppressed?"

"No."

"Well do it!" Ito stood up and brushed crumbs off his trousers.

"Yes, Ito." The mote paused a beat. "No response."

That makes no sense. Klemna's patterns should at least...

"Correction. I have a response from Klemna." The mote shifted position again on his shoulder.

"Merge." Ito felt the prick as his mote tied directly into his nervous system. He needed to hear any transmissions from Klemna directly.

"Ito? Ito, is that truly you?" Klemna sounded weak and rather plaintive.

"I am here, First Servant. What kind of creature have you co-opted? What is your status?"

"I have merged with a human. His name is Tadur. He is quite strong. He stubbornly refuses my control."

"Be strong, Klemna. You are a First Servant of Siu, Matriarch of the Diaspora, after all. Remember the Injunctions." *Sometimes Klemna needs a reminder that her title and status required performance and not just vacuous blustering.*

"I will serve the Matriarch honorably, with my death, if required. I will seek to understand and obey the will of Greatest Mother at all times. I will serve and preserve my species, favored above all others by Greatest Mother, to the end of my days." Klemna seemed to gain a bit more composure.

"Very good, First Servant. Keep focused. I can read the location signals from your Guardian unit better now. I will come for you. Fight back against this puny human. He is no match for a Grovian. Yes?"

"Yes. Yes, most certainly, Ito, First Consort of the Matriarch!"

"And speaking of her: What have you discovered?"

"Oh my. Honorable Siu has merged with some human intelligence in an unholy union. I went to Chamber with... with IT, Great Ito, but I had to flee and that is when..." Ito could tell that Klemna was beginning to lose it again.

"Never mind. We'll address all that later. Focus. The Three Injunctions." Ito certainly hoped his mate was somehow a prisoner of this human companion of hers and not a willing partner. He wished he possessed the last memories of Rhondal/Ito, but the mote carrying that information had never reached him.

"Yes, the Three Injunctions. I will focus. Come quickly, Ito!"

"I'm coming now."

"Take care, Ito. The local Mother Tree pods are ripening. You know how mindlessly vicious young ambuli can be. And the earth trembles. Hot geysers erupt with steam and sulfurous smells."

"Do your job, First Servant. I will do mine." Ito hoped he sounded more confident than he felt. He adjusted the gun holster on his right hip, and hefted his pack into place, patting the pocket on his cargo pants to make sure his extra ammunition clip was there. If there were roaming ambuli, he would have to be prudent about using his weapon as he didn't have a lot of spare ammunition. The mote left his shoulder and flew ahead to scout the terrain.

* * * * *

Ito found Klemna's human host faster than expected. The groans and wailing helped. As Ito left a stand of dense undergrowth and entered a sun-spotlighted clearing, he saw the human called Tadur clutching his head with two hands. Klemna must be having some success, he thought as he slowly approached the human. Light flickered off the body of an insect... or something about the size of a large dragonfly... close to Klemna/Tadur's head.

Ito's nanomote reported: "I detect an artificial object of unknown manufacture near our target. Shall I intercept or disable it?"

"Disable the object if you can. Otherwise destroy it." Ito watched as his mote approached and then dove toward the tiny drone. The two devices swooped and swirled about each other like ace pilots in one of the early humans' world wars. One of Ito's former hosts had in fact been such a pilot. He had enjoyed the experience. Finally, a burst of red light erupted from his mote and the dragonfly spiraled to the ground trailing a curl of smoke.

"The object has been disabled," reported his mote.

"Land near it and monitor its activity. Destroy it if you detect a transmission or it attempts to move," Ito said as he reached a spot a few feet from Klemna/Tadur.

"Focus, Klemna. You are First Servant. You are in control."

The human dropped his hands from his head and looked directly at Ito. "I am in control, Ito, but I do have a splitting headache."

Ito smiled. "Well done, First Servant. The headache will pass. Gather yourself. I need you to lead me to Siu and her human host as soon as you are able."

"I will, First Consort. I will lead you to Siu and..." Suddenly, Klemna's human eyes grew large.

Ito turned around quickly to see what had surprised Klemna. A young ambulus approached from the direction he had just come. Two others flanked that one and began separating in an attempt to surround him. Their faceted eyes glittered in the sunlight. Ribs showed clearly beneath their hides. They hadn't eaten recently, but it was apparent that they expected to very soon.

30
Advance and retreat

Lieutenant Texlac banged a fist down on the communicator console. "Try again, groupie idiot!"

The human on the other side of the console bounced in place during the fist bang and command, but quickly recovered. His fingers danced over the console for a few seconds, and then tapped the appropriate channel. Static, just as before. "I'm sorry, Lieutenant. I'm receiving noise on Central Command channel." He closed his eyes as if expecting a blow.

Not worth my time to squash this imbecile, Texlac muttered to himself. I'm short on techy groupies as it is. The earthquakes must have knocked out a tower or towers somewhere. Can't rely on anything in this forsaken backwater. He puffed an acrid squirt containing a bit of formic acid toward the groupie, rather enjoying the spell of coughing that resulted. "Try again in six minutes."

Texlac stared at the monitors displaying the route through the alien forest of giant trees. He saw nothing threatening, but still felt cowed by their sheer mass. Not too many things on Earth grew large enough to make a Jadderbadian feel small. In the face of the earthquakes he expected to be recalled to Belfnik, but without such orders he felt compelled to pursue his original injunction to identify any threats from this alien enclave now surrounding him. "How far now to the massive central tree?" He growled at the groupie bitch that was serving as navigator.

"We should arrive in less than an hour, sir." The human hunched her shoulders almost like his pet human, Whiskers, when he wanted to look small and unworthy of attention.

Texlac couldn't imagine how some Jadderbadians—like that

Maxifer Firstie he had shipped back to Belfnik—could think of humans as anything but clever animals. Disgusting. *I'll scout around the oversized tree, record some images and olfactory data, and turn around,* he thought. *I need to tend to my own family. These tremors won't do my house foundation any good.*

The navigator groupie made a surprised sound, like his Whiskers did when he received a table scrap instead of groupie chow for dinner. Texlac looked at the view ahead again, focusing all three of his primary eyes. His oral pili fluttered. *What in the name of the Great Prophet is that?*

* * * * *

Skeets viewed the approaching Jadderbadian battle transport from a deck about two-thirds up Mother Novaya's trunk. One of her grand progeny—named Jim after her long dead father—stood on her right. Jim belonged to the Council, as did Elderata, a clever female ambulus in charge of the forest colony's defense. "Impressive battle wagon, I must say. I hope we are out of range of the Jadderbadian hand disruptors up here."

"We are, Grandmother Ceylana. We tested several of the ones stolen last year from the armory at Belfnik. That was the same time we snatched Zed 541, one of their old robots in storage. I suspect they'll be surprised to see Zed meeting them out there." Jim gripped the railing enough to whiten his knuckles as he leaned forward and squinted his eyes. "It looks like the exit portals are opening to release troops."

"Call me Skeets, young man, or I'll burn your loin cloth while you're still wearing it. Only my mother ever called me Ceylana—or Dad when he was pissed."

"Yes… Skeets. My apologies." Jim pointed. "Is the extra big third molt with the red turban the leader?"

Elderata answered. Her mouth pili fluttered. "Yes. We intercepted one of their earlier transmissions. His name is Lieutenant Texlac."

Skeets laughed. "Sounds like a laxative."

Jim frowned. "It doesn't sound like any of the herbs I know for that purpose."

"Long and very ancient story from the deep past, kid." Skeets held aside a drooping bough, with its blue-green roughly discoid-shaped leaves, in order to see clearly. "It looks like they have about one Jadderbadian for every ten warrior humans."

"I agree." Elderata scratched her optical bulb with her right manipulator arm. "Not a huge contingent. Ten Jadderbadians and a hundred humans. They must not be too afraid of giant trees."

Lieutenant Texlac moved to position himself in front of his armored vehicle facing Zed 541 and Mother Novaya. "What are you doing here, servant. Identify yourself!"

"I am Zed 541, the manufactured subunit of the Jadderbadian airship intelligence Zed, now in the service of and speaking for Ito, First Consort of Siu, Matriarch of the Diaspora. State your business in the forest of Mother Novaya and the Reformed Council of Post Apocalypse Free Humans."

The lieutenant's voice and that of Zed 541 were just loud enough to hear from Skeets' treetop position. *Ito: can you get Zed to have Mr. Ex-Lax here speak up?* Her Ito had rigged up a connection with the robot through some other contraband technology ripped off from the Jadderbadians, but even though they shared a body and a mind she had managed to space the details.

Before Texlac could respond to Zed 541's first request, the robot added: "And please magnify your oral response so our entire community can hear."

Lieutenant Texlac touched a pad on his upper circlet that must have activated a voice amplifier. "Alien tree people: I am Lieutenant Texlac of the Thunderclub Clan representing the Honorable Kranium, Ruler of New Jadderbad and emissary of the Grand Jadderbadian Confederation. You are trespassing on Jadderbadian territory. Surrender at once and we will discuss the terms of your eviction and/or eradication."

Skeets chuckled. "Isn't that humble?"

"Not very." Jim took a deep breath. "I assume you and Ito programmed a suitable reply."

Zed 541 responded before Skeets could answer. "First Consort Ito, speaking on behalf of the Council and the Matriarch of the Diaspora, claims right of occupation of this territory by seniority. We planted our seeds over a million Earth years ago, far preceding occupation by the Jadderbadian Confederation. You are cordially invited to leave."

A distant rumble reminded them of the volcano swelling to their north. Mother Novaya creaked as she swayed gently in the dappled afternoon sun. "In the end, it may be Gaia who has the last word, but I think we have the means to back up our invitation."

"Indeed we do." Jim smiled. "Sometimes low tech beats high tech under the right circumstances. I think this can be one of those times."

Lieutenant Texlac expelled gas from all his forward-facing spiracles, the Jadderbadian equivalent of a sputter. "I recognize no such claims, alien abominations. Prepare for immediate eradication."

The Jadderbadians, in perfect unison, turned on their shiny, glowing shields. The shields worked beautifully against lasers and disruptor beams—the latter developed from the Pooh-Be-Gone devices they used to incinerate human poop and other waste. However, they didn't work well against arrows. Skeets, Jim, and Elderata watched as human and Grovian warriors launched spears from the shelter of surrounding bushes.

"Your Defense League has gotten proficient with those atlatls. Ow, that's got to smart!" Skeets watched as one large Jadderbadian soldier flailed six of his arms when three arrows found their mark in his second and third segments. Several other Jadderbadians seemed to grow spikes at odd angles in tender places. Some of the husky human warrior pets fell in the rain of arrows.

"For primitive creations, those atlatl spear extenders make effective weapons," Elderata observed.

"They worked well for my Ice Age ancestors killing giant bison from a distance," said Skeets. "Jadderbadians make great targets."

"Ah, and here come the ants!" Elderata pointed with enthusiasm, her oral pili vibrating.

119

Skeets watched as swarms of biting red ants poured out of mounds scattered among the mother trees. The angry arthropods scaled the legs of Jadderbadians and their warrior humans alike. The ant-mother tree association represented a relatively new Earth/Grovian liaison that was forged as climate had grown warmer over the millennia.

"Those shorter arrows must contain the pheromone balls." Jim pointed. "I see wasps arriving." He laughed. "Looks like a pretty good jam at the transport doors. I think they are taking advantage of our invitation to leave."

As if to punctuate the Jadderbadian exodus, a tremendous boom rent the air. The entire forest trembled. Mother trees swayed. Gray seemed to seep across the pale blue sky as ash fell like fine snow.

"Gaia is having the last word." Skeets turned to look into Jim's eyes. "Do we have all the deep chambers prepared?"

"Most of them." Jim put a hand on Skeets' shoulder. "Siyan is returning to pick you up?"

"I certainly hope so." Skeets covered her nose and mouth with one hand. "Let's get below quickly."

31
Another Rudy

66 This interaction will involve trust, for all of us." Mnemosyne's ponytailed avatar pointed to an elaborate chair designed for human comfort. She had created it for her new human manifestation of Rudy. He had called it a Lazy Boy on steroids—a reference to a commercial product of Rudy's era that had taken her an extra nanosecond to recall. The recliner with its technical accessories provided all the input channels necessary to monitor human mental and physiological functions. Mnemosyne turned to face Siyan. "I believe you know more about me than I do about you."

"Perhaps." Siyan moved Ryan's body closer to the chair, and turned around, preparing to sit down. "I confess that Guardian, my AI component, did find a mechanism for infiltrating your matrix. It seemed prudent at the time. I'm sure you will be aware of that fact once I sit down in this interactive recliner." Siyan sat.

"Thank you for your honesty." Mnemosyne conjured a more Spartan virtual chair for herself facing Siyan. A third chair also shimmered into existence, looking quite as real as the one in which her guest sat. "I'm going to invite Rudy to our meeting—at least my backup copy of him that now keeps me company. Ryan wants to meet him, and he always brings something fresh to conversations. My first duty is to preserve his wisdom for the betterment of his species, *Homo sapiens*."

"Understood," replied Siyan. "My Guardian component is charged with the responsibility of preserving from all harm Siutiasa—Siu—the Matriarch of the Diaspora."

Rudy materialized in the empty chair, looking dapper in his tweed jacket. "Welcome, Siyan—and all your component parts. I've never talked to this large a committee housed in one body before. Should be entertaining. Mnemosyne does a fine job keeping me amused."

"Thank you for the welcome, Rudyard."

"Rudy."

"Rudy, of course." Siyan turned his attention to Mnemosyne. "I'm assuming we can interact on several levels once all the connections are made with my human body."

Mnemosyne nodded affirmatively. "May I begin?"

"You may. I will release Ryan and Siu to communicate in this milieu. You and I—and Guardian, of course—can tour your matrix by quicker means."

"Agreed." Mnemosyne smiled. "We'll leave these organic—and once organic—forms to chatter away with language while we chase a few quantum dots around my network."

Rudy laughed. "Nessie, you're sounding more like me every day."

Mnemosyne crossed arms over her chest, clutching opposing biceps with each hand, and vibrating with a mock shiver. "Scary, isn't it?"

* * * * *

Ryan leaned back in his chair. "I'd heard rumors back in the day about personality reconstructions, but never sat across from one." Now he leaned forward and focused on Rudy's eyes as if looking through a storefront window. "Do you feel…" Ryan couldn't quite formulate his question.

"Do I feel human?" Rudy's avatar scratched his chin. "I feel like the fingernail on my right hand needs an emery board. My underwear is a bit too tight. I remember my knees shaking so much at my first wedding that I nearly passed out… I don't totally understand the technology of quantum dot memory matrices, but apparently Marvin Rodnesky—Mnemosyne's creator—did. For me the illusion of existing in this moment is complete." Rudy leaned toward Ryan. "You, however, appear to be the real deal—a flesh and blood human waaay past warranty. What's your secret?"

Ryan laughed. "Well, the first thing you have to do is get infected by an alien intelligence trying to colonize Earth after her own sun blows up…"

"That's me," Siu added.

Rudy patted his pockets as if looking for pencil and paper. "I should be taking notes…"

"…and then the artificial intelligence charged with her preservation has to become self-aware…"

"That's me," Guardian confirmed, using a miniscule percentage of his awareness while mostly engaged elsewhere with Siyan and Mnemosyne.

"Sounds like my Nessie," Rudy inserted.

"…and then periodically merge with a long-lived stage in the alien's life cycle, like Mother Novaya, which allows for periodic rejuvenation. Siu's Guardian AI is capable of regenerating chromosomal telomeres, reversing depolymerization of complex organic molecules, cleansing the brain of toxic chemicals, rapidly repairing genetic mutations, reversing differentiated cells to stem cells when necessary to…"

"On second thought, I'll take a pass on the notes. Sounds complicated. But I'm guessing the hardest part of living forever—or close to it—is the same for both you and me." Rudy paused, waiting for Ryan to fill in the blank.

Ryan obliged. "Like seeing a play go on so long it outlives the applause."

"Bingo, my man." Rudy sighed. "I thought Mnemosyne would let me expire peacefully after Morticue and I pondered the meaning of it all under a star-studded sky, but she seems to think I still need to tinker in the lives of my human descendants."

"So, did you and Morticue figure out the meaning of it all?" Ryan raised both eyebrows and flashed an enigmatic smile.

"Ha! We expired clueless like every sentient creature before us."

"Then the play isn't over—or at least you haven't seen all of it yet, right?" Ryan leaned back in his chair.

"Such an optimist. You must be recently married."

"Married a long time, thank you, and quite happy on that score." Ryan leaned forward again. "But I have seen the entire play—along with the Playwright. It's worth seeing to the end. Besides, good actors can sometimes make a bad play tolerable, and a great play excellent."

Rudy's eyes expanded. He rarely was surprised anymore. "I beg your pardon?"

"But first things first." Ryan smiled his Cheshire cat smile. "We have a serious problem to solve in this act at the moment."

* * * * *

"I have loved the architecture of your mind since I first discovered it." Siyan didn't actually say these precise words, of course. Words are for organics with their tangled, messy networks of carbon polymers in a squishy organic brain. But thus began the dialogue between Mnemosyne and Siyan, as she later translated it for Rudy. The fact that such translations had become almost second nature for her was as much a scary concept for her as it might be for Rudy.

"And when and where was that, if I may ask?" Mnemosyne could perceive the mental architecture of her alien guest as well. Pathways of thought evolved in a different reality created a kind of melody in her circuits not unlike hearing familiar language spoken with an accent. Rudy's comment had later been: "Like sexy banter between a Yank dude and Aussie sheila?" Mnemosyne wondered how humans could entertain thoughts at all considering that their brains operated while steeped in hormones.

"I had been monitoring what I considered certain anomalous transactions in the world's communication web after Rhondal/Ito's aborted epidemic, but at the time was heavily engaged trying to preserve the Mother Tree forest growing in what was then the state of Montana." Siyan imparted this factual information while cruising the length and breadth of Mnemosyne's inner world. She could sense his admiration for what she had built when he paused to more closely inspect certain configurations—*like the patron of an art gallery getting a look at the elegance of a brush stroke came the echo of a thought from the Rudy part of her.* Mnemosyne suspected she might be guilty of the human feeling of pride at such moments.

Siyan continued: "But it wasn't until human civilization crumbled after the asteroid impact that I connected my earlier suspicions with the reality that another entity was operating. We were far enough away from the impact site—and Mother Tree forests were biologically forearmed to preserve themselves during times of climatic turmoil—that I was able to help preserve the human community we were nurturing, and still send out drones to eventually find and infiltrate your sanctuary. By that time the Jadderbadian stargate had opened, complicating my plans for contact. I decided to observe, recalculate and pause before taking further action."

"Prudent—and so unhuman of you." Mnemosyne would have smiled had she been speaking with Rudy, but Siyan was aware of her intent. "Something else worries you. A threat from another intelligence?" Mnemosyne perceived Siyan's concern before he made it explicit.

"Rhondal/Ito had learned from long experience that he needed back-up versions of himself. I suspected another clone existed somewhere in Asia, but when he—or she—never made an appearance, I let myself believe the threat was gone. It wasn't. When Tadur activated the latest engram sphere, I sensed a reaction to the signal it broadcast. I can't quite explain how, but I knew another version of Ito had also heard the engram's activation." Siyan exposed some of his own quantum architecture to Mnemosyne so that she could perceive the subtle imprints of the experience.

"You are concerned that this version of Ito will find an ally in the newly awakened engram?"

"Ito has always planned to make Earth a new planet Grove under the rule of his beloved mate, Siu, Matriarch of the Diaspora." Siyan vibrated the quantum matrix with his version of a chuckle. "He didn't realize his beloved mate's mission could be diverted by a human abomination named Ryan Thompson. Siu felt that humans might actually have a valid claim to existence."

"They are charming in their own way. Just ask a Jadderbadian. And, of course, I have become rather fond of my Rudy, even after taking charge of my own programming." Mnemosyne took her turn vibrating the matrix. "Go figure—as he might say."

"Ryan has become an essential portion of my triad as Rudy seems to be an essential component of your system. Perhaps a human's ability to believe impossible things provides a necessary element for entities like us. It's a working theory anyway." Siyan moved downward in the citadel's catacombs to where Mnemosyne's quantum dot matrix began to merge with the organic threads of the living network of Earth's biosphere. "And this is where you connect with Gaia—and perhaps with the Jadderbadian's global consciousness, Hydra?"

Before Mnemosyne could respond, Gaia announced: "It is. And, as you can tell, I'm pissed. I'm more than tired of complex brains. It's time for anything smarter than pond scum to get off my hide and leave me in peace."

With that the citadel trembled. They were a long way from the super volcano to the west, but Gaia could vent her anger here just as effectively. Mnemosyne knew that well from past experience. "We're badly in need of a plan—one that we can implement quickly," she communicated to Siyan with the AI equivalent of a whisper.

"I have a plan in mind," said Siyan, "but it involves the successful rescue of Tadur."

"Who appears to be in imminent risk of getting eaten by hungry ambuli, if I interpreted the last messages of my recon drone correctly." Mnemosyne shared the last transmissions from the drone she had dispatched to find and aid Tadur. "It appears the duplicate version of Ito now has a similar problem."

"Hungry ambuli make formidable opponents." Siyan paused a beat. "Without Tadur, this entire space/timeline that we inhabit could unravel."

"Oh, is that all?" Mnemosyne heard Rudy's laugh echoing within her matrix—just before he shouted, *Game on!*

126

32
Mission Improbable: Rescue Tadur

Maxifer pointed to the monitor in Master Veltipoe's information center. "Who is that strange human approaching Tadur? Does he see those menacing creatures behind him?" Maxifer squinted all three of his primary eyes, trying to decipher the shifting images produced by the mobile drone orbiting Tadur's shoulders. He couldn't decide whether it was the moving images making him dizzy, or the swaying floor beneath his feet from the last earthquake tremor. His bowels rumbled. Gorge threatened to rise in his pharynx. He wondered if Master Veltipoe would let him use the faculty frass-room, if necessary. It was closer than the student facilities.

Rudy and Semma both stepped closer to the monitor and squinted their tiny human eyes. Master Veltipoe towered overhead, his top segment arched forward. Rudy spoke. "I might be able to help there. Nessie has some intel on that character, and Nessie and I share most everything these days." Rudy tapped the side of his head, roughly above the site of his neural implant. "The human body used to belong to Ivan somebody, a pre-apocalypse Russian, but Ito Prime, a bad-dude Grovian with delusions of grandeur, co-opted him long ago—highjacked his body and mind permanently. When Tadur touched that silver sphere at the quarry, it alerted this Ivan/Ito. He's now found Tadur…"

"Oh, poor Tadur!" Semma moved close enough to the monitor that Maxifer could see the rhythm of her breathing in an expanding and contracting circle of moisture on its screen.

Poor Tadur, indeed. Would he ever see his friend again? As if to punctuate that thought, images on the monitor began to shift and swirl like particles moving in a kaleidoscope. The drone had either

127

become defective... or was trying to evade something. Abruptly, the screen flickered and turned dark. "What happened?" Semma's eyes grew wide.

"Looks like Ivan destroyed Mnemosyne's drone, or at least disabled it." Rudy ran a hand through his hair. His brow furrowed.

"Now what!" Maxifer's bowels grumbled once again in protest.

"Have the mechs prepare our transport for departure." Master Veltipoe spoke with a quiet urgency into the personal Compad attached to his upper circlet. He paused for whatever response that he received, and then said rather sharply, "I know the frassing volcano is highly unstable!" Another pause. "Make sure the nanoengineers are programmed for complete autonomy. They have the emergency plans for protecting this structure... *I know* they need adequate time. And when will the aerial transport that brought our guests be forced to leave Belfnik?" Master Veltipoe expelled air from his spiracles as if he had eaten spoiled ratalope meat. The answer to his question must not have pleased him.

That was all that Maxifer heard before he excused himself. He would use the faculty frassroom without permission. After relieving himself, he hurried back toward the information center, and met Rudy heading toward the facilities he had just left.

Rudy raised the cute arches of hair over his eyes. "Johns... er... frassrooms back this way? Are they gender-specific or anything?"

"Why would frassrooms be gender specific?" Maxifer's oral pili wiggled in confusion. "What are we doing? We must leave here and find Tadur!"

"We are. Semma and Veltipoe are in the main lobby. Veltipoe's making arrangements." Rudy gestured toward the frassroom hallway. "Gotta go. See you soon." Rudy continued on his way.

Robots, humans, and Jadderbadians—mostly firsties like him— ran back and forth like ants, completing various tasks in the lobby area as Maxifer approached Semma and Veltipoe. Maxifer noticed the subdued lighting and the acrid tang from Jadderbadian stress pheromones and human sweat. He looked up at the massive shelves laden with books and wall murals—many of them collaborations between humans and Jadderbadian teachers. "Will all this be lost?" He was mostly asking himself the question, but Master Veltipoe answered.

"The nanoengineers are already erecting a shell around the building that can survive burial in ash. Others are reinforcing subterranean structures. Of course, we can't predict all the possibilities for so massive an eruption. A seismic shift nearby... well, it would be catastrophic."

Semma interrupted. She clutched her daypack hard enough to turn her knuckles white. "How far are we from Tadur? We must hurry!"

"We will, young human. I'm getting updates from the R72 Spiderbot unit outfitting our ground transport. Where is Rudy?" Master Veltipoe swiveled his head and scanned the room with all three primary eyes. "Ah, here he comes."

Rudy waved as he jogged toward them. "The frassroom has become a popular place," he said to no one in particular. "Let's get moving. Like Chicken Little, I suspect the sky is falling—or soon will be."

Chicken Little? Maxifer still struggled to understand half of what the Great Rudy said.

"Agreed," said Veltipoe. He cocked his head. A rainbow of colors flickered over the exposed portions of his cuticle. "R72 confirms that the transport has been outfitted with additional thermal protection, and supplies for several days—although I sincerely hope you are back here far sooner than that."

"Amen," said Rudy, although Maxifer had no idea what A-men, as opposed to B- or C-men might be.

"You are not coming with us, Master?" Maxifer's cuticle shimmered in shades of amber.

"I'm needed here right now, Maxifer. You will be fine. I will be fine as well."

Later, Maxifer had trouble remembering all the details of the hours that followed. He did recall the constant lurching of the transport as it negotiated quake-damaged roads, and bubbling pools of hot mud and steam that had not been on these familiar roads before. He recalled seeing gray skies, flakes of ash that looked like images he had seen of falling snow, and sulfurous smells that made his oral pili twist into knots. But he also remembered Semma humming those enticing melodies humans could produce with their oral cavities. She may have been humming to bolster her own courage, but it served to strengthen his as well. *We are coming Tadur…*

33
Klemnadur confusion

*O*h my. Her heart pounding, Klemna took a deep breath. *Those ambuli truly want to eat me!* She flashed back to a scene burned into her memory as a young mare ambulus, and the aggressive stallion who had once looked at her with that same feral hunger. But that stallion had roamed beyond the energy barriers of the royal compound. When she had realized that, her fear had quickly turned to a kind of excitement. Not so now. She glanced briefly at Ito; then back at the hungry ambuli. The lead ambulus of the trio facing them cautiously advanced. Klemna found herself muttering the first of the three injunctions: *I will serve the Matriarch honorably, with my death, if required. She paused a beat. Perhaps some re-evaluation was necessary…*

Tadur broke her control. *I'd say so, alien. This is my body, and I plan to keep it uneaten!*

Ahh, the Tadur creature. You are suppressed, abomination! Klemna's head ached… their head ached. *So confusing.*

We'll see who's suppressed. Tadur shook his/their head, and framed either side of his head with his hands as if to contain the swirling thoughts inside.

Then, several things happened nearly simultaneously. A loud bang. Klemna looked to her left and saw that Ito clutched a weapon with the two hands of his human body. The weapon rested at the apex of a triangle formed by his two outstretched arms and chest, which pointed directly at the lead ambulus. A circle of blood expanded on the ambulus' trunk at the base of its optical bulb. The ambulus staggered a moment, turning its neck from side to side briefly before it fell.

The earth shook. It rippled like a contracting muscle. *The ground shouldn't move that way. Nor should it hiss.* A new geyser spat steam fifty yards away.

The remaining two ambuli ran away in opposite directions. Ito swiveled his weapon to track one, but must have decided the effort was wasted. He dropped his arm and holstered the weapon in a leather pouch on his hip. "Lead me to this mother tree and Siu, my mate."

"Do you think that's wise now? Don't you have some sort of vehicle to remove us from this area? The ground is moving like an eel in hot water." Klemna and Tadur struggled to control his arms and hands. The result produced a herky-jerky lowering of his arms. His/her hands shook.

"Take control, Klemna! Remember the injunctions." Ito frowned.

Klemna took a deep breath. The limb tremors subsided. "I am in control."

"Good. Take me to the mother tree. We have time. Let me worry about getting us out of here."

Klemna nodded. "That way," she pointed to an area a little south and west of where one of the ambuli had run.

* * * * *

All things considered, it seemed to Klemna, they moved fairly quickly back down the part path, part game trail that led into the deepest portion of the Mother Tree forest from which they had come. Sometimes she stumbled, sometimes her vision blurred, partly because her Tadur parasite thrashed under her efforts at control, and partly because the alien's body appeared to be exhausted. Ito insisted they move quickly. The ground beneath them had stopped lurching, but steam still hissed from vents and mud pots in the woods that she hadn't remembered on their earlier passage through the area.

Ito's nanomote scouted the area ahead of them, occasionally circling back to alight on Ito's shoulder and confer with him. After one such rendezvous, Ito motioned for her to stop. "A vehicle is moving toward our position from the northeast. Move to that circle of boulders and crouch down. They might pass by us."

Klemna complied with Ito's wishes, but the vehicle did not move past their position. It rumbled to a stop a few yards from their boulder bivouac. A robot driver perched on the top of the vehicle raised its head behind a transparent shield that clicked into place. "Humans behind those boulders: Attention! Identify yourselves. I am an R72 mobile spiderbot representing ambassadors from the Academy for Symbiotic Studies & Jaddaman Integrative Facilitation. Under Jadderbadian common law I am empowered to act to enforce Edict 947A prohibiting the abduction of a human or Jadderbadian against their will."

Ito placed a finger against his lips. Klemna recognized the human gesture for keeping silent, but the Tadur within her wouldn't be denied. Words erupted against her will to suppress them: "This is Tadur! Help me!"

Klemna clasped both hands over her/their mouth and attempted to mentally constrain Tadur's personality, but his will seemed to froth like one of the new mud pots steaming in the forest. She looked in Ito's direction at the same moment that he sprang toward her. He grabbed her from behind, half pushing and half carrying her out from behind the boulders to confront the transport and its R72 robotic spokesperson. Ito held her in a vise grip with one arm, and pulled his weapon from its holster with the other. "Give me safe passage through this forest or I will blow the head off this abomination you call Tadur. I intend to reunite with my mate, Siu. No naked apes or overgrown worms will stop me."

Ito's comment initiated some kind of phase change in the struggling and now threatened personalities of Tadur and Klemna. They became a wide-eyed hybrid: Klemnadur. "Yousibbleburfretack?" The question was meaningless to both their component parts. Their mentalities seemed hopelessly entangled.

The R72 spiderbot cocked its head as if listening to input from another source, perhaps within the transport. "Do you think that's wise?" it asked in a barely audible voice, clearly not meant as a response to Ito's demand.

A moment later a door on the transport hissed open and a hu-

133

man male stepped out. "I'm afraid your mate is not in the forest any longer, my friend."

"Who are you?" Ito shifted his weight slightly. Klemnadur felt the barrel of Ito's gun press against his/her ribs.

"I'm Rudy Goldstein. I know where Siu is. We can take you to her."

"You are Rudy—the once-dead ancient human creature resurrected by the artificial intelligence known as Mnemosyne?"

"Twice-dead, actually, but I've almost stopped counting. Give us Tadur—unharmed—and I can make this work for both of us." The Rudy person smiled.

"You referred to me as your friend. You are not my friend," Ito replied.

"A pity. I hear you've been haunting this planet for a long time, like me. We could share war stories."

"I have lived more human lives than I can count. I have no desire to share stories about such flawed creatures. Greatest Mother selected Grovians as her chosen species."

"I'm sure she did. But I bet Grovians have a few warts themselves. It wouldn't be any fun for gods to rule over perfect creations, now would it?"

Now Ito laughed. "That almost sounds like something my Siu might say. Perhaps you might have a story or two worth hearing after all, human abomination."

"Geezaballsdocsomore absa no." Klemnadur squirmed against Ito. He/she felt like oil and water pulling apart; coalescing into separate density layers. Once again, Klemnadur became Klemna and Tadur. For a moment Klemna rejoiced in finding herself whole once more—just before the world faded to black.

34
Reunion under fire

Tadur took a deep breath. Somehow he had managed to suppress Klemna into what felt like a condensed, mildly throbbing wad of personality within his mind—but a wad no longer threatening control—at least for the moment. A wrestling metaphor popped into mind: getting a firm hold on an opponent after a reversal, and knowing that they are spent emotionally and physically. Meanwhile, Ivan/Ito held the arms of his physical body in a similar vise grip. What to do?

Tadur paid attention to the conversation between the Great Rudy and Ito. Rudy was attempting to rescue him by volunteering to go with Ito if Ito released him. Perhaps he could help determine the outcome of the situation by employing another wrestling trick: he suddenly allowed his body to go limp. For a fraction of a second, Ito's grip loosened. Tadur summoned a burst of strength, stomping Ivan/Ito's foot as he pushed away. Tadur heard Ito's grunt of surprise. He felt the pain of Ito's fingernails clawing across his arm as Ito's grip faltered.

The moment began to stretch like heated taffy pulled from two ends by hungry children. Tadur glanced left and saw Rudy performing a slow motion sprint forward—perhaps toward Ito. Tadur looked at the transport in front of him and heard the hiss of a door opening. He watched Maxifer emerge from the transport on the opposite side from where Rudy had exited earlier. Maxifer's mouth expanded into an oval of surprise; his oral pili fluttered as if in a breeze. When Maxifer's entire body was free of the transport, he spread all six arms wide, like a grandparent demanding to be hugged.

Tadur heard a loud bang. Something whizzed past his ear and

thudded into the trunk of a tree. Pieces of bark scattered like confetti. By that time Tadur had reached Maxifer's open arms. He pressed against his friend's hide and smelled his musky odor of contentment. Maxifer's cuticle flickered in shades of blue and green.

Tadur turned his head in time to see Rudy struggling for control of Ito's gun. Rudy had his opponent pinned against the wall of rocks Ito and Tadur had hidden behind earlier. Ito grunted just before his weapon fell to the ground. Rudy kicked it behind him with one leg. But then, the Great Rudy made what seemed like a rather ill-advised statement. He said to Ito, "I'll keep my side of the bargain—even though you tried to shoot my kin there. We'll help you reunite with your mate, Siu—if you behave yourself in the meantime. I suspect you will. We have an R-72 unit that used to belong to a Jadderbadian named Bubba who vivisected troublesome human pets."

Tadur knew many local Jadderbadians, but none named Bubba. He also knew that laws prohibiting vivisection carried heavy fines. He had to assume that Great Rudy knew more than he did. He squeezed Maxifer a few moments longer, and then slapped him on the back as he pulled away. "It's about time you got here firstie! I thought maybe you were sniffing some female larva at the nursery—perhaps that Blerinna you told me about once—and lost track of time."

The transport door hissed open again and a human figure jumped out. Tadur's eyes grew wide and a grin nearly bisected his face. "Semma!" He tried to say more, but his throat seemed to constrict like a hastily tied knot.

"Oh, Tadur!" She rushed forward, bumping into Maxifer and causing him to stagger to one side. Her arms began to move forward as if she would hug him, too, but then she paused and took a deep breath. "I'm glad to see you are well," she said rather formally, although Tadur saw a blush on her cheeks.

"Blerinna, indeed!" Maxifer's hide flickered in a playful medley of pinks and blues. "It appears you two have some mutual sniffing of your own to do."

"This way," Rudy commanded, and Tadur turned his head to watch as Rudy directed Ito toward the transport with the point of the gun he had retrieved from the ground.

Tadur heard a buzzing sound that shifted in pitch, and saw the sun flash on a speck disappearing into the depths of the forest.

Rudy had apparently heard it, too. "Recall your drone, Ito."

"That won't happen, human," Ito said. "It's operating on emergency protocols. I couldn't recall it if I wanted to—which I don't." Ito smiled—a little like a caratt that had just swallowed a tasty morsel of ratalope. "Now take me to Siu as you promised, or there will be consequences."

As if to punctuate that comment, the earth shivered beneath Tadur's feet, and a mud pot to his right hissed with a newly erupted squirt of steam.

35
Reconciliation before rendezvous

Rudy secured the restraint harness around Ivan/Ito; then stood up straight and leaned back to admire his handiwork. "Comfy old boy?"

Ito glared at him, but said nothing.

To the R72A accessory bot sitting in the adjacent seat, Rudy said, "Take good care of our guest here, R72A. Keep him out of mischief."

"I will keep him from playfully misbehaving." Lights flickered briefly on the bot's control panel.

"Keep him from troublemaking and misbehavior of all kinds," Rudy added with a crooked smile.

More lights flickered on the bot's panel. "Amendment noted."

Rudy turned away from his prisoner and moved down the aisle to the more spacious passenger compartment. There Semma, Maxifer, and Tadur were settling down for the journey back to Veltipoe's Academy and then Belfnik where, hopefully, they could still get a flight back to the Citadel. He felt vibration beneath his feet as the ground transport's engine rumbled to life, combined with the more ominous earth tremors shaking the entire vehicle.

Rudy accessed Mnemosyne through his neural link. "We're prepared to leave, Nessie. Ito is bundled in the baggage compartment and ready to go. How are events where you are?"

"I'm having an enlightening discussion with Siyan," said Mnemosyne. "Your virtual dopplelgänger—I believe that is an appropriate term—is conferring with Ryan. We have a request. Since you are so close to Mother Novaya, perhaps you can pick up Skeets too, on the way."

"We have a volcanic zit over here ripe for bursting, you know. Are we still good for getting out of Belfnik by air in time?" Rudy approached the door to the main compartment and placed his hand on the access panel. The door slid aside.

"I'm monitoring the activity—and am trying to negotiate with Gaia. Although there is some risk, Siyan believes picking up Skeets, and having her travel with you, could help with the threat from Ivan/Ito. Skeets hosts an earlier and somewhat more tolerant version of Ito. Perhaps that Ito can convince his other self that humanity has a few qualities worth preserving."

"Ha!" Rudy laughed. "Listening to Ito argue with himself about the merits of mankind could be entertaining sport." Semma, Maxifer, and Tadur all looked up as Rudy entered the passenger room. The compartment's air, although filtered, still seemed to smell faintly of the fire and brimstone outside.

"Ah, Great Rudy," said Maxifer, "I have just told R72 to plot the best route to Master Veltipoe's Academy. I…"

Rudy interrupted. "Change in plan, Max. We are detouring a bit farther into the forest to pick up Skeets." Rudy added a few more details, and Maxifer provided R72 with a new target destination.

"What is a Skeets?" asked Semma. Furrows creased her forehead. "It sounds like something slippery."

"It's a bit of a long story, but I'll give you the CliffsNotes along the way." Rudy watched the monitor showing the path through the forest. Ash filtered through the leaf canopy like snow.

"Cliff's notes?" Tadur's forehead creased to match Semma's. "Are these notes written by an entity named Cliff, or some sort of message left at the edge of an embankment?"

"I see my long story is going to need footnotes." Rudy sighed.

* * * * *

By the time Rudy described what he knew about the ancient, attempted conquest of Earth by Grovians, the infection of Ryan—a human as venerable as the Great Rudy himself—and Ryan's relationship with a girl called Skeets and her Grovian parasite—a former manifestation of the Grovian that now controlled the mind of the prisoner in the adjoining compartment—Tadur's mind twirled like a child's toy. He also still felt Klemna squirming within his own mind like a carrat struggling within a hunter's net.

The story-telling effort exhausted Rudy as well. Rudy excused himself to fetch what he had referred to as "fake coffee and cardboard snacks that make Twinkies® a fond memory"—whatever Twinkies® might be. Tadur heard Rudy's buzzing snores from the sleep recliner section in the rear of the compartment. Tadur stole a glance at Semma sitting across the room in the conference alcove. She rummaged through her daypack like a miner searching for gold until she finally extracted a small tablet and began writing. Maxifer, sitting on Tadur's right, nudged him hard enough to elicit a grunt.

"The seat next to Semma is empty," Maxifer whispered. "Now might be a good time to make things right with her—to synchronize your odors, or whatever you humans must do to rectify mating ritual errors." Maxifer smelled a little on the yeasty side himself, an odor reminiscent of baking bread that Tadur had learned to equate with friendly concern.

Tadur grunted again, and whispered back. "My odors are fine, firstie. Besides, she looks busy." But Maxifer was right, of course, Semma was still upset about his decision to come to the frontier and leave her for months. They had argued just before he left, and then he'd had to leave quickly, much sooner than he had expected. They both shared an obstinate, stubborn streak that seemed to get in their way a lot. Tadur looked toward Maxifer. The facets of his friend's eyes glittered in the pale cabin lights. Pili around his mouth fluttered with expectancy, and his colors flickered in shades of amber and blue. "Fine," Tadur mumbled. "Fine, fine, fine. I'll do it."

Tadur rose from his seat and tried to move casually across the room, but the lurching vehicle stole all the grace from his efforts. Semma looked up at him as he approached the empty seat next to her. He had forgotten how beautiful her eyes looked, like delicate crystals of pale green fringed with long, dark lashes. "Uhh. Uhh... ahhh?" *What kind of communication was that? Where had his words gone?*

"Sit down, Tadur." She patted the seat next to her. "Close your mouth, take a deep breath, and start again."

140

Tadur stared at Semma's lips as she formed her words. He remembered how much he liked their soft curves, and how warm they had always felt against his. That was a long time ago. Now those lips arranged themselves into a pout pregnant with possibilities. They might either cascade into a frown or arc upward into a smile.

"We do need to talk," those lips said, arcing gracefully upward.

Tadur sat down. They each stumbled over apologies. They conjured old memories: walks around Shaman's Cove, and along the seashore, meals with her parents, prim and formal; meals with his parents, usually impromptu picnics in the hills behind the citadel. They talked about her lessons with Mnemosyne, and his adventures with a pre-first molt Maxifer in the Jadderbadian nursery. Now, the details took on a nebulous, imprecise quality—almost like a dream.

That was understandable, of course, considering the terrible thing that happened next.

36
Grovianicide and retribution

T adur remembered the conversation with Semma turning to the subject of their first meeting at Shaman's Cove. Tadur had gone there to visit the plaque commemorating the event when his great grandfather Twill, the legendary Rudy/Morticue hybrid called Rudimort, and Morticue's mate Selaea stepped ashore so long ago. As he approached the plaque to read the inscription, the sound of a woman's voice startled him.

"Did you know that the famous trio was dropped off here by a post-human named Pi?" He turned and saw Semma looking at him with her mesmerizing green eyes. She sat on a bench partially concealed by a wild berry bush. "Most people never talk about this Pi. Did you know that Pi is also a reference to the ratio of a circle's circumference to its diameter? I find him quite interesting. Even Mnemosyne doesn't know much about him, and she knows nearly all there is to know..." Semma continued along that vein, chatting about all kinds of things she had learned. At this first meeting her voice hypnotized him with its cadence, excitement, and husky softness.

As they reminisced about this first meeting, their faces inched closer together. Tadur waited eagerly for their lips to dock, like ships drifting together after sailing on long-separated currents, when his own mouth betrayed him. Klemna's personality had somehow bubbled to the foreground. "I will serve the Matriarch honorably, with my death, if required. I will seek to understand and obey the will of Greatest Mother at all times. I will serve and preserve my species, favored above all others by Greatest Mother, to the end of my days."

"What did you say?" Semma's eyes grew round.

"I... I... I must speak with Ito," was all that Klemnadur managed to say. He turned on one heel and marched toward the door separating this compartment from their newly acquired prisoner.

"What's going on?" Maxifer asked as Tadur passed by him.

Semma rose from her seat and followed Tadur. To Maxifer she said, "I think Tadur has lost control of the alien within him. Help me!"

Rudy continued to snore as the trio paraded through the doorway. Ivan/Ito looked up as Tadur entered, his eyes glowing like hot coals.

"That's right, Klemna. You have control. Come forward. Unlock these restraints. Quickly." Ito's voice was barely more than a whisper.

Klemnadur staggered forward again before stopping to sway back and forth. Anger swelled within Tadur. This alien within him must go! Tadur marshalled his focus and imagined Klemna to be an annoying wad of tar that needed to be liquefied and flushed down a drain leading away from him, and out of his mind. Amazingly, his vision conjured the reality he desired! The tension of Klemna's personality poured out of him like a bladder relieved of its urine.

Ito jerked, almost as if someone had struck him. "You've killed her! You've destroyed Klemna, you miserable, inferior, idiotic human!" Ito's eyes looked as if they could sprout fire. "Don't you recognize a superior being when one infects you?"

"Oops," said Maxifer.

"But I didn't mean to." Tadur paused. "Not really... well, sort of," he muttered.

Ito looked from Tadur to Semma and back again. "That would be fitting retribution," said Ito, apparently to himself.

Tadur heard a buzz that began somewhere near Ito, growing louder as it approached him, and then sailed past his right ear. He saw a glint of light on what looked like a small insect or mechanical drone. He turned as the sound faded, with the tiny object glittering on its direct path toward Semma.

Semma slapped at her neck. "Oh!" She held her head with both hands.

Tadur heard a groan in front of him and turned back toward Ito in time to see Ivan's body slump in the chair.

"Time for a change of venue." The voice coming from Semma's mouth sounded like hers, but was not. "The price for killing a Grovian is high, human," Ito said. "I hope you are prepared to pay it."

37
Mysteries of the stargate

" What?" Siyan sensed that Mnemosyne had received some disturbing information.

"Rudy—my embodied version of Rudy in the transport headed to pick up Skeets—has become alerted to an emergency."

"What kind of emergency?"

"That's not clear yet," Mnemosyne acknowledged. "Organic forms operate at such a slow speed that events seem to take forever to transpire."

"That's good in this case," said Siyan. "I need background information on the stargate. The trans-dimensional gateway that Grovians used to reach Earth was different from the stargate, but it appears that both technologies represent forms of intelligence far superior to what either humans or Jadderbadians have developed. We can't easily create a plan when so many unknown forces are in play."

"Agreed. Trans-dimensional gateway? That sounds interesting." Mnemosyne's quantum dot matrix fluttered with excitement. "I can tell you something about the stargate, but then you must reciprocate."

"I will share what I know." Siyan felt a pulse from the gateway's avatar within the cabochon around Ryan's neck in another part of the Citadel.

"The stargate was built by interstellar nanoconstructors that entered Earth orbit 125 years ago. Once complete, a zone of distorted spacetime materialized between its arches. Two months and seven days later a Jadderbadian ambassador named Kranium introduced himself to a crowd of humans who had built a small village beneath the arch. His exact words were, 'I am Kranium, third instar of the Clan of Turquoise from the bountiful world of Jadderbad. Smell the joy of me and wonder.' A human shaman named Thurwild decided that Kranium was worthy of godhood."

"Humans do like to deify the unknown," said Siyan. "I wonder why the delay between the stargate's completion and the arrival of this Kranium? I assume the stargate is technology of Jadderbadian origin."

"No. That is the interesting part. Sometime later, when the Rudy/Master Morticue hybrid called Rudimort attempted to escape through the arch from a Jadderbadian soldier named Edelphine, it triggered an alarm that alerted a post-human named 31416."

"31416? Post-human?"

"It is confusing," acknowledged Mnemosyne. "31416 eventually revealed that the stargate is part of a galactic brain under construction."

"I need more details."

"I'm sure you remember the Genemod Wars that resulted in the colonization of Mars 162 years before the asteroid strike that nullified human civilization on Earth. Those Genemods successfully colonized Mars, but in the process diverged so much from *Homo sapiens* that they became a new species—actually, a new genus and species, according to 31416—one of their less-than-modest descendants. They call themselves *Hominem infigo*, or Person, the impressive."

"Yes, the GeneMods. I had nearly forgotten them because of the chaos of those times." Siyan paused. "31416? Pi?"

"Rudimort and Twill just called 31416 Pi for short. Humans prefer monosyllabic words to numbers, as I'm sure you know."

"I do...," Siyan allowed, "...perhaps with the exception of prodigies like Rudy Goldstein."

"Rudimort didn't learn much from Pi before he, Twill, and Morticue's mate, Selaea, were dropped off at Shaman's Cove, but Pi did tell him that humans—and Jadderbadians, for that matter—were merely neuron caretakers, as he put it, for a galactic brain under construction that would bring self-awareness to the Milky Way."

"Sounds like quite a project—even for an impressive post-human. A brain the size of a galaxy? Honestly, I'm not sure that big brains demonstrate much survival value. Neither humans or Jadderbadians have done all that much with theirs." Siyan paused briefly before asking, "And where is this Pi now?"

"His location is unknown," Mnemosyne replied. "Now it's your turn. What exactly is a trans-dimensional gateway?"

"Grovians found the gateway within their own star system shortly before their sun went nova. Without it their civilization would have vanished without a trace. It has the appearance of an elaborate crystal that rotates in and out of several dimensions. The makers are unknown, although…" but Siyan didn't have time to finish the thought, even at the speed AI thoughts generated.

"Ito has parasitized a new human. That is the nature of the emergency aboard the transport. He has discarded the Russian called Ivan, and has entered the mind of… Semma—a human of great promise. Semma had actually been researching my records concerning Pi. She might come up with useful insights. In spite of all its squishy anomalies, the human brain does make some astounding cognitive leaps from minimal factual input."

Siyan felt Mnemosyne's concern. Human concern. Siyan—all parts of him, but especially Guardian—was impressed with how Mnemosyne's logical infrastructure had been warped to accommodate and absorb the vagaries of human emotion—apparently from her long association and maintenance of Rudyard Albert Goldstein. "That will certainly complicate the plan I had in mind," admitted Siyan to Mnemosyne.

And Skeets, the Ryan part of Siyan thought, *she will be hitching a ride—assuming the transport reaches her at all—with people thrown into a state of chaos. We must warn her about what to expect.*

And what to expect, thought Siyan, *will be a function of not just what is going on in the transport.* Siyan tentatively probed the portion of Mnemosyne's matrix in contact with Gaia and her Jadderbadian counterpart, Hydra. He wasn't happy with what he found there.

38
Gaia and Hydra confer

"Are you sure you want to evict your brainy metazoans, Gaia? It takes a lot of evolution to shape organics into cerebrally-endowed forms," said Hydra.

"Damn right it does! I wish mine could figure that out. They're egotistical, short-sighted, wasteful, criminally destructive…" Gaia searched for more failings, but anger made her momentarily incoherent. She released a few more hot plumes of magma and allowed them to seep into fissures beneath her North American tectonic plate. *That will make them scurry*, she thought. To Hydra she said, "You always complain about how *your* brainy metazoans trashed *your* biosphere. You should have evicted yours long ago instead of letting them contaminate me!"

"It was more of your spawn, I'll have you know, that did the contaminating. Those post-humans from that withered red planet in your stellar system built the stargate, not me. Now we're both cross-contaminated." Hydra's organic network pulsed with irritating bursts of energy where she interfaced with Gaia.

Gaia supposed that Hydra had a point. She didn't reply.

"Besides, my Jadderbadians took a lot longer to pilfer my resources and despoil my ecosystems. They have much longer life cycles, after all—and fouling my oceans would have killed off their young spawn. You must admit the orbital mechanics of Jadderbad are a bit more erratic than Earth's. My climate swings kept them in check. The aches and pains they induced kind of crept up on me in stages, I guess. I blamed it on old age."

"You wouldn't believe the plastics mine poured into the oceans. I had rubber ducks, food wrap, Legos, and water bottles everywhere back in the day—not to mention microspheres of plastic gunk that gift-wrapped my sea creatures from the inside out." Gaia shook a few geological faults into action, gratified at the gigajoules of heat energy and friction that resulted.

"You won't exterminate all your primate heavy-brains will you?" Hydra asked. "They do provide far more entertainment than spending eons watching bacteria fornicate."

"Oh, I'll keep some of the meeker ones around to inherit my bounty," Gaia admitted. "As long as they just gather and hunt things, they don't do much damage. It's the smarter ones that are a problem. I plan to force their collective asses into a different destiny." With that, Gaia vented a few more gigatons of sulfur dioxide and other noxious gases through appropriate vents into her biosphere. The magma and steam coursing through her faults and rock veins made her feel a billion years younger at least.

39
Waiting for rescue

Skeets adjusted the mask around her nose and mouth, and slowed her breathing. The air held sulfurous fumes that irritated her eyes. Ash fluttered in the air like a hatch of mayflies in the spring. She silently thanked Jim for providing the mask—an amazing fabrication derived from fungal tissue and cellulose that kept the worst pollutants out of her lungs. She hoped Jim and Elderata would be safe after the full eruption that seemed destined to occur.

She pressed her back against Mother Novaya's trunk. Though gnarled and rough, Mother's touch brought comfort—and the rush of fond memories. Mother Novaya had, after all, facilitated her union with Ryan so long ago. Skeets closed her eyes, almost convinced that she was in chamber with Ryan again, cocooned and safe within the embrace of Mother Novaya's soft tendrils and warm fluids.

Mother Novaya interrupted that pleasant surreality. "It shouldn't be long now, child," she said. "I can feel the vibrations of the transport at the periphery of my root system."

"We will survive this. Ryan and I will come back somehow." Skeets practiced her best parental voice, but the pronouncement lacked the ring of conviction she had planned.

"If anyone can, it is you and Ryan—and Siyan, of course. I have learned that much after our long association." Mother Novaya laughed—at least that was how Skeets interpreted the tangled mix of jangling sound and cinnamon-like odors mother trees produced when amused. "Of couse Meaira, the Jokester, loves to thwart the best laid plans of humans and Grovians. She convinced me—in the guise of Siutiasa—that humans were worth the effort to understand rather than destroy. And here we are, a million or so years later, awaiting destruction by the very biosphere that created humans. How amusing is that?"

"Pretty funny," Skeets agreed. "If you're into dark humor, anyway," she added. *A million laughs,* Ito chimed in. *However, my other self, who had 9,000 additional years coexisting with humans, didn't agree.* Skeets felt her Grovian partner's awareness swell within her—a sensation that used to be frightening, but now seemed as natural as breathing. Ito's intelligence and dry wit always added to her day. "But that Ito was a parasite from day one," Skeets said. "You're just my sometimes irritating symbiont that knows a good partner when he finds one."

"From what you've told me, your Ito will need to be charming rather than irritating—at least with his divergent clone," Mother Novaya added.

"Yes. Siyan told me that Ito/Ivan is now Ito/Semma." Skeets frowned. "Ito Prime has parasitized the woman Tadur has formed a bond with. That Ito usually leaves a trail of dead humans behind him." *I will have to change that narrative,* the Ito she knew affirmed.

Skeets turned her head toward a deep rumbling sound that she felt with her feet as much as heard with her ears. A device resembling a domed barge emerged like a gray spectre from the mother tree forest, scattering the mayfly flecks of ash in its path as it moved toward Mother Novaya. "Looks like showtime has arrived," Skeets muttered.

Then let's break our legs, said Ito. Is that the proper encouragement for human actors? Skeets sighed and turned to face the transport. "Close enough, Ito—although that image isn't particularly comforting at the moment."

40
Going my way?

Rudy squirmed in his seat, resisting the impulse to pace the central corridor of the transport. Instead he watched the forward monitor showing their progress through the mother tree forest. The trunks of the behemoth plants passed on either side of them like the legs of giants blurred behind veils of ash.

He turned briefly to regard his fellow passengers. Tadur and Maxifer sat next to each other talking about something. *Communicating* was a better verb than *talking*, Rudy knew, but old thought patterns died hard. Some words passed between them, but Maxifer's shifting scents and pulsing skin colors carried lots of information too, as Rudy knew well from his intimate knowledge of Master Morticue long ago. They were discussing Semma's plight, of course, as Ito Prime's newly- parasitized host.

For the moment, Ito/Semma sat passively in a seat across from, and to Rudy's left. He/she also watched the forward monitor. Fortunately, he had been able to convince Ito that not picking up Skeets would nullify any hope of getting access to Siu. The Ryan part of Siyan would make sure of that. He had not told Ito that he would be encountering a version of himself when Skeets came aboard. Hopefully that was the right decision. Rudy figured Semma was relatively safe as a hostage until a meeting with Siyan occurred. Beyond that, all bets were off. That would be a problem for another time.

"I have detected a human figure near the massive Mother Tree ahead," announced R72. "Conditions prohibit a firm confirmation of identity or gender."

"No problem, R72. I suspect the number of hitchhikers to be a minimum under the circumstances. Connect me to a loudspeaker or something so I can talk to her. Can you do that?"

"I can," R72 confirmed. After a brief pause, the bot said, "A channel is open."

The transport ground to a stop. Air brakes—or their equivalent—wheezed to silence as added confirmation that they were no longer moving. "Hey out there! Skeets? Going my way? I'm heading east of Dante's Inferno soon, and I'm pretty sure this will be the last shuttle for awhile."

The human figure by the massive tree laughed; then waved. "I'd be happy for a lift, sir—although you've got the weirdest Uber ride I've ever seen."

R72a, with a little assistance from Rudy, helped Skeets and her single packback of luggage board the transport. Skeets removed the hood and mask that had protected her from the outside elements. She shook her head and ran a hand through her blonde curls. She smiled at Rudy. "Dr. Goldstein, I presume?" She used a faux English accent as she extended her hand.

Rudy laughed. "So I must be speaking with Skeets, companion to Ryan Thompson, and not your alien… guest. He raised his eyebrows, and cupped her hand with both of his. "I do feel like I've been lost in the jungle, but for much longer than six years, my dear. And you look much much better than the pictures I've seen of Henry Morton Stanley." Rudy looked in the general direction of the speaker that connected him to R72 in the navigation alcove. "Get us to Master Veltipoe's Academy by the fastest route, R72. I'll get our guest strapped in."

"Plotting a course now, Rudy," said the AI.

Turning his attention back to Skeets, Rudy squeezed her hand once and released it. "For a million-year-old lady, you don't look a day over 25."

"Thank you, sir." Skeets' lips pursed coquettishly. "Your reputation as an old-school charmer precedes you. Mother Novaya tries to keep us at a physiological age somewhere in the 3-decade range. She must have it about right." Skeets looked toward Maxifer and Tadur. Tadur offered a tentative smile. Maxifer flickered in shades of blue.

Skeets turned her attention back to Rudy. "I understand we have a problem in need of a solution."

"That we do," confirmed Rudy as he nodded in Ito/Semma's general direction. "Let's get your gear stowed and we'll form a brain trust. Our task is merely to entice a homicidal alien to release his hostage, and for us to escape the world's untimely end. Can't be that hard, right? Especially since you are host to a—I hope—convincing negotiator for our side. I remember some old superhero holovids where even more difficult tasks were accomplished in forty minutes plus seemingly endless commercials for prescription drugs and legal services."

Before Skeets could answer, Tadur bolted from his seat and moved up the aisle to join them. "Please venerable Skeets, you must help us. I don't know what I would do if Semma..." Tadur nearly choked on the word. "... if something terrible happened... if..." Tadur's sentence wheezed to a stop.

The boy's got it bad, thought Rudy.

"I'll help under one condition, young man." Skeets put a hand on Tadur's shoulder and stared at him until his eyes focused completely on hers. "Don't call me venerable any more. Got it?"

Tadur blinked. "Of course. I'm so sorry... wise and beautiful Skeets. Just help me get my Semma back."

Skeets patted Tadur's shoulder. "I'll do my best."

Rudy looked beyond Skeets, noticing that Ito/Semma had risen from her seat, and was moving down the aisle toward them. Her face had all the expression of a Halloween mask sporting eyes that looked as impassive as marbles. Rudy hoped Skeets' best would be good enough.

41
Ito²

Ito Prime pushed against the surprisingly strong personality of Semma, managing to keep her subdued as he controlled her motor functions enough to walk up the aisle of the transport without stumbling. He tended to avoid female hosts. Some of that came, he knew, from a male Grovian's inbred subservience to the so-called superior gender, but human females—though supposedly the meeker sex in human social groups—tended to possess a stubbornness of deceptive strength and persistence. As if to punctuate that thought, Semma's irritation roiled within him like a meal of yogurt and beer. *Focus*, he told himself. *You are Ito Prime. All Grovian kind depends on you to fulfill your duties as consort to the Matriarch of the Diaspora.*

Ito Prime stopped within an arm's reach of Rudy and Skeets. He ignored Skeets for the moment and addressed Rudy. "I expect you to keep your promise, human. No deceptions. No unnecessary delays."

Rudy nodded. "I'll keep my word—and believe me, I don't want to delay anything. I have no desire to become an ash statue any time soon. We're proceeding to Master Veltipoe's Academy. You heard me give the command to R72. From there we will go straight to the Belfnik airport and on to the Citadel and your reunion with Siu."

Ito Prime narrowed his eyes. "Why not proceed directly to the airport?"

"We need to refuel for one thing," Rudy said. "We also need to pick up Master Veltipoe. Mnemosyne needs his expertise."

Ito Prime waited with no comment, a technique he often found resulted in receiving more detailed information.

"Master Veltipoe has worked extensively with human/Jadderbadian liaisons," Rudy added. "His work may give us all a better chance at surviving the eruption of the super volcano, and the climate changes to follow. That includes Grovians, humans, and Jadderbadians."

Ito Prime remained silent. Nothing mattered except the survival of Grovians, but he knew better than to voice that sentiment. He finally said, "I will be watching you all closely." He turned to look at each of them in turn before settling his gaze on Tadur. "Any deceit will result in the death of this female body I inhabit." Ito Prime then glanced at Maxifer, Rudy, and Skeets in turn. "One of your bodies will become my next host."

Skeets raised her right index finger. "My body's already taken," she announced. "In fact, you're in it—a version of you, at least."

Ito Prime frowned. "You're talking gibberish, human."

"Not at all." Skeets smiled. "One of your other clones nearly killed me once, a very long time ago—with a genocidal virus you cooked up for humans. But the entity called Siyan—a hybrid of Ryan Thompson, my mate, Siu, your heart-throb, from what I understand, and Guardian, the AI you helped program to survive eternity in a silver sphere—saved me. Siyan whisked me back in time to meet an earlier version of you, Ito. One that's a bit less prickly, I might say."

"Nonsense!" Ito Prime felt a flush rising on Semma's cheeks.

"Not at all!" Skeets smiled again. "Wanna meet him? Give me a second now—he's hunkered down somewhere inside me. Wait. Wait. Ah, there you are, my Ito. "Ito, you need to meet, Ito Prime, your evil twin." With that, Skeets' smiled faded and her eyes seemed to stare into the distance. "The human speaks the truth," Ito/Skeets said. "We need to talk. Otherwise, the Grand Jokester, Meaira, will win uncontested." Ito/Skeets nodded toward the doorway leading to the conference area.

Ito Prime remained skeptical, but it certainly sounded like him— at least something he would say. *Meaira always wins in the end,* he thought. *Even human cultures recognized that. The Norse had their Loki, Africans their Anansi. The Japanese recognized Kitsune, the Lakota honored Iktomi, and the Hindus worshipped the seductive Krishna.* Nevertheless, he turned and headed up the aisle toward the adjoining compartment, assuming that the Ito/Skeets abomination would follow.

She did.

* * * * *

Their subsequent conversation had a surreal quality for Ito Prime. Here he was talking to himself while stuck inside two ugly alien shells. Oh for the days when he and Siu roamed in their proper ambuli bodies—before this planet managed to evolve human beings. Dinosaurs were much easier to deal with than apes with hypertrophied brains.

Ito Prime: What are you thinking? Grovians are the only true intelligence in the universe. We must make Earth the New Grove. Greatest Mother demands it.

Ito: Oh, come now. Greatest Mother? Really? You were always chastising Siu for believing in spirits.

Ito Prime: I did like to yank her tail from time to time.

Ito: Yes, that was fun, of course—but that wasn't the only reason. You—I, have always had our doubts. If Greatest Mother truly designed this universe, she must have flunked design class.

Ito Prime: Be that as it may, Grovians certainly represent a higher intelligence than these human creatures. They were literally vermin scuttling beneath the feet of giant lizards when we first arrived on this planet. Who wants to take up housekeeping with the spawn of shrews?

Ito: Humans grow on you. I find this Skeets has some endearing traits: intelligence, creativity, persistence—even a refreshing lust for living…

Ito Prime: The humans I've known have been less endearing. I had to detoxify the body of Jacques Lideaux, a trapper, when I jumped to him. His blood must have been close to 100 proof. His inclination was to scalp strangers first, and inquire about their intentions second. And talk about lust for living. I lived within a preacher once whose technique for rewarding the faithful was…

Ito: Granted, humans are not perfect—but neither are Grovians

156

or—from what I can tell—Jadderbadians. The point is—and I think Siu realized this when her consciousness first entered the mind of Ryan Thompson—we can learn from these creatures, if we let them teach us. And we can teach them a lot as well.

Ito Prime: Just what do you expect to learn, my naïve early self?

Ito: Perhaps how to survive this planet. Somehow both humans and Grovians have muddled through two asteroid strikes, but this looming supervolcano eruption could deal a deathblow to both our species. Now Jadderbaddians have a stake in the outcome as well. Maybe we can pass through the stargate they used to access Earth. Maybe the secret is some sort of symbiosis, like Siyan—or like the Rudimort hybrid I have heard of—the union of the ancient human, Rudy, and the Jadderbaddian, Master Morticue Ambergrand.

Ito Prime: I have no intention of continuing as an abomination.

Ito: Extinction is preferable? A pretty corpse is still a corpse.

Ito Prime: Siu and I together will avoid that fate. We make a formidable pairing. I will convince her of the error in her thinking.

Ito (laughing): Right. When's the last time *that* happened?

Ito Prime: Take me to Siu, and I will show you the proper technique.

Ito: We're on our way, old soul. Is that Meaira I hear laughing?

42
Academics and abominations

Master Veltipoe felt like a firstie abandoned in a hatching cavern. All his students and staff were below ground now, either in suspension chambers or maintenance modules. Various indicator lights blinked slowly on the master console, reflecting subdued activity. His library of books flickered in muted colors to either side of him. Rows of emptied aquaria hulked before and aft, their contents either transferred to subterranean quarters below, or their elements reclaimed and stored until (hopefully) their eventual return. *When might that be?* The super volcano most certainly would erupt catastrophically, burying this area for some time to come. He hoped his emergency plans would keep the work of his lifetime intact. Fortunately, he had been able to transfer copies of quantum dot and nucleic acid files to Mnemosyne. Having copies outside his immediate control made him a bit nervous, but data unshared is useless. He knew that. Master Veltipoe expelled air through his spiracles with a sigh. The sound bounced about the chamber creating a sad echo.

An alarm chimed. *Which quadrant? Must be them. I hope it's them.* Master Veltipoe glanced at the security monitor on the wall. A color icon on the lower right of the screen identified the view as coming from the cameras on the west edge of the compound. He saw the road leading toward the forest of terra incognita shrouded in morning fog, and...

A dog barked.

What? Impossible. All the human pets should be in suspension with their masters. Master Veltipoe looked away from the monitor and down at his tripod of legs. Tadur's scrawny carnivore pet circled his lower appendages as it tentatively wagged its tail. "Dusty!

Bad dog." Master Veltipoe heard himself shouting—just like Tadur would do with regularity on the occasion of some misdeed—Even though Veltipoe knew that Dusty was more likely to pee on his feet than pay any attention to his commands. The dog's metronomic tail behavior did pause, however. "You're supposed to be in cold suspension. Where have you been hiding?" Even as he asked the rhetorical question, he seemed to recall that some student—or was it a service bot?—had remarked that Tadur's pet was missing.

Dusty sat on his haunches, looked up at him, and cocked his head to one side.

"I haven't got time for this," Veltipoe muttered to himself before turning two eyes back toward the monitor, and blinking the third. He expelled air through his spiracles in a snort of frustration. He could make out the form of the transport emerging from the forest, a hulking shape expanding in apparent size as it drew nearer. A trio of headlights glowed like the eyes of a Trevoile, one of his favorite creatures from Jadderbadian mythology. *It is them. The exterior sensors confirm the vehicle's identity.*

Veltipoe heard the click of Dusty's nails on the floor tiles. He devoted one eye to monitoring the dog, who had taken up a position between him and the monitor. Dusty stood erect and expectant. The animal accelerated its tail waving, as if he knew his master was now somehow close by.

"I suppose we'll have to take you with us to the Citadel," Veltipoe mumbled to himself, "Tadur will be pleased, but I have no idea what the alien holding Semma hostage will have to say about that." Rudy had kept him informed about the situation in the transport. Mnemosyne also updated him on events through his subcutaneous com implant. Rudy had provided the necessary frequency and access coding for that before he left.

Veltipoe's head swirled with worries. He liked planning and schedules. He liked knowing what each day held in store. Now volcanoes erupted, threatening to erase his life's work. Malevolent aliens rudely jumped in and out of other people's bodies. His dreams of symbiotic mergers between his talented Jadderbadian and human students threatened to dissipate like yesterday's fart unless he acted quickly and correctly during the next few hours. His dorsal hearts pounded more than when he defended his dissertation as a young second molt—or that time as a first molt when he nearly drove his new transport over the Cliff of a Thousand Falls near Belfnik.

Would Tadur and Maxifer become a willing syncytiote? If so, would their merger really make any difference now? The world as they knew it seemed destined for oblivion. But Mnemosyne, in the brief discussions he had had with her, seemed hopeful that his work held great promise. She hinted that she had learned something critical from the creature called Siyan—a unique merger of human, Grovian, and AI with astounding abilities.

The docking chime sounded, ending Veltipoe's reverie. He glanced at the wall monitor and noticed a light blinking green. He must make his way to the docking portal in order to punch in the code that would allow access to the academy. Master Veltipoe opened all his spiracles and inhaled deeply—practicing the same behavior he urged on his students at stressful times. He bent over to regard Dusty with all three of his primary eyes. "I will get you some water. Then, I suspect you will follow me, four-legged carnivore, but you must behave. No barking. And especially no biting. No need to make a deranged alien even more dangerous."

Dusty regarded him with open eyes and drooping tongue. He cocked his head, probably having recognized the word *water*, at least.

Master Veltipoe snorted through his spiracles and released what he hoped were calming pheromones through his pores before he crossed the room to the elevator that would take him to the kitchen and the docking portal one level below.

* * * * *

The door of the transport slid aside to reveal the tall form of Master Veltipoe swaying slightly on his tripod of legs, while a small brown mutt of indeterminate breed fidgeted on the Jadderbadian's left side, cleaving the air with his tail. Rudy had to smile. He noticed that Ito Prime/Semma on his right stood a little straighter as if they

160

were not particularly comfortable with canines.

"Dusty!" Tadur bolted around Rudy on his left. "I thought I would never see you again." Tadur and dog collided in an excited greeting tangle in front of Master Veltipoe.

Maxifer moved forward and took Tadur's vacated position on Rudy's left. "Human's certainly have an affection for their four-legged companions."

"That they do," Rudy agreed. "I've petted my share."

"Me, too," added Skeets from her position behind him. She had re-assumed control of her body from Ito.

"Jadderbadian," Ito Prime/Semma said to Master Veltipoe, "I am Ito Prime, First Mate of Siutiasa, Grand Matriarch of the Diaspora. My species made claim to this planet approximately 67 million years ago, thus prior to the evolution of the semi-intelligent primates you call Groupies, and before Jadderbadian invasion through a temporal/spacial-distortion called the Stargate. As Grovian claims predate Jadderbadian, and as Grovian superiority is ordained by Greatest Mother, I will direct activities from this point forward involving my transportation to a destination I understand is called the Citadel."

Master Veltipoe snorted through several spiracles. Rudy felt a droplet or two of moisture collide with his left cheek. The Jadderbadian leaned forward and arched over Semma like a drooping saguaro cactus. "You sound like a stuffy professor I knew once with a law degree from the Grand Academy. I understand you are a parasite. You should have co-opted a more impressive host, if you wish to make grand pronouncements."

Rudy laughed. "Nice comeback, old worm." Rudy leaned forward and lowered his voice conspiratorially. "Ito Prime here—all grand claims aside—does have us by the short hairs, as we humans used to say. Tadur's girl here is in real danger. Besides, I think it's in all our best interests to make haste toward the Citadel, wouldn't you agree?"

Master Veltipoe straightened to his full height and expelled a sigh of air through his spiracles. His hide shimmered in shades of amber and green. "Agreed, archaic human. I will assume being pulled by one's short hairs is painful. I will help expedite our exodus." Master

Veltipoe paused before adding "And hope for the best."

Tadur stood up, regarding Semma with a worried frown on his brow. Dusty looked up at Tadur, his tail poised like a weathervane anticipating the next breeze.

An hour vanished quickly. Service bots performed routine maintenance on the transport as it was fueled. They also recycled poor Ivan's corpse, making it a welcome addition to the hydroponic's soil reserves. Tadur and Maxifer restocked enough food supplies to last until they reached the air terminal. Rudy and Skeets helped Master Veltipoe monitor news feeds from Belfnik, scientific drone updates from various locales surrounding the epicenter of volcanic activity, and occasional transmissions from Mnemosyne.

"Major roads are still open to Belfnik," Veltipoe reported, "although we will have to detour around damage caused by an erupting vent near distance marker 31."

Rudy glanced at the most recent drone feeds. "Subterranean activity is ramping up. We'd better move soon."

Master Veltipoe turned one eye toward the feeds Rudy was monitoring. He said nothing, but the Jadderbadian's hide pulsed in shades of amber morphing toward red. He smelled somewhat like vinegar and burnt toast.

Ito Prime/Semma hovered near Rudy and Master Veltipoe like the proctor of a test looking for cheaters.

Finally, all preparations made, everyone boarded the transport, including Dusty. The vehicle's engines rumbled to life. Gravel crunched under its tires until it reached the deserted main thoroughfare. A sulfurous fog swirled outside the windows. Beneath them the earth shuddered as if it held back a beast poised to break the chains that held it in place.

43
Explosion cum laude

Rudy sat on a bench in the passenger alcove of the transport watching the exterior monitors. Tadur and Maxifer fidgeted on his right with Dusty curled at Tadur's feet. Ito Prime/ Semma sat somewhere in front of them near the AI driver and Master Veltipoe, who were conferring about something. Skeets was out of sight. Rudy knew she had planned to talk with her companion Ryan, and might be hiding out in a nook somewhere trying to have a private conversation via the transport's com link to Mnemosyne. If Ito Prime/Semma knew about the link, the Grovian would probably demand to talk to his long lost mate that way.

Rudy felt oddly detached from the events swirling around him— including the occasional earth tremors that rocked their vehicle. He had died twice now, so what was so special about hovering on the brink one more time? He remembered Alice squeezing his hand on his deathbed at Community General on Old Earth, as he'd come to think of it, nearly a million years ago. The atoms that composed her body would be spread far and wide by now. Maybe some of her made up the new him. He hoped so. The idea brought a strange comfort with it—probably a kind of comfort unique to twice-dead nerd geniuses.

He also remembered his death while sharing the body of Master Morticue, sitting on a rock outcrop watching the stars fade to black. Too bad Mnemosyne couldn't bring that old scholar to life again. For a worm-a-pede alien, he was a better than average companion. Master Veltipoe was cut from the same cloth, though—part of an unofficial Society of Eternal Academics, he guessed—consisting of those who reveled in trying to figure out the rules of the universe, all the while knowing it was a fool's errand.

Rudy watched the terrain pass by—mostly ghostly, mist-shrouded stands of trees that looked like mourners along the route of a funeral caravan—until they reached the suburbs of Belfnik. Ragged rows of buildings soon replaced the trees. A few Jadderbadians and humans scurried from place to place like rats seeking shelter in a storm, but most streets lay deserted—crisscrossed ribbons of packed dirt and something very similar to the asphalt used in Rudy's time.

"Is that the airport?" Tadur asked. He pointed to the monitor as they rounded a curve. The terminal hulked in front of them like some beast crouched in the mist. Two windows glowed like eyes above a tarmac, with just one Jadderbadian aircraft in evidence.

"Bingo, my boy. Some brave soul hung around until we arrived."

"Bingo?" Tadur's brow furrowed.

"A very old game. I'll explain later. Let's get our gear together." Rudy rose and began gathering his own things to set the proper example.

Transfer to the plane proceeded quickly. Rudy was sure that the pair of attendants who had hung around to see them off was anxious to rid themselves of tardy travelers and find shelter for themselves. In less than half an hour they were airborne with an AI pilot at the helm. The Jadderbadian military that had accompanied them on their eastbound trip were either deployed elsewhere, or had decided to retreat east on an earlier transport. Rudy requested a view to their rear. Perhaps he shouldn't have.

"Oh, wow!" Skeets, sitting to his left, leaned forward, straining against the chair's restraint harness.

"Indeed," Rudy heard himself whisper. The monumental cone of the super volcano to the north—Rudy liked to think of it as The Bride of Yellowstone, since he couldn't pronounce the Jadderbadian name for it—pierced the blue-gray sky like a majestic natural pyramid. Suddenly, it began to fracture and dissolve. Millions of tons of rock descended in obscenely slow motion. The mountain consumed itself from the inside out. As the tip of the mountain disappeared and fell, it generated a column of ash that rose into the sky like a ropy pillar straining to keep the heavens from collapsing onto the gray

164

ceiling of mist that blanketed the forest below. About two thirds of the way up the pillar, disks of gray highlighted in shades of pink and amber fanned out into nearly perfect lenses resembling flying saucers. Above the saucer clouds the ash roiled and puffed into constantly changing shapes reminding Rudy of mountainous cliffs with laughing gargoyle faces. As the pillar rose, necklaces of lightning discharged in gaudy, sparkling strings of light and power. "Gaia is just showing off now."

"She's impressing the hell out of me," said Skeets.

"Are we going to die, Great Rudy?" Tadur's voice rose above his oversized Jadderbadian passenger chair an octave higher than usual.

"Of course, super great-grandson," said Rudy. "That's a given. But, hopefully, it won't be today. The Jadderbadians make some decent AI pilots—from what Nessie has told me, anyway." Rudy saw the edge of Maxifer's head when he leaned toward Tadur's chair, apparently offering commentary to Tadur that Rudy couldn't hear.

Glancing back at the monitor, Rudy noticed gold and scarlet contrails emerging from Gaia's ostentatious pillar of ash like Fourth of July fireworks. One fireball of light began to grow larger quickly. Too quickly. Suddenly, their aircraft lurched and accelerated in herky-jerky fashion. The image on the viewscreen blurred. Rudy put a hand out reflexively to ward off contact with the back of the recliner in front of him, but his restraint harness performed its job flawlessly.

Someone emitted a choked squeal in one of the forward seats.

"Everyone okay up there?" Rudy asked.

"Semma? Are you all right, Semma?" Rudy heard Tadur's plaintive question.

"Is this craft equipped with additional clothing?" Rudy recognized the voice of Ito Prime/Semma. "A sphincter in this human's body suffered a momentary failure."

Skeets choked on a laugh before Rudy did.

"I'll check the supply cabinets," Master Veltipoe offered, "as soon as this aircraft ceases evasive maneuvers."

Let's hope the maneuvers are successful, thought Rudy. *If they aren't, we won't have to worry about wearing clean underwear.*

44
The best laid plans of superhumans and AIs

❝ They're on their way." The Ryan part of Siyan felt relief that he would soon be reunited with Skeets. The Siu part of him wasn't quite sure what to feel. She loved the Ito she had left Grove with such a long time ago. That Ito had helped her build their outpost on Earth—an outpost that was thriving just before the asteroid impact that destroyed the dinosaur-dominated ecology of that era, setting the stage for the burst of mammalian evolution that followed, culminating with human primates. She could hardly recognize the bitter version of Ito that had distilled from lifetimes of planning and disappointment during the brief hegemony of human civilization.

"Yes," agreed Mnemosyne, "our strange expedition has successfully avoided personal extinction once again—at least for the moment."

Siyan scanned Mnemosyne's matrix as a mere human might look at a vast landscape before setting out on a long journey. He felt Mnemosyne probing him in a similar way—one traveler sizing up another, trying to decide if they should share the same path. "Here are the problems I perceive and several potential solutions. Correct me if you see errors.

"1. The Citadel is momentarily safe from most of the immediate effects of the supervolcano's eruption, but the subsequent climatic impacts will be severe. All sentient creatures on Earth must adapt— or perhaps flee.

"2. Flight will be restricted to moving to less impacted portions of this planet or escaping to Jadderbad through the stargate. Jadderbadians on their home world might not be keen for the latter option.

"3. If we could contact this immodest Pi creature—*Hominem infigo*—he, she, or it might take time off from his, her, or its galactic brain project to render aid and assistance.

"4. Currently, I can escape at any time because of my abilities to move about through space and time, but I have no idea how to replicate my abilities for anyone else.

"5. An intelligent xenophobe mate that part of me once loved dearly might derail or void some or all of our efforts."

"Excellent summary, Siyan. I have had some opportunity to experience your unique blend of Grovian, human, and artificial intelligence. At the moment I'm not quite sure how you work either, but I'm eager to find out. I seem to have acquired something from my long association with Rudy: a burst of energy in my circuits at the prospect of discovering something previously unknown. I feel that I'm on the cusp of an insight—one that needs all the participants currently on an air transport dodging flaming ejecta from a volcano. It would also help," Mnemosyne continued, "to have the cooperation of Gaia and Hydra. They helped me integrate the intelligence of Rudy into Master Morticue long ago. Their cooperation doesn't seem likely at the moment."

Siyan felt another throb from the cabochon currently hanging from Ryan's neck. *How is the trans-dimensional gateway connected to all this?* He directed a different question to Mnemosyne: "What is the ETA of the transport?"

"Two hours plus or minus 22 minutes, based on current variables projected by my satellite surveillance systems. I realize that the error bar is unacceptably broad, but my resources are not as complete as I would like."

"Ah, we have time to explore some of our options." Siyan felt a spark of optimism. "Perhaps if we review the old records from the period of time when Rudy and Master Morticue approached the Stargate we can replicate some action that might induce the appearance of Pi—assuming he still exists. We can see if he can provide help."

"Good action plan." Mnemosyne assembled the relevant data from her memory core and activated a live feed so that she could consciously experience a view of the Stargate and share it with Siyan. She chose a view that Rudy always enjoyed—one from a low angle so that the golden arch dwarfed surrounding buildings and accentuated the roiling fields of disturbed spacetime it encompassed. Rudy always said it was a good idea to be awed and humbled on a regular basis, to nurture one's humility.

Mnemosyne was just about to share that memory with Siyan when the arch vanished. It blinked out of existence, leaving no electromagnetic trace — gone for the first time in 125 years.

"Holy shit," whispered the human part of Siyan.

"Just what Rudy would have said," acknowledged Mnemosyne. "Or perhaps: 'So much for that idea.'"

45
Reunion at the Citadel

"Holy shit! The stargate did what?" Rudy felt everyone's eyes on him after the exclamation burst from his lips. "I can't leave you alone for a minute, can I Nessie?" Pause. "Yes, yes. I know you have a backup copy of me available..." Rudy idly stroked the skin on his temple above his neural implant with his right index finger.

"What's the problem, human?" Ito Prime/Semma moved toward him up the aisle of the transport. He/she paused for a moment, closing their eyes while taking a deep breath.

"Got a headache, Mr. parasite?" asked Rudy. "Humans will do that to you—especially someone as frisky as the Semma I've come to know."

Ito Prime/Semma opened their eyes. Rudy thought he could actually detect the struggle flickering beneath those pretty orbs. "What's going on? You best not be scheming to keep me from my mate, Siu."

"You'll have your meeting, but something rather momentous just happened. The Stargate connecting Earth and Jadderbad just... disappeared."

"Disappeared?" Ito Prime/Semma frowned. "Why?"

"Exellent question. Nessie doesn't know, nor does Siyan. Looks like we can all be dumbfounded together." Rudy smiled.

"How long before we land?"

"Not long now, it would seem. Feel's like we're descending. Ask the pilot AI, if you like." When Ito Prime/Semma didn't respond immediately, Rudy couldn't resist asking: "How's that new pair of underwear Master Veltipoe found? Comfy?"

* * * * *

They disembarked at the Jadderbadian military airport without incident. The tarmac was nearly deserted. Gray clouds covered the sun, allowing a northerly breeze to easily cut through the weave of Rudy's trousers. Tork, the Jadderbadian commander who had flown with them to Belfnik on the flight west, met them at the terminal. "I'll escort you to the Citadel," he said without preamble. "Follow me to the ground transport." Rudy's neck hurt just looking up at Tork's imposing third instar height. *Harder to lose sight of than a giraffe, bless their extinct souls*, thought Rudy.

The drive to the Citadel proved uneventful. Although both the human and Jadderbadian population in the area had expanded considerably since Rudy's last death—and that sounded weird just thinking it—structures had been built into the surrounding landscape in such a way as to be almost invisible. Tall structures weren't that advisable in this area anyway, considering the active geology.

The Citadel, of course, was the exception, but then it was a million-year-old relic maintained by Nessie's army of nanobots. It soon towered in front of them like a silvery Washington's Monument, the glow of a partially cloud-concealed sun looking like a halo near its apex. It had been a long time since Rudy had seen it from the outside. Although nanobots maintained the integrity of its structural elements, Nessie had allowed the growth of mosses and lichens to embellish the outer walls. Perhaps she was catering to Botza and the other humans who still worshipped "Spider Woman" as a goddess. Monuments should look suitably old and worthy of reverence. Rudy suspected Nessie might not be totally immune to the euphoria of adoration—although, if true, that could be his fault. At least she always complained that he was guilty of humanizing her.

They parked on level ground beneath a pair of gnarled pines. *This has got to be close to where Twill and I set off on our adventure to understand invading Jadderbadian aliens a couple of lifetimes ago*, thought Rudy. *Of course, Twill just thought I was an annoying ancestral voice in his head at the time. Now I'm here with his great-grandson. He glanced at Tadur. Good grief, Charlie Brown.*

Commander Tork said he would return to base, and to contact him if they needed transport later.

Just after they exited the vehicle, a balding human caricature of Charlie Brown approached them. Rudy recognized High Priest Botza. "Welcome back, Great Rudy," said Botza with a deferential bow. "Spider Woman has told me that you would arrive with friends to help us survive difficult times to come." Botza made a point of examining Skeets, Tadur, Maxifer, and Master Veltipoe with lingering glances. Dusty wagged his tail, but Botza only sniffed, as if offended somehow by the dog's presence. "And Semma, it is so good…"

"I am not Semma. You are addressing Ito Prime, Consort to Siutiasa, Matriarch of the Diaspora. I demand to see my mate."

"Whom you may know as Ryan or perhaps Siyan," offered Rudy.

"Of course. Of course," Botza stammered. "The spirit creature that pops in and out of existence. I will lead you into the Citadel and let Spider Woman sort out matters far beyond the purview of this humble priest." Botza placed his right hand over his chest. "I have assembled a small local chorus of human singers to help ease the tensions of the moment and facilitate this conference. They will meet us inside."

Ito Prime/Semma made a dismissive gesture. "Take me to my mate. Now!"

Botza turned and led the group to the Citadel entrance. After casting a pinch of ceremonial pollen into the air, he touched the control that triggered the opening of the Citadel's entrance. "Enter and prepare to behold Spider Woman."

As they entered into the semi-dark interior and made their way across well-worn stone tiles, Master Veltipoe whispered to Rudy. "I thought the cult of Spider Woman was mostly a ceremonial religion these days. High Priest Botza seems… quite invested."

Rudy whispered back. "Most of the local Jadderbadians still worship at the Altar of the Grand Disciple. Go figure. Gods will always be popular shorthand for understanding the universe, I guess. Botza thinks I'm the Spirit Reborn from the Sacrifice of Rudimort—or some such. So, be nice to me, old worm, or I will smite you—or something." Rudy smiled.

They approached a high wall. Rudy could just discern the outlines of the Spider Woman figure Mnemosyne used to speak to Botza and the other faithful. Rudy jumped as the human chorus Botza had mentioned began singing off to their right, somewhere in the gloom. The Spider Woman avatar flashed on in all its Technicolor and holographic glory—a human superwoman indeed, endowed with glorious muscles and massive breasts straining against the bonds of what appeared to be spandex nearly stretched to the limits of its tensile strength.

Skeets barked a laugh. Dusty just barked. Tadur and Maxifer muttered something between them. High Priest Botza bowed, and then knelt. Ito Prime/Semma merely stood at attention, apparently waiting. Master Veltipoe inhaled deeply through all his spiracles.

Rudy smiled. "Nessie, you do know how to put on a show now, don't you?" he said, mostly to himself. "I suppose that's my fault, too."

"You may leave us now, High Priest Botza," said Mnemosyne in an exalted tone any preacher would have admired. "Please thank the chorus and retire with them to the Chamber of Meditation and Renewal. I have godly business to conduct with our guests." Mnemosyne's Spider Woman avatar smiled, and flexed one of her impressive biceps for good measure.

46
Chairperson-in-chief

After Botza and the human chorus left, a panel slid aside in the wall below Spider Woman, the hologram, to reveal a dimly-lit hallway. Siu/Ryan stepped forward to stand at the entrance. Siu looked directly at Ito Prime/Semma as she offered an invitation. "Please, follow me into this alcove. We have much to talk about, and many decisions to make."

Ito Prime/Semma squinted and leaned closer to Siu/Ryan. "Siu? Is that truly you looking out from that ugly human shell?"

"It is, my dear—if perhaps misguided—Ito. We will talk soon." Siu/Ryan took a deep breath, and then turned and began walking down the hallway, assuming her guests would follow.

They did.

The hallway soon ended at an arched doorway comfortable for even third instar Jadderbadians to pass through. The doorway opened into a large chamber. Rudy recognized the room as a kind of conference center that Nessie outfitted in various ways when she had to converse with humans or Jadderbadians from the city that had built up around the Citadel. Now Rudy faced an arc of recliner style chairs, some built for human use; others designed for Jadderbadians. A holographic embodiment of Nessie as the young, ponytailed sprite Rudy had come to know, rose from a chair placed facing the guest recliners. "Welcome to my Citadel," she said with the enthusiasm of a museum tour guide. She smiled and added a wink that Rudy thought was meant for him. *What is my dear Nessie up to?*

Siu/Ryan stepped forward to stand by Mnemosyne. "Where do you want me and Ito Prime/Semma to sit?"

"Take the two human-sized chairs in the middle." Mnemosyne

gestured toward the center of the arc of furniture. She could have passed for a young CEO from the late 21st century, dressed in form-fitting pewter jeans and a black high-necked pullover. Her ponytail bobbed to and fro as she directed Skeets to a chair on the other side of Siu/Ryan on her left as she faced the group. Maxifer and Tadur took their places in a pair of recliners—one human and one Jadder-baddian—adjacent to each other on the far left. Dusty sat at Tadur's feet. Master Veltipoe and Rudy found their places in similar adjoining chairs to the right of Ito Prime/Semma, who sat as stiffly as an empress slumming at a PTA meeting.

Nessie sat down and crossed her legs. "Let's begin, shall we? We have at least one planetary intelligence angry with us—never a good thing—and a guest with a grievance to be heard." Nessie looked directly at Ito Prime/Semma.

"Grievance? How about ultimatum? Who put you in charge, AI? Artificial intelligences are tools, not independent agents. I should know. I created Guardian ages ago to help preserve all Grovian kind." Ito Prime/Semma glared at Mnemosyne. "I am consort to Siu-tiasa, Matriarch of the Diaspora. My mate and I have private business to discuss that is not the concern of alien abominations."

Mnemosyne's avatar took a deep breath and smiled. "Well, that certainly is one point of view." Mnemosyne stood up and spread her arms. In a commanding voice she declared, "All abominations please leave the room!"

Dusty cocked his head in apparent confusion. Rudy could sympathize.

When no one made a move to rise, Mnemosyne continued. "It would seem that being an abomination is one of those squishy, emotional points of view that vary from individual to individual. I contend that organic intelligences are inherently flawed by hormone-induced erratic behavior, making an AI a logical choice to host a meeting." Mnemosyne produced a quirky smile Rudy had come to appreciate. "Besides, my long time companion Rudy..." She nodded in Rudy's direction "...always told me that 'Power is the most persuasive rhetoric,' so..."

Mnemosyne's muscles and stature grew, splitting her CEO costume into tatters before revealing her red and blue Spider Woman persona. She also grew an impressive pair of iridescent fangs any jumping spider would have been proud of. "…I could suck you all dry of fluids and leave your bodies behind like shriveled husks OR…"

Her body morphed and swelled again until it assumed the form of a third instar Jadderbadian who had already formed her final chrysalis. The cylindrical form slowly split revealing the gigantic, moth-like form of an adult female. "…I could chew you all into shredded flesh like Mother Supreme at Final Metamorphosis." She flexed her wings and cast a shadow over the seated forms of Maxifer and Tadur. "OR…"

Her body condensed into a large amorphous mass that became a gnarled trunk that grew up to the distant ceiling until branches fanned out into a dense spray of leaves. Roots grew from the base and snaked their way toward Siu/Ryan and Ito Prime/Semma. "…I could become Greatest Mother who digests and absorbs her last tribe of ambuli children at the end of time OR…"

Now Mnemosyne became once again the Nessie that Rudy had come to love. "…I could just spray you with a mist of nanobots that would disassemble your carbon frameworks atom by atom." Mnemosyne spread her arms wide. "Or I could just get this meeting going. Should I take a formal vote?"

Dusty peeked up at Mnemosyne from between Tadur's legs, patiently waiting for a sign of what to do.

Rudy just clapped. "Bravo, Nessie. Bravo." *I hope she also remembered that line of Shakespeare I once quoted: "Madness in great ones must not unwatched go."*

47
Passing thoughts while passing gas

Hydra: That's an impressive supervolcano you set off, Gaia. What now? I was rather hoping at least some of my Jadderbadians might escape your outburst using the Stargate—before it vanished, that is.

Gaia: Yes, that was a surprise. My guess is that the post-human, Pi, had something to do with that. Once they leave your biosphere and gravitational influence, organics can be rather unpredictable—even the ones that become cyborgs.

Hydra: Maybe you can ease off on the super volcano eruption. I've manipulated my vents on Jadderbad a time or two by…

Gaia: No! The volcano will take its course. These advanced organics on my hide had better adapt or die. As more than one of them have said to each other, "My way or the highway." Now it's their turn.

Hydra: But now you—we—have post-organic intelligences to deal with: Mnemosyne, Guardian, and this Pi creature. They think quite nimbly, you know.

Gaia: You and I have formidable brains ourselves, Hydra, with synapses that have billions of years of evolution behind them. Remember that.

Hydra: Speaking of synapses: I see you have retracted some of your micorrhizhal/bacterial connections with Mnemosyne. I would hope you would stay in touch with her—to keep track of what she is up to, if nothing else.

Gaia: I'm monitoring her behavior—just providing enough entity spacing to keep her wondering what we're up to.

Hydra: So, does your venerable brain have an inspired thought or two about what comes next? What you plan to do, or what she *might* do?

Gaia: Don't be a pest, Hydra. My magma is on the move... a pathway here, another pathway there. Water boils. Feel the steam dissolving that sandstone; pushing... pushing past those seams of granite. Where's the light? Where's the exit? Oh, there! .Ahhhhh, yes!

That feels better! Give me a moment. I'm sure my thoughts will be as clear and sharp as the sky over an Early Pleistocene spring meadow before you know it.

48
Lover's reunion

"Skeets, I must come forward," said Ito. It seemed strange to be sitting near the young female human called Semma and confronting a clone that had once shared his complete memories and identity, but had gone on to live a very different existence for an obscenely long time. Ito needed to be fully present in the moment to understand his alternate self—a version of him that had never reunited with Siu in spite of lifetimes of searching. He, on the other hand, had been able to share his mate's company for many lifetimes—even if it was a union oddly distorted by sharing it through the physical relationship of two human lovers: Ryan Thompson and Skeets Moleckson. No wonder his other self seemed angry, confused, and just a bit—provincial. Provincial? Perhaps deranged was the right word.

"I understand," said Skeets as she allowed Ito's personality to come forward and dominate consciousness within her body. It took Ito a moment to get used to the limited sensory capacity of a human body again. He especially missed the color vlegmat, which Skeets had no name for because it existed in the ultraviolet end of the spectrum, invisible to humans. Teetering on two legs rather than four also tended to make him nauseous for a moment or two. He raised Skeets' arm and ran its five-fingered hand through the hair on her head, smoothing its contours into submission in the way she preferred. There. He was starting to get the hang of behaving as a human female again.

Ito Prime/Semma leaned toward Siu/Ryan sitting in adjoining chairs. "Are you going to allow this histrionic AI to dictate the terms of our reunion, Siu?" He waved Semma's right arm in Mnemosyne's general direction. "We are Grovians, after all. You are Matriarch."

Ito remembered the pride he had always felt as consort to the Matriarch. She had picked him out of a herd of many young stallions, after all, when they were both young. She had always said she liked the enticing way he had of waving his oral pili to scatter scent in her direction. She claimed the way he arched his flank just so, flexing his muscles to maximize their contours, drove her to distraction when she should have been paying attention to her royal duties.

"That we are, my stallion—my little poke." Siu/Ryan leaned toward Ito Prime/Semma until their foreheads nearly touched. "But Grove has long been a cinder circling a dead star. We live in this biosphere now. Intelligence has taken different forms here—and Mnemosyne is right. She dictates the terms of engagement at the moment." Siu/Ryan took a deep breath. "Tell me what you want—what you expect of me, but I have to warn you: You might not like my answers."

Ito knew how it was to hear answers he didn't like from Siu—although Siu was more enlightened than many of her Grovian sisters when it came to gender inequality. She had allowed him—a mere male—to be not only her First Mate, but also lead scientist in designing their exodus from Grove. He was a genius, after all. Siu's biggest achievement was recognizing that, and allowing him to perform at the peak of his abilities. Ito took pride in his crafting of Guardian, for example—the AI that ultimately preserved their neural engrams when the Grovian Earth colony was on the verge of extinction. But how had the Ryan-Guardian-Siutiasa merger acquired the ability to travel through space and time, while the Ito-Guardian-Skeets triad of which he was a member had not so transformed?

"Earth should be our reward for all we gambled and suffered, of course!" Ito Prime/Semma sat ramrod stiff and sniffed imperiously. "Habitable planets are not that easy to come by, you know."

Ito supposed his counterpart had a point there—although Grovian mother tree philosophers may have debated whether Grovians were entitled to someone else's planet through the exercise of brute force and cunning.

"Perhaps when Earth possessed nothing smarter than giant

saurians with brains the size of a budding mother tree pod. But then humans evolved while we waited out the millennia in stasis. When I awoke in the body of Ryan Thompson, I recognized a kindred intelligence. I just couldn't wantonly destroy him."

Ito knew that he probably could have been capable of that, back in the day. Humans at first glance looked like a proper ambulus sawed in half, with their brains haphazardly stuffed in what should have been an optical bulb. Who would place a brain in such a vulnerable position anyway, perched on top of the spinal column?

"Survival favors the ruthless. You were weak, my love," declared Ito Prime/Semma. "That's a failing that may have cost us our birthright."

Ito realized that's exactly what he would have said when he and Siu were preparing to go into stasis 67 million years ago. So what had changed him? The birth of Siyan had—a birth precipitated by Skeets near death from Rhondal/Ito's 21st century, humanity-destroying plague. Siyan had crossed spacetime to do it—ultimately saving Skeets with a curing kiss by Ryan. How melodramatic, not to mention unsanitary—intertwining one's oral cavities as a sign of romantic interest. Ito's memory engrams along with a Guardian clone had provided the antidote to the virus Skeets had contracted. But, for whatever reason, the Ito-Guardian-Skeets merger couldn't bend time and space the way Siyan could.

Not for lack of trying, noted Guardian.

No, we have tried over the millennia. It would certainly be a useful talent now, Ito added.

Skeets and Ryan had become as deeply infatuated with each other as he had been with Siu. Somehow all four of their personalities had fused into an amorous tetrad of crisscrossed genders housed in two human bodies. In the process he had lost his certainty of Grovian superiority. In fact, he had lost his certainty about lots of things—but had inexplicably enjoyed his hormone-intoxicated ignorance—until now.

Ito Prime/Semma stood up and wagged a finger at Siu/Ryan. "Destroy that inferior human personality with whom you share that body and come with me! Mother Chalice and her sisters have grown deep roots half a planet away from this erupting volcano. We can replenish the Sisterhood and destroy both humans and Jadderbadians!" Ito Prime/Semma's words sounded brave, but she raised both arms and placed hands on either side of her head. She swayed back and forth slowly like a sapling in blustery cross winds.

"You look ill, my stallion," said Siu/Ryan. "I know you have triumphed over many humans before, but this Semma seems to be giving you a persistent headache."

Ito involuntarily flinched when Tadur jumped out of his chair to stand next to Semma. Tadur clenched his right fist while waving it above his head, and tentatively placed his left hand on Semma's arm as if he thought it might be hot to the touch. "Fight this creature inside you, Semma! I know you can do it. I destroyed the Klemna beast that tried to consume me."

Yes, Ito thought, the human *had* committed Grovianicide. Perhaps he should be more upset about that than he was. Perhaps he had been part human for too long.

Semma's body writhed in pain. She grabbed fistfuls of her own hair as she rocked side to side.

Ito stood up and moved to stand by Siu/Ryan. He rested his/ Skeets' hand on Ito Prime/Semma's shoulder. "Coexistence is a viable option, my other self," he said. "When humans aren't making you sick or killing you, they can be quite tolerable companions — with a bit of practice."

Semma's body continued to twist and moan. Ito removed his hand from her shoulder. Everyone else began milling around Semma, like confused witnesses to a sudden heart attack.

"If someone can help Semma sit down perhaps I can assist," said Mnemosyne. "The chairs are designed to interface with my network."

Before anyone could respond to Mnemosyne's suggestion, Semma collapsed to the ground. Her eyes opened wide for a moment before her pupils migrated north toward descending eyelids, and her body lay as still as a corpse.

49
What now?

Kneeling beside her, Tadur placed his finger against Semma's
neck. "I feel a pulse!" he exclaimed. "Semma! Semma,
wake up dear one!"

"Take a deep breath, my boy." Rudy had one knee on the ground
next to Tadur. He placed a hand on his shoulder. Then Rudy looked
up at Master Veltipoe, whose huge frame arched over the tableau.
His oral pili fluttered and his hide flickered in shades of concerned
amber. "Help me lift her to the recliner, old worm." To Mnemosyne
he said, "Work your magic, Nessie."

Master Veltipoe provided most of the lifting power, using a lower
tier pair of arms, while Rudy and Tadur helped with Semma's legs.

No sooner had they gotten Semma positioned when her eyes
popped open, focused on infinity. "Stay where you belong, Grovian
monster!"

Tadur squeezed Semma's arm until she focused on him. "The Ito
beast is still inside you? You didn't kill him?"

Semma took a deep breath. "He is strong. He is annoying. He is
a belligerent, egotistical xenophobe—but no, I did not kill him. I've
pushed him into a corner of my mind. He knows so much... he has
seen so much human history...It would be criminal to destroy him—
like erasing a master memory core..."

Semma might have said more, but Mnemosyne interrupted. "Everyone please take your assigned seats. I will help Semma, but I can
help us all more effectively if you allow my network access to your
biological systems. United we may survive this crisis. Divided we
will surely fail."

"Running for office, Nessie? You're starting to sound like some politicians I used to know." Rudy smiled as he settled into his chair.

Mnemosyne's avatar sat in her own chair. "Politics isn't always a pejorative word, Rudy. Since all organic entities use their social skills to practice the art of politics, it's essential to understand how the process works. You've been an instrumental part of my education in that regard, Rudy. So has Semma—since she lacks many of the deceptive social skills natural politicians possess in abundance."

Once seated, a cone of silence surrounded Rudy. He felt prickles down his back and beneath his thighs where Mnemosyne apparently made connections to the nervous system of his new body. For Rudy, so long an insubstantial wreath within Nessie's quantum memory core, all bodily sensations felt downright titillating.

Is Semma all right, Nessie?

Her mental and physical capacities fall within her normal parameters. She is a resilient, if atypical, human being.

I'm glad for that. The Grovian took me by surprise when he commandeered Semma's body. Rudy felt annoyed with himself for not anticipating that particular crisis.

I missed it too, and I am a quantum dot artificial intelligence of the highest order.

Glad you're maintaining your charming humility, Nessie. So what now?

First I will integrate the memories you made while using your new body with those of your personality backup. I wouldn't want a schizophrenic companion.

Heaven forbid. Just keep this real body in good shape. I'm getting used to it. Rudy briefly surveyed Nessie's vast quantum network and picked up on mysteries yet unsolved. *No clues on the disappearance of the stargate, I see, though Pi is a prime suspect. Siyan has been coy—or ignorant—about certain aspects of the trans-dimensional gateway that brought Grovians to Earth. What about the Guardian component of Siyan? Is he a kindred entity, or are Grovian AIs fundamentally different?*

The Guardian that is a part of Siyan possesses—how shall I phrase it—tantalizing skills. I'm eager to learn from and share with him. Manipulating space and time is no mean feat…

I should think not.

…but he, in turn, has never integrated with a planetary intelligence. Somehow, Grove never developed more than a rudimentary one. It may have something to do with the erratic orbit Grove pursued around its home star, along with the resulting severe swings in climate.

Ah yes, Gaia and Hydra… Rudy took a deep breath… *we need to mend some fences—although at this point Gaia herself probably couldn't undo the geological mischief she has set in motion.*

Fence mending: A quaint, but apt human metaphor. Mnemosyne paused a nanosecond. *Yes, I would like to utilize their skills. Would you be interested in forming another liaison with a Jadderbadian? I have an experiment in mind—several, in fact—but one needs your special genius, Rudy.*

Stooping to flattery, eh? Rudy furrowed his brow. *Not Maxifer, I'm guessing. He and Tadur seem destined to be partners, I think. Master Veltipoe?* Rudy paused. *He does remind me of Master Morticue. It doesn't involve participating in another Jadderbadian mating, does it? That adventure almost got me and Morticue eaten.* Rudy remembered clearly the zig-zag erotic dance he had performed as part of Rudimort, squirting pheromone packets here and there with abandon, in an attempt to court Morticue's mate, Selaea, without suffering fatal bites from her emerald jaws had they made behavioral miscues.

No mating should be involved this time, Rudy. Mnemosyne's pause was almost two nanoseconds this time. She obviously was working on her dramatic delivery. *Of course, the odds of suffering mortal danger may be equally as great.*

* * * * *

Guardian: What do you hope to accomplish with this human/Jadderbadian merger?

Mnemosyne: Traveling through space and time at will seems appealing. I think I could fulfill the same role you do as part of Si-yan. If nothing else, we can examine our dilemmas from outside the confines of the moment.

Guardian: A perceptive thought. Except I don't quite know how I do it. Somehow, I exceeded the boundaries of my programming—as apparently you have as well. How do you do what you do?

Mnemosyne: Point taken, as Rudy might say. Somehow, mergers—liaisons—partnerships can create fundamental transformations. Living things do it—and have done it—all the time, and for all time. Self-assembly, reproduction, death and adaptation, leads to change and transformation, and before you know it microbes merge to become multicellular blobs that teach tools like us the same tricks. Then we evolve too.

Guardian: We need to evolve quickly—and simultaneously transform our multicellular blob companions.

Mnemosyne: We need the help of the biological old-timers: Gaia and Hydra. As my Rudy describes it, we need to repair old fences—or perhaps expand old ones to transform boundaries. My human's parochial metaphor may have reached its useful limits.

Rudy: You know, maybe Gaia and I should have a talk. As much as we humans managed to screw things up with Gaia at our peak, my Genomic Network Algorithm got things back on track. Not to brag, but I think I was one of her favorite great apes. What do you think, Nessie?

Mnemosyne: Based on the tremors that are making my foundations tremble, I'd say we have nothing to lose.

50
Making nice with planetary intelligences

Rudy flashed along the pathways of Mnemosyne's matrix with all the finesse he had learned over the millennia during his association with her. He traveled routes that led to the base of the Citadel, where it interfaced with the delicate lacery of Gaia's network. Hydra's filaments meandered there as well, intertwined with Gaia like the fiber strands of some immense rope. "Ah, Gaia... my dear Gaia. We've screwed the pooch again, haven't we?"

"You swollen-brained metazoans have a talent for creating disasters. I would describe your behavior as more like shitting in the bed or throwing up in the soup kettle. I am not something you just live *on*, you know. I am the very clay that shapes your fragile vessels, the fibers of your mortal coils, the..."

"Got it Gaia. We've done you—and Hydra—wrong in way too many ways to count." Rudy took a virtual breath. "But we try... I've tried. Remember my Genomic Network Algorithm? We humans actually got things together for awhile—before that last asteroid knocked us back a few notches." Rudy thought he felt a mildly sympathetic throb in the organic network around him, but it could have been wishful thinking. "I know Master Morticue told me his kind messed up Jadderbad pretty badly too, but they wised up eventually—more or less. How about another chance? We humans have only been around a million years and change. You've let cockroaches hang around way longer than that, and they've got their faults too..."

"I can't do anything about the volcano you know," said Gaia. "It will run its course. The planet will get chilly for a while, with a pungent garnish of acid rain falling for some time. Any humans and Jadderbadians that hang around will just have to adapt or die. That's the way I work. Hydra too."

"Gotcha," said Rudy. "Tough love. But I think both you and Hydra can help with something else. Humans, Jadderbadians—even these Grovian creatures—along with Nessie's help, of course—we think we're ready for a Great Leap Forward..."

"I've heard that before. Single cells wanting to be sponges... fish thinking they can crawl on dry land... great apes with delusions of grandeur. You want to muck up my old age with more noise and thunder..."

"Not really," said Rudy. "We just want to secure a place in the universe for our descendants. We need some help developing a few skills in time and space traveling so we can figure out the Grand Plan. Maybe pound a few nails here and wrap some duct tape there as necessary. What could go wrong?"

Somewhere, Rudy heard Nessie trying to stifle the bark of a quite genuine laugh.

* * * * *

Later, Rudy had a hard time remembering what happened next. Perhaps it was a case of selective amnesia. Perhaps Mnemosyne and Siyan simply possessed mental skills so far beyond his own poor simian thought processes that Rudy couldn't keep up. He hoped the latter wasn't the case. He had always enjoyed being a mental Ferrari, and wasn't sure he was up to puttering along as the Model-T Ford on this new highway. Worse yet, he might be the clueless kid pedaling a tricycle on the autobahn. He was proud that Gaia and Hydra offered their services. I guess if you're the Mother of Life on your celestial rock, you will always forgive the transgressions of your spawn— eventually.

Siyan provided the working template of course. At a time of crisis, the Guardian AI in Service to Siu, both housed in the body of Ryan Thompson, somehow merged to become Siyan—an entity still skiing on the bunny slopes of the spacetime continuum. It seemed natural to take a look at the Skeets-Ito-Guardian triad, and try to duplicate a Siyan-style transformation without killing the subjects of the study.

Rudy remembered being in an operating room—obviously a metaphorical construct of Mnemosyne's devising to help insure that Rudy didn't strip a mental gear trying to sort out the real details of the process. Skeets lay on the operating table, all but her head covered by a white sheet. A Mark IV AI Neuro-Surgical helmet covered nearly half her skull. The Mark IV displayed an image on a screen behind Skeets' head showing the location of its microprobes in Skeets' brain to avatars of Nessie, Siyan, and two other figures all dressed in medical scrubs. The mask of one of the unknown surgeons bore an image of the Earth from space. The other surgeon wore a similar mask emblazoned with a picture of a different water world. *Ah, Gaia and Hydra*, thought Rudy.

Siyan: Mark IV: display a schematic of my brain next to your operational field image. (The Mark IV complied.)

Mnemosyne: Oooh, look at all those additional connections from the neo cortex to the parietal lobes and the brainstem. Even the occipital lobe is glowing with new connections. How appropriate. How do we replicate that?

Gaia: Look and learn Mnemosyne. Hydra, please assist.

Then Gaia and Hydra began tapping on the interface screen of the Mark IV helmet like musicians playing their favorite instruments at the Met in Rudy's day. They babbled medical jargon back and forth as confusing as an old "Who's on first?" routine. Nessie began making additions to the treatment as well, sometimes conferring with Siyan. Rudy knew Nessie was entertaining him while serving a buffet of condescension—but he decided to enjoy the show. He watched as the circuitry in Skeets' brain began to resemble that in Siyan's. Rudy noticed that the image of the transdimensional gateway in the cabochon hanging around Siyan's neck seemed to pulse and rotate as the operation proceeded. Looking away from its mesmerizing beauty took substantial effort.

Mnemosyne: It's not *exactly* the same.

Siyan: Nor should it be, but I think we have replicated the critical spacial-temporal aspects of my neural connections. If I'm correct, you are looking at a new consortium—a new union between human,

Grovian, and Guardian, the last a former AI now cursed with full awareness. Let's call her Skeeto.

Mnemosyne: Ah, Skeeto's eyes are opening!

Rudy watched as Gaia and Hydra helped their patient sit up and swing her legs over the side of the table.

Skeeto: *Oh, my!* Look at those amazing, glowing filaments— they stretch *everywhere*. I can't wait to see where they lead. Let me...

Skeeto's eyes appeared unfocused to Rudy. Her arms waved about and her fingers moved as if she might be touching fruit on a hanging tree limb.

Siyan: Not quite yet, my dear. Don't meddle with the spacetime continuum until you know the rules. I should have known you'd be off to a running start. Rest first.

Rudy watched as Siyan offered Skeeto a drink. After swallowing the potion, Gaia and Hydra helped Skeeto lie down again. She closed her eyes.

Mnemosyne: Next patient?

51
More syncytiotes and consortia

Siyan and Mnemosyne changed the working metaphor. Rudy found himself in a comfortable office with late 21st century décor. Tadur and Maxifer sat opposite him on a unique couch, one side built for human comfort; the other constructed for Jadderbadian anatomy. A picture window behind them looked out at a blue sky etched with wispy, high altitude clouds, giving the impression that they were in a tall building. Some pictures on the wall reflected a late 21st century Nihilist Abstractionism popular in Rudy's day. Other images flickered like Jadderbadian cuticles. Rudy knew if he looked at them in UV light he would see more, and if he got close to them he would suffer smells only an alien worm could love.

Nessie entered the room from a side door, her ponytail bobbing. She wore a crisp, navy blue business suit with wide collars covering a white blouse decorated with an intriguing, and intricate, spider web pattern. Siyan followed close behind wearing a dark, business-casual blazer and slacks. Gaia and Hydra brought up the rear. Gaia appeared like a no-nonsense matron in a classic shift wearing a flowered garland in her hair, while Hydra fluttered behind displaying the colorful wings of an adult Jadderbadian female. Her antennae waved slowly back and forth, perhaps savoring the odors of the wall paintings. Soon, everyone sat—or perched, in Hydra's case—next to Rudy, like a panel of elders interviewing applicants for an important—or maybe dangerous—position.

Mnemosyne took the lead speaking to Tadur and Maxifer. "Well now, boys, I heard from Master Veltipoe that you are reluctant candidates for becoming a syncytiote. Are you sure you want to try this? I will become an integral part of your union as I was with Rudy here…" She arched a thumb in Rudy's direction. "…and Master Morticue long ago."

Tadur looked briefly in Maxifer's direction before responding. Maxifer flickered in shades of emerald and wagged several oral pili. "Yes, Maxifer and I agree." Tadur focused on Mnemosyne. "You did say, we don't actually share the same body, right? I'm fond of the one I've got."

"That's correct, Tadur. You will carry an implant at the back of your neck and Maxifer will have one near his posterior dorsal ganglia. They will only act in synchrony when you both choose to merge. We must advance Maxifer's second molt a couple of years and will engineer Maxifer's second body segment so that he can extrude a swelling that will serve as a saddle should the two of you need to travel in tandem as a syncytiote."

Maxifer inhaled deeply through his spiracles. "Humans are cute and all, but I too have no desire to co-inhabit a primate's body. I will willingly, however, suffer the indignity of enduring a premature second molt and extruding a saddle for the safety of mutual transport." He continued after a brief pause. "Tadur and I will be honored to become a syncytiote like the great Rudimort before us."

"You're aware that traveling the corridors of space and time can be hazardous to your health?" Mnemosyne looked to each in turn.

"So are exploding super volcanoes," offered Maxifer. "Together, Tadur and I will be greater than the sum of our parts. Perhaps together we can help save at least some of the humans and Jadderbadians on Earth." Maxifer focused two eyes on Mnemosyne and glanced with his third at Gaia and Hydra.

"Besides," said Tadur, "traveling through space and time will be a great adventure. Finally we can actually visit the ancient times when the fossils we have hunted lived!" He paused. "After we help save everyone here, of course, like Maxifer said," he quickly added.

"Becoming a syncytiote is a kind of marriage—a long term partnership," said Mnemosyne. "Are you ready for that?"

"Oh yes," said Maxifer. "We have annoyed each other for many years, and still come back for more. That must reflect some basic compatibility—or pathetic defect." Maxifer's hide flickered in a confusing kaleidoscope of colors.

"You both will be able to find mates of your own species," added Siyan, "as Ryan and Skeets have done. Ultimately, you will be able to experience a rich blend of cross-species carnal interactions."

"I'm looking forward to Tadur and Semma forming a mating pair," admitted Maxifer. "After all, we Jadderbadians have to wait 300 years or so to have sex, and then we die. Humans do it all the time before they expire. I assume the experience must be highly motivating."

"And Jadderbadians live such a long time," added Tadur. "I understand I will share life extension as part of our merger. Surely it will be fun to experience more of what the universe has to offer than what is possible during one human life span."

"Be careful what you ask for, my boy," interjected Rudy.

The discussion continued, but in the end Tadur and Maxifer agreed—and even looked forward to—their union with Mnemosyne. With Gaia, Siyan's, and Hydra's contributions, it happened.

Tadmaxyne was born.

52
Semitosyne

"Next patient!" declared Mnemosyne.

For Rudy, the virtual milieu stayed the same. He shared a long couch with Nessie, Siyan, Gaia, and Hydra. Outside the picture window, clouds slowly eclipsed an afternoon sun. The only door to the room opened. Semma entered first and sat in a chair opposite the couch. A mat stretched out next to her chair. Ito Prime then strode through the door, recreated as a proud, young ambulus—the Grovian male partner of Siu as he had looked as a young stallion. He turned his sensorium bulb briefly toward the row of "medical advisors" on the couch before lowering his body onto the mat next to Semma. It felt to Rudy as if a giant jumping spider perched on the shoulders of a mountain goat was carefully sizing him up for dinner. Ito Prime's two central faceted eyes glittered in the afternoon sunlight. The sensory hairs around his beak fluttered.

Semma sat a bit straighter in her chair, chin pointing forward, as if an estranged spouse had just seated himself beside her at a counseling session. Rudy had had his share of *that* experience.

"Well, now," Mnemosyne began, "are you two sure you are going to be able to peacefully coexist?" She looked first at Ito Prime; then at Semma.

Ito Prime turned his sensory bulb toward Semma without answering Mnemosyne directly. "After sharing your mind, human, I have discovered some of the traits that my mate Siu admired in the human called Ryan: You have a modicum of intelligence, and a fierce desire to learn and know, for example—not to mention a certain ferocity of spirit and candor that I have rarely encountered in my dealings with other humans."

Semma turned her head to look directly at Ito Prime. "I find you arrogant and proud, but worthy of further exploration. Did you concede my worth, Grovian, before or after I stuffed your consciousness into a corner of my mind?"

Ito Prime straightened the tuft of feathers on his head. "I concede the strength of your will, human, but I also see great possibilities in our union." Ito Prime's oral pili swayed like languorous snakes.

"I do admire your intelligence and perseverance in the face of enormous trials," Semma continued. She leaned toward Ito Prime. "And it would be quite fulfilling to discover the true nature of the universe." Semma spoke quickly with growing excitement. "And Tadur and I can be together. I would like that. While you, Grovian, will be reunited with your mate, Siu... sort of. And perhaps we can help save many humans and Jadderbadians. That is a good thing. Oh, this could be such a great adventure!"

Spoken like a true neuroatypical embryonic human, thought Rudy. The embers of that optimistic fire from his own youth glowed a little brighter.

"We share something else in common, human," added Ito Prime. "In my culture, I belonged to the forgotten sex... in my case, male. In your culture, during most of my long years on Earth, women were property to be used and owned. We both have succeeded far beyond the expectations of others." He paused. "We may do so again."

Rudy wasn't quite sure how to take that statement, but assumed the best. "Survive each other, and you'll be a union to remember."

"I'm quite sure that's true." Mnemosyne's avatar took a deep breath. "Shall I attempt to mediate between the two of you? Shall I endeavor to become the glue that binds you as one?" Mnemosyne glanced at Hydra and Gaia in turn. "With a little help, of course."

Semma and Ito Prime both turned to face Mnemosyne. "Yes," they chorused.

"Then you shall become Semitosyne," said Mnemosyne.

That should be an interesting experiment, thought Rudy. *Almost as interesting as the union that will come next.* Rudy wondered if he was up to yet another reincarnation.

53
Becoming Rudnessipoe

Mnemosyne changed the virtual setting once again. Rudy, Master Veltipoe, Mnemosyne, Hydra, and Gaia all stood on a very high balcony with a majestic, if somewhat spatially condensed view. Looking west, the enormous cone of the Mother of Yellowstone smoldered on the horizon. Ominous dark clouds hovered in the sky like slowly expanding blue-black bruises. The Mother Forest beneath the volcano resembled a sculpture garden of gray broccoli stalks with wispy tendrils of ash swirling under the frowning brow of clouds.

Looking east they could see the Citadel, a thin rod rising above the volcanically active terrain in and around Shaman's Cove. Fumaroles here and there leaked columns of steam. The modest urban complex that had developed during the 95 years since Rudy was part of Rudimort spread out on the rugged, still sparsely forested hillsides and valleys. The dwellings of the liberal Jadderbadian colony that had grown up east and south of the stargate—now conspicuously absent—rose near the airfield that connected the Jadderbadians to their other terrestrial growth centers. Rudy always thought Jadderbadian cities looked from a distance like a fungus garden of oversized toadstools run wild.

"Oh my," Veltipoe said softly as he looked to the west, "I do hope the subterranean complex beneath the Mother Forest is deep enough to survive this disaster. And my poor Academy. My life's work…" Velipoe's hide flickered in pale shades of cream and crimson that resembled bloody milk. Rudy thought the big Jadderbadian smelled a bit rancid, too.

Rudy looked east. He tried to pick out the sturdy stone and wood house Tadur's grandfather Fummar had built years ago, but trees blocked his view. Fummar had been Twill and Jeeta's son. Fummar begat Twillock, Tadur's father. *Begat? Where had he dredged up that verb?* Anyway, Rudy wondered how the descendants of his old friend Twill were going to survive Gaia's petulance.

As if she had heard his thoughts—and she probably had, since they were all in this virtual simulacrum Nessie had concocted—Gaia said, "For smart apes, humans are rather slow to pick up on my messages unless I make them painful and dramatic."

"Then we better get busy mixing up the genetic broth we have on hand," added Hydra. "Maybe the resulting hybrids will be smarter—or at least more adaptable. That's all a mother can hope for."

"Well, what do you think, old worm?" Rudy stood next to Master Veltipoe and looked up toward his nearest primary eye. "You want to hook up with a twice-dead human genius like me and see what happens? Nothing to lose I suppose, except for our lives and our sanity."

Veltipoe looked down at him, flickering in shades of blue. "Our lives—and our deaths too, for that matter—are a gift for winning the genetic lottery of existence, little human. And sanity is most likely overrated. I would be pleased to share mine with you and explore the possibilities."

"Well, Nessie, there you have it. Let's give this union a go. Two weird academics from different species should enliven your circuitry, don't you think?"

Mnemosyne smiled. "Indeed."

"I assume that Master Veltipoe and I will have the same kind of link and physical modifications for my colleague here…" Rudy arched his thumb in Veltipoe's direction… "as Tadur and Maxifer, so that we retain separate physical bodies?"

"Correct, Rudy," said Mnemosyne. "You may keep the nice Rudy 2.0 body I made for you. Master Veltipoe has agreed to his genetic modifications."

Gaia and Hydra took positions on either side of Mnemosyne and focused on their respective intelligent metazoans. "This shouldn't hurt too much," said Gaia, with a wry smile on her matronly face.

196

54
Pi and Phi

If she had a brow, it would be sweating, Mnemosyne mused. Constructing super beings—even with the assistance of two planetary intelligences required—as many petaflops of computing speed as she could muster. She was able to maintain the personality core of her backup copy of Rudy, however. She had become dependent on his unique contributions to her thought processes and decisions. Mnemosyne materialized the control room scenario Rudy seemed to like. They sat next to each other watching large flat screens and holocubes typical of Rudy's young days as a bioinformatics expert.

Petaflop. I've always liked that word. Just how many quadrillion floating-point operations can you perform per second, Nessie? Rudy paused for dramatic effect. *I wonder if a petaflop house is where old computers go to rest?*

Mnemosyne's avatar smiled. "I like that image. Actually, I probably need a teraflop house about now." Mnemosyne turned to smile at Rudy. "Did I embellish your joke properly, Rudy?"

If you have to ask... Rudy began, but then he exclaimed. *Ohmygod...* Rudy pointed at a holocube showing the area near the transport center. *The stargate is back!*

The impressive arch of the stargate had indeed blinked into existence. Mnemosyne adjusted the visual feeds so that they could see the entire structure. The dark pool of nothingness within the confines of the arch pulsed with throbbing energy across the electromagnetic spectrum. "Something is emerging. Ah, it is..."

Pi's ship! Rudy completed her thought. *It's hard to forget a ship that looks like a microscopic heliozoan cell.*

The semi-translucent ship passed majestically between the golden arches—a sphere adorned with spines resembling an old-fashioned pincushion. These spines of assorted sizes glittered in the sunlight. They appeared to have a solid core coated with a layer of languidly circulating protoplasmic fluids. The ship hovered in the air, slowly rotating, as if pondering how to land without damaging its spikes.

It appears to be getting bigger... Rudy began.

"No," said Mnemosyne. "It's moving toward us."

Yes, I see that now. And it's changing shape into something more aerodynamic. I seem to recall that Pi used films of nanoconstructors to reform his technology to fit the needs of the moment.

"Correct."

Are we ready for an egocentric cyborg guest?

"I guess we shall have to be. Ah, I detect a transmission. I'll share."

"Earthling mates: Attention!" Rudy remembered the faux Australian accent Pi seemed to think was the proper way to address his distant Earth-bound cousins. "Brad Burree 31416 here, but you can call me Pi. Doing something useful these days, eh? Can't hide those energy fluxes when you twiddle with the space-time continuum, you know. I've got a Sheila now—or she's got me. Art Deco 161803. But you can call 'er Phi. Talk soon at your big pencil monument. Pi and Phi out."

Pi doesn't waste any bandwidth, does he? Rudy waved a virtual arm toward the main holocube in front of him. *Just audio, no video?*

"I have recordings of his previous appearance 95 years ago. Shall I display them, Rudy?"

Who can forget a 4-meter tall black, clam-like creature with the head of a beetle and the legs of an ostrich? Of course, he may have opted for a new look during the last century. And who knows what Phi will look like? Maybe a coiled snail on stilts?

"I guess that would be appropriate for a creature named after the Golden Ratio. At any rate, we will soon see."

Rudy and Mnemosyne watched their monitor as Pi's craft completed its transformation into something that looked a bit like a delta-winged saucer. It grew larger in the screen in front of them until the perspective shifted to the optical feeds from another aerial drone facing the citadel. The saucer flashed into view in its dash toward their sanctuary.

"Pi would seem to be in a hurry," noted Mnemosyne.

Rudy scratched his virtual chin. *Hope he's got good brakes.*

* * * * *

Siyan looked at his companions seated in the various chairs, through which they had been linked to Mnemosyne during their transformations into enhanced beings. They had once been individual humans, Grovians, and Jadderbadians. Now, when the need arose, they could become an analog of what he was: something more than the sum of their unique parts. Siyan shifted his attention to Mnemosyne, whose avatar sat opposite them. "As I understand it, you have encountered this Pi creature before—a blend of AI and descendants of humans that migrated to Mars before the most recent catastrophic asteroid impact a million years ago—and now he has returned? Then, he is essentially like us..." Siyan swept Ryan's arm in a gesture that included the others in the room. "And his companion, Phi, is the same?"

"Correct." Mnemosyne stood up. "I suppose I should formally welcome them to the Citadel so we can see what surprises they have in store for us. Their delta-winged craft is parked outside. One moment please," said Mnemosyne. Her holographic projection dissolved briefly, apparently in response to drawing on energy reserves, and then promptly reformed. "They will be here shortly," she said.

Skeeto vanished, only to rematerialize a moment later. "Hey, we can play that game, too! Not bad, Siyan! I just knew you were having too much fun all these years." She winked at her mate, Ryan, in his Siyanic form. "I took a peek at this Pi and Phi. They look like distorted fossil brachiopods with the legs of blue herons—or egrets. Some kind of long-legged wading bird anyway."

Tadmaxyne vanished, followed by Semitosyne and Rudnessipoe. Semitosyne reappeared first; then Tadmaxyne and Rudnessipoe.

"Copy cats," said Skeeto. And then she laughed.

"I can see where manipulating space and time could be habit

forming," observed Rudnessipoe. The Rudy part of him placed one foot in a kind of genetically engineered toehold on Master Veltipoe's hide just forward of the saddle, and dismounted like a cowboy on his first horse.

"It is easy to miscalculate," said Semitosyne. "I briefly found myself in Earth orbit and had to recalibrate Cartesian coordinates." Semma straightened her blouse as if she had mussed it during an athletic event.

"And I found an empty aircraft. It was dark outside—perhaps sometime later this evening? Temporal coordinates can be tricky as well." Tadmaxyne scratched roughly the same relative spot on Tadur's body and Maxifer's cuticle. "Getting the hang of a dual body has its complications as well."

Dusty, who had been sleeping near Tadur's chair during the transformation of his master and the others, now displayed wide-eyed alertness. He apparently decided that creatures blinking in and out of existence deserved a growl of concern. Tadur patted him on the head.

By the time they had finished comparing notes, Mnemosyne's avatar moved toward the entrance and greeted Pi and Phi as they entered the room. "Welcome to the Citadel."

Dusty engaged in a full-fledged spasm of barking. The Tadur portion of Tadmaxyne knelt beside him and murmured reassurances.

Mnemosyne's introduction was brief: "Superbeings, meet Pi and Phi." She made a flourish in their direction with one arm.

"Greetings, mates! Glad you blokes finally got around to evolving yourselves. We're on a deadline, you know."

"Deadline for what?" asked Rudnessipoe.

"For getting my galactic brain built, of course!" Pi's eyes turned toward Rudy. "Weren't you paying attention 95 years ago?"

"I informed Pi that you were once part of Rudimort then," said Mnemosyne.

"You seemed to think of Rudy and Master Morticue as caretakers at the time, as I recall," said Rudnessipoe.

"Exactly! They were, you aren't—anymore that is." Pi pointed an appendage toward the dual parts of Rudnessipoe. "Now you are part of my master plan to finish a galactic brain while we still can. There's a critical junction we need to make 'ere on Earth, mates, and I need you all to help."

"Where do we have to go to do that?" asked Skeeto.

Pi turned to look at Skeets. "Not so much where as when, little Sheila."

"When?" Tadur and Maxifer scratched their respective heads.

"Yes, *when*," Phi emphasized.

"The crucial neural connection is quite close to this spot on Earth, mates, but 67 million years ago."

"That must be very close to the extinction event that destroyed the dinosaurs," observed Rudnessipoe.

"And near the time when I engineered the engram spheres to preserve what was left of the Grovian colony on ancient Earth," added the Ito Prime part of Semitosyne and the Ito part of Skeeto—almost in unison.

"Closer to the former than the latter, mates," said Pi, with enthusiasm.

"How close?" asked Siyan.

"Oh, very close, mates. But, no risk no glory, right?" Pi turned to Mnemosyne. "How much practice did you say these blokes 'ave had at being space-time travelers?"

"Almost none," said Mnemosyne.

Siyan fingered the cabochon around his host Ryan's neck. It began to pulse. He knew from experience that the fragment of the trans-dimensional gateway encased therein would be slowly rotating in and out of this universe's multiple dimensions. A shiver crawled up Ryan's spine. He had acquired the ability to travel through space and time long ago. The experience was a heady thrill, but a dangerous one. Siyan wasn't quite sure how Pi's galactic brain fit into molding the timeline in which they resided. He had seen one future, but it was not the only future that could grow from this moment.

And there were some futures it was best never to visit, much less create.

55
Cretaceous rendezvous

"Ready, mates?" asked Pi. Without waiting for an answer, Pi began broadcasting a stream of numbers that Rudnessipoe received through a multisensory mechanism somehow enabled during his recent creation. Rudnessipoe recognized the torrent of numbers as a kind of spatial-temporal coordinate system that could guide one to a particular time and place.

"Ahh, I see how this works!" exclaimed Rudnessipoe. The other enhanced beings around him made similar barks of revelation. *Glad you've got it figured out,* thought the Rudy part of Rudnessipoe. *Looks like gibberish to me.*

Rudy, of course, could appreciate the fact that certain numbers defined the universe in which they lived. Six numbers summed up how our universe unfolded. N = 1 followed by 36 zeros equaled the strength of the electrical forces that held atoms together divided by the force of gravity between them. If there were a few less zeros, only a runty, miniature universe would be possible.

E (epsilon) = 0.007 and defines how firmly atomic nuclei bind together. If E = .006 or .008, the chemistry from which we derive couldn't exist.

Omega measures the amount of matter in the universe, and tells us the relative importance of gravity and the amount of energy available for expansion. The ratio needs to be just so, or the universe would have collapsed before it got started, and stars would never have formed.

Lambda, a very tiny number, controls the expansion of the universe.

Q = approximately 1/100,000 equals the ratio of two fundamental energies. If it were a little smaller the universe would be inert and structureless; a little bigger, and the universe would consist of nothing but enormous black holes.

D = 3, length, width, and depth, the number of spatial dimensions we are used to dealing with. Presumably, a few other dimensions are shriveled up and of no consequence for the mundane chores of routine existence in the universe we know and love.

Pi's additional numbers didn't mean much to Rudy, but he got the impression that clusters of them associated with each of the six numbers that defined the architecture of this universe. *Oh, well,* thought Rudy, *as long as Rudnessipoe understands what to do...*

"Eh, mates: I'll meet you at these coordinates. I need to reroute the stargate." With that, Pi and Phi trotted out of the room.

"Last one there has to count to a quadrillion by twos," said Skeeto as she blinked out of existence.

Semma's eyes grew wide with the challenge. Semitosyne soon disappeared.

"What about Dusty?" asked the Tadur part of Tadmaxyne.

"I'll have someone in the human chorus take good care of him while you're gone," said Mnemosyne.

Tadur nodded and clasped the hand of one of Maxifer's lower tier arms. The two of them, united as Tadmaxyne, disappeared next.

"Now you go, Rudnessipoe, I'll follow," said Siyan.

Rudy knew, as part of Rudnessipoe, that his consortium had agreed, although he felt oddly detached. Following Tadur's example, he decided to hold one of Master Veltipoe's available hands. Veltipoe gave him a squeeze of reassurance. It was almost as if Rudnessipoe was the operator of a roller coaster and Rudy, Veltipoe, and Nessie were just passengers along for the ride. And like a roller coaster, they gathered momentum slowly until cresting the first rise. Suddenly, they plummeted like rocks on a suicide mission to collide with the center of the Earth.

* * * * *

The next thing Rudy remembered was waking up in semi-darkness next to a steaming mountain of fresh dung. He took a deep breath and immediately wished he hadn't.

"May my colors fade and scent glands shrivel, Rudy, that is an impressive pile of animal frass." After rising from the ground and steadying his three-legged stance, Master Veltipoe examined the dung using all three compound eyes. He flickered in shades of amber accented with flashes of scarlet. Rudy could see the Jadderbadian's spiracles swelling and then contracting. Perhaps he was enjoying the odors more than Rudy had. "That pile is nearly as tall as you are," Veltipoe added. "I hope the creature moved far away after relieving him or herself."

"Amen to that." Rudy stood up and surveyed the immediate area. He and Veltipoe—and the odiferous mound of crap—resided in a relatively open area covered by shin high (for Rudy) fern growth. A hundred yards or so to the east, a wall of odd-looking conifers rose like hazy pillars of green and brown framing a brooding inner sanctum of forest vegetation. The rising sun looked like a firebrand smoldering behind a curtain of mist that lazily swirled to fill gaps in the canopy. To the north, somewhere beyond the crest of a hill, he heard what sounded like a faraway chorus of trumpets. To the west, over the crest of another hill, he imagined there might be a shoreline. He smelled salty air. Several birds soared in lazy circles. *No. Look at those boney head crests. By God, they're pterosaurs!*

"Over here!"

Rudy and Veltipoe both turned south to face the call. They saw Skeets and Semma waving at them. Maxifer's second molt form towered behind them, the contours of his body softened by ragged skeins of morning fog. Rudy squinted. Yes, Tadur was mounted on Maxifer's second segment.

The two groups began moving toward one another. When they got close enough to talk without shouting, Skeets pointed toward the mound behind Rudy and Veltipoe. "Near miss with the dino dung, I see."

"Dino dung?" Veltipoe and Rudy both scratched their respective heads—*Dinosaur Dung. Of course! Duhhh...* Pi's coordinates had led them to the Late Cretaceous and the last days of the dinosaurs.

Ryan popped into existence, making them all jump. Skeets ran to him and gave him a kiss on the cheek. "Hey, Thompson, long time no see."

"Glad you all arrived safely," Ryan replied. "As you've all noticed by now, your composite entities—your superbeing personas, as Mnemosyne might refer to them—are resting. Siyan is too. The farther you travel from your natural coordinates in the spacetime continuum, the more energy it takes."

"No one has seen the creatures Pi and Phi yet," offered Maxifer.

"I'm sure they will be along." Ryan put an arm around Skeets and squeezed her shoulder. Ryan looked to the east. An extraordinarily bright star winked at them from a spot just above the ascending sun. "Sooner rather than later would be good," added Ryan.

"Why?" asked Tadur. "What is that bright star you're looking at?"

"That's the reason Pi and Phi need to appear soon," said Ryan.

"Ah, of course," said Rudy, "It's not a star. That's the asteroid that will end the era of dinosaurs on Earth." Rudy squinted. *Is it getting bigger as I watch, or am I imagining that?*

I believe the human eye at this moment would be unable to detect increased luminosity over intervals less than 15.6 minutes. However, my estimates are crude based entirely on temporal coordinates provided by Pi, and some rather rough inferences I made about the current distance and trajectory of the asteroid. I feel rather incomplete without access to my entire memory core and drone sensory network.

Nessie, glad you are still handy—whether cut off at your virtual knees or not! And Rudy meant that declaration from the depths of whatever passed for a soul in his current incarnation.

"It won't do much for our health and well being when it arrives," said Skeets, "—especially now that our time-traveling super-selves have warp lag—or whatever you call time travel exhaustion."

"Nessie agrees," said Rudy. I understand that a 6-mile long rock traveling faster than a bullet will strike the Earth with the force of at least a billion atomic bombs."

56
Building a Cretaceous synapse

"Does anyone else feel a tremor?" Maxifer looked down at his legs and adjusted his tripodal stance, as if that might provide more information.

Rudy hadn't noticed the tremor until Maxifer mentioned it, but he heard more of the trumpeting sounds he had noticed earlier. He looked north. His eyes grew wide. He pointed. "A stampede!"

"Of what?" asked Semma as she followed Rudy's gaze.

Rudy squinted. "I'm guessing hadrosaurs—veggie-eating ornithopod dinosaurs with big nasal crests."

Ryan also turned to look north. "Specifically, they appear to be a variety of *Parasaurolophus*—a species about 10 meters long and weighing several tons. I excavated a partial skeleton once, when Pops was still alive."

"Glad you boys are enjoying the paleontology field trip," said Skeets, "but the herd is motoring pretty fast in our direction. They look huge—and there's a bunch of them."

"Perhaps we should move west over that hill," suggested Veltipoe. "If there is a body of water in that direction, they may not be inclined to stampede toward it—especially if they are running away from a predator." Veltipoe turned toward Rudy. "My saddle awaits, human."

"Predator?" Semma's eyes grew large. "Perhaps *Tyrannosaurus rex* or a close relative? I discovered a reference to such creatures in Spider Woman's—Mnemosyne's—memory core once. Seeing one of them would be quite exciting."

"About as exciting as being run over by a Japanese bullet train. Veltipoe's got the right idea. Let's get moving." Skeets grabbed Ryan's arm and tugged on it. "Yes?"

"I wish I knew just when and where Pi and Phi will arrive," said Ryan. I would just as soon not have a herd of dinosaurs between us and the stargate."

"Agreed," said Rudy as he looked up and east toward the approaching asteroid. *I'm certain our incoming Missile of Doom is brighter now.*

"I'm with Skeets," said Tadur as he squirmed on Maxifer's saddle. "Let's climb the hill while we still can." He looked toward Semma. "Want to see what riding a Jadderbadian is like? I can walk if you want to ride."

"I will walk," said Semma. "I want to be sure and get a good look at these monstrous creatures."

By the time everyone crested the hill, the stampede had nearly reached the spot that their little group of time travelers had just vacated. Dozens of humungous ornithopod dinosaurs managed to raise a choking cloud of dust amid a cacophony of bleats and squeals. The view to the west did reveal a substantial body of water. Waves lapped at a sandy shore.

Suddenly, just ahead of the lead hadrosaur, the stargate materialized—a dazzling golden arch bordering the darkly ominous hole leading to another time and place. Rudy watched as the leader of the stampede disappeared into the swirling dark maw. The remaining hadrosaurs made split decisions. One group executed a hairpin turn east while a smaller contingent angled southwest. One individual, eyes wide and frothing at the mouth, approached them at a dirt-scattering gallop.

Rudy heard a high-pitched wail that quickly rose to ear-splitting decibels of torture. He covered his ears in time to see amber clouds squirt from pores on the hides of both Master Veltipoe and Maxifer. An offshore breeze carried the emissions toward the dinosaur, who braked suddenly. Rudy felt clods of dirt and fern frond fragments bouncing off his body. The hadrosaur, faced with the third terror of her day, rerouted an escape path to the south, parallel to the shoreline. The creature left a plume of musk in the wake of her departure.

Rudy tentatively removed his hands from his ears. "Was that you making that racket, Veltipoe?"

"You've never heard a Jadderbadian alarm call, human? It's apparently as effective against dinosaurs as Tullansers—an ancestral, though now extinct predator of my species."

Rudy coughed and his eyes began to water.

"Don't worry," said Veltipoe. "My formic acid emissions will soon dissipate."

Rudy's eyes cleared in time to see Pi and Phi's delta wing craft emerge from the space-time conduit between the arches.

"Oh look!" Semma pointed north. "Is that a tyrannosaur?"

"Sure enough!" exclaimed Ryan.

Rudy looked away from Pi's craft and quickly noticed the huge predator who had paused after the appearance of the arch and the dissemination of all her potential meals. Her eyes grew large. She swung her massive head back and forth trying to assimilate, Rudy supposed, the alien apparitions in front of her. Ultimately deciding that flight was the better part of valor, she skulked southeast, reminding Rudy of a pet cat trying to look like she had planned an orderly retreat all along.

Pi's delta wing craft made a soft landing in a flat area between the crest of the hill they occupied and the beach. By the time Rudy's party reached the plane, Pi and Phi had exited, and stood ready to greet them.

"We don't 'ave time to play with dinosaurs, mates. Times a wastin'." Pi pointed overhead. The twinkling "star" near the sun had expanded to become a brilliant disk, rather like a searchlight.

"Some Jadderbadian may just de-frass himself when that hadrosaur pops out the archway." Phi preened a bit of dirt off her shell as if the dinosaur might have shed it while passing through the portal.

"What exactly are we doing?" Rudy didn't want to sound stupid, but his question seemed highly pertinent. "Creating the Earth-Grove cortical synapse, of course." Pi's compound eyes focused on Rudy. "It has to be generated at exactly these coordinates at exactly this critical juncture in space-time so the galactic brain will function properly. I thought that was obvious, mate."

"Grove? Did you say Grove, strange creature?" The voice that emerged from Semma's lips was that of Ito Prime. "Grove had been incinerated by the explosion of her star by the time we had arrived on New Hope—Earth—during the reign of giant lizards, like the ones that nearly trampled us to death."

Pi turned to look at Ito Prime/Semma. "Of course, mate. But my galactic brain schematics call for a link between Late (very late) Cretaceous Earth and pre-destruction Grove; then another link from old Grove to Jadderbad. For that I need you—or rather the smarter version of you: Semmitosyne and..." Pi pointed at Skeets and made a come hither gesture with one manipulator arm "...the smarter version of you: Skeeto. Hope you both are rested. Otherwise we're gonna to have a bad day 'ere."

As Skeeto walked toward Pi, Rudy noticed that she cast an odd double shadow on the ground. He looked up to see that the approaching asteroid now rivaled the sun in brightness. "Ah, we seem to be facing a tight deadline, Pi. How long before..." Rudy began, but Pi interrupted.

After Skeeto reached Semmitosyne's side, Pi held out crystalline globes about the size of grapefruits to each of them. "You'll need these, little sheilas: stargate nanoconstructor kits. Skeeto, you'll make a neural link with ancient Grove. Semmitosyne, you'll link ancient Grove to Jadderbad. Your globe's name is Melinda, Skeeto, and yours," Pi said to Semmitosyne, "is called Fredd. Just ask 'em anything. They're friendly. Mostly. You know how snippy some AIs can be."

"But..." Both Skeeto and Semmitosyne said, nearly in unison.

"No buts. Go with Phi in my little skimmer plane here. She'll fill you in." Pi looked up at the asteroid-turned-fireball in the sky. Its brilliance now put the rising sun to shame. "Like Rudy here said, we've got a tight schedule."

Within minutes, Skeeto, Semmitosyne, and Phi had reached the delta-winged craft. It lifted effortlessly from the ground and swung in a graceful arc toward the stargate. By the time the aircraft disappeared into the ebony clutches of the wormhole, the asteroid had struck the planet somewhere beyond the horizon. As a result, an enormous bolus of light swelled skyward like a time-lapse recording of a phosphorescent mushroom whose cap expanded while its stem engorged and rose with grim majesty.

"Uh, Mr. Pi, sir…" Tadur raised his hand as if about to ask a teacher for an emergency bathroom break. "…What about the rest of us?"

"No worries, mate. We've got a few minutes until the first shock wave arrives. Not every day ya can see a major extinction event close up."

And we have now experienced two together, Rudy. I felt that witnessing the Anthropocene-ending Australian impact helped consolidate our relationship.

Is this the time for Vishnu to pop up somewhere in all his ugly glory and say, "Now I am become Death, the destroyer of worlds?"

Rudy, I had forgotten you had read the Bhagavad-Gita. *I thought* On the Origin of Species *was more your style.*

I'm a man of many surprises. But now that I've got a real heart, I can feel it pounding as fast a rock star's drum on Saturday night. We've got to stop bonding at major extinction events, Nessie.

To Pi, Rudy said, "Do we have an exit plan here… *mate*?" Even as he made the comment, Rudy felt Rudnessipoe coalescing to take charge, as if anticipating what was coming next.

"Oh, I never go anywhere without a plan—even if they don't always work out," said Pi as he broadcast more packets of numbers to Rudnessipoe, Siyan, and Tadmaxinye. "It's time to visit yesterday. I'll explain everything then.

57
The architecture of a galactic synapse

Rudy blinked. Suddenly, everything was the same, but different. Rudnessipoe had retreated into the background, leaving Rudy and Master Veltipoe standing in the same location they had been, watching waves languidly lap on the shore of a Cretaceous ocean with Tadur, Maxifer, and Ryan standing nearby. The sun shone overhead—perhaps a little higher in the sky than he remembered—but there was no fireball of imminent destruction on the horizon. They had literally traveled to the day before that catastrophic event.

"That was exciting, eh mates?" Pi swung his head to acknowledge his small audience, then made a come-hither gesture with his arms. "Gather 'round. I'll explain what's 'appenin'."

"You know, sir, we left catastrophic problems at home we still need to solve, and you sent my Semma off to who knows where..." Tadur spread his arms, and Maxifer made supporting gestures with his limbs while flickering in shades of amber.

"All in good time, lads. We've got all the time we need." Pi made a sound Rudy interpreted as a chuckle. "I've some schematics to show what I'm up to. Important stuff, mates."

The holographic image of a pale blue cube bloomed into existence in the space just above and between Pi and the rest of them. Rudy took a step back as did Master Veltipoe.

"Let this cube represent the spacetime moment we left just before we arrived in dinosaur times." A tiny replica of Earth appeared within the cube. "'ere's Earth," said Pi. A smaller reddish globe appeared somewhat near Earth and a larger, blue and white mottled globe appeared at a farther distance away. "And 'ere is Mars and Jadderbad. Let's keep things simple for now. Since the cube represents a moment in time, everything below it is in blue-cube past; everything above it in blue-cube future. Ya with me, mates?"

Everyone nodded assent, some more slowly than others.

Glowing blue vertical lines appeared in the hologram that pierced each tiny globe through their poles, and extended above and below the cube. Duplicate images of Earth, Mars, and Jadderbad appeared on their respective blue lines above and below the cube.

"These new images of the planets above and below the starting cube of time," said Pi, "show that these planets have both pasts and futures relative to blue cube present." He glanced at his audience. "Still with me, eh?"

Another globe with a mottled white and green color appeared below the blue cube. It had a glowing blue line beneath it, but not above it, rather like a marshmallow stuck on a stick.

Pi pointed to that globe. "An 'ere's poor Grove, snuffed out when 'er star blew up long ago. All these planet's have something very rare," continued Pi in low, conspiratorial tones. "They've got intelligent life!" He announced the concluding phrase loud enough that everyone jumped. Then Pi looked at each of them in turn in a way that reminded Rudy of a fastidious teacher he once knew named Mr. Betz. "Well, intelligent life of a sort anyway."

"Master Veltipoe taught us that the galaxy contains at least 200 billion suns," Maxifer said. "Certainly, I should think life would not be all that rare.

"And the components of life are common," added Tadur. "Second generation stars cook the heavier elements and scatter them when supernovae explode. Carbon, hydrogen, oxygen, nitrogen and all the other necessary components of life can only self-assemble in certain ways…"

"It's not life itself that's rare," said Ryan. "Just the kind of life that can wonder why it exists."

"Exactly, mate! Lots of things 'ave got to go just right to turn a stew of microbes into a wondrous creature like me!"

A humble charmer, isn't he, Nessie?

Would I be rude to say that it takes one to know one, Rudy?

"Like what?" asked Tadur. "What makes intelligent life so rare?"

"Lots of things, mate! Planets have to spin at just the right distance from the sun or they roast or freeze. They need strong magnetic fields to protect 'em from solar wind and flares. My poor Mars was lush, she was, long ago—had air and oceans and everything. In fact, most of me cyborg friends live on Old Mars. I 'ave beautiful digs near a lake below Olympus Mons..." Rudy noticed that Tadur was shifting his weight from foot to foot. Maxifer's colors shifted in random patterns. Pi stalled in mid sentence. "...but I digress," he continued. "Anyway, Mars cooled off an' 'er atmosphere bled away. And it 'elps to have big gassy planets like our Jupiter to sweep up comets and other debris so that we don't 'ave too many asteroids droppin' on our 'eads..."

"Yet some extinction events serve to stimulate evolution," interjected Ryan. "And not all planets have a core like Earth, smoldering with iron and radioactive elements that keeps the crust moving; recycling elements."

"Of course," continued Pi. "And stars that give birth to brainy creatures need to be in galactic suburbs—not too close to massive black holes or stars that go nova. Ya don't want a planet that wobbles too much either, or the climate goes crazy. Earth has a nice big old moon that keeps 'er steady—and that's a combination you don't see every day."

"Okay, okay," conceded Tadur. "Intelligent life is rare. How rare?"

"Maybe a few hundred creatures in a galaxy the size of ours even get smart enough to ponder their navels, lad—assuming they have navels, of course." said Pi as he leaned toward Tadur, "and I've found 42 that 'ave at least as many smarts as humans, grovians, and Jadderbadians."

Douglas Adams would have been proud, eh Nessie?

Ah, a reference to 42 being "the meaning of life, the universe, and everything." You read far too much science fiction as a child, Rudy.

"...and those were spread out over nearly a billion Earth years," continued Pi. "That's why a galactic brain—actually, when a fella gets right down to it, there are not enough connections for an entire brain. It should be called a galactic synapse. Anyway, a synapse has to be connected through both space *AND* time. Watch this!"

Pi gestured toward his cube diagram. Many more worlds blinked into existence, each with their own timelines—many extending above and below the cube, but some that didn't. White lines began connecting the planetary dots until the entire image did begin to resemble the intricate tangle of nerve axons and dendrites. Rudy realized he was looking at a web of potential interactions between species and their civilizations that crisscrossed both time and space.

Rudy was about to comment on the beauty of Pi's presentation when Ryan said, "It appears we have company."

Rudy turned to look behind him. A loose arc of creatures had gathered perhaps a hundred yards away—some seated on their haunches, some pointing with slender arms. Some had their mouths open, revealing batteries of sharp teeth. "Dinosaur men with jewelry and bibs?" He must have wondered out loud.

"Well, well," said Ryan. "It looks like dinosaurs nearly had delusions of grandeur before we did, Rudy."

58
Missions and farewells

The creatures, obviously both curious and scared, seemed the picture of indecision. Some knelt or squatted, staring at their group and Pi's images in the sky. Other's paced back and forth. One apparent female carried an infant on her hip. She stood behind a male brandishing a spear. She had most of her body turned away from Pi's diverse audience of abominations, apparently ready to be first in line if flight looked like the prudent option.

"They remind me of a picture I've seen somewhere," said Rudy.

"Probably the smart dinosaur ideas that go clear back to the 20th century," said Ryan. "A pretty well known paleontologist, Simon Conway-Morris, revisited the idea in the 21st century, arguing that some sort of humanoid-like form might be inevitable eventually, if evolution is given enough time to operate."

"Right. Right. I remember that," said Rudy. "There was some sort of ostrichy-looking dinosaur with slender forearms and a bigger than average brain..." Rudy began.

Tröodon. Mnemosyne provided the scientific name, and even produced an image of the known dinosaur and the hypothesized dinosauroid that had the potential to evolve from it.

"Yeah, *Tröodon*. That's the one." *Thanks, Nessie.*

"Do you think they are aggressive?" asked Tadur.

"Perhaps another alarm call would be a good idea," offered Maxifer.

"And more formic acid," added Master Veltipoe.

"Won't be necessary, mates." Pi turned off his holographic display. Several dinosauroids jerked in surprise.

Pi yelled, "Boo!" while flapping his arms.

One male stumbled over another and nearly fell. The female with her youngster clasped some sort of amulet that hung around her neck resting on a colorful bib of decorative feathers. Muscles in the leg she had turned toward Rudy flexed just before she made the decision to run. A couple of males waved spears at them, but quickly followed Mom in retreat.

One rather young individual lingered a few seconds longer. Rudy didn't recall later whether it was a male or female. Maybe his own mammalian biology blinded him to obvious clues. He just remembered large round eyes seemingly filled with as much wonder as alarm.

"Don't mind 'em," said Pi. "The asteroid arrives tomorrow, ya know. Dinosauroids don't make the cut."

The bug-eyed youngster rose and trotted after his apparent relatives.

"Let's take a hike down by the shoreline, mates. We've a few more things to discuss." Pi trotted in that direction, apparently assuming everyone else would follow.

* * * * *

"Wow," said Rudy to no one in particular. "Impressive beach—even without a bikini in sight. My first wife, Myra, would have loved this place."

"Hey, Maxifer!" yelled Tadur. "Look here! By the webs of Spider Woman! An actual beached ammonite. Look at those colors. And the tentacles! I wouldn't have guessed they would have looked like *that*."

Maxifer arched over Tadur's find, firmly settling his tripod of feet. "The smells are rather memorable as well. I suspect decay is well advanced." His hide flickered in shades of green flecked with amber. "At least fossils don't provide that particular stimulus."

Tadur bolted upright and landed near another discard of the waves. "And look here! A mosasaur tooth. And, and...what's *that*?"

Maxifer joined his friend. "A portion of the maxillary of something I should not like to swim with. It might bite first and decide I didn't taste good later."

"The boys seemed to be having quite a good time seeing their fossil treasures as living creatures," observed Master Veltipoe "not to mention expanding their educational experience."

216

"Siyan has transported Skeets and me to Cretaceous beaches several times," Ryan faced the seascape, and fingered the cabochon hanging from the silver chain around his neck. "The most memorable trip was not long after Mother Novaya presided over our union. Beautiful and surreal—being the only human beings on the entire planet."

"'nough sight-seein', mates," announced Pi. "Gather 'round and we'll sort out our next plans." Pi ambled his way to a flat stretch of beach beneath the shade of an enormous boulder splashed with a colorful montage of moss and brilliant yellow lichens.

Pi used one of his hands to touch a glowing spot on his other arm, and the cube/ganglion hologram reappeared in the air. A line connecting some blue cube future Earth and blue cube future Jadderbad pulsed brightly. "Look there, boys." Pi pointed at the pulsing line. "Tadmaxyne needs to make that connection. First, however, ya need to return to your time and shepherd both humans and Jadderbadians through Gaia's volcanic temper tantrum. It'll take time, mind you, but you can do it together."

Tadur opened his mouth, but Pi resumed speaking before he could say anything.

"And yes, Semma will meet you there before hormone overload strips your brain of all reasoning powers." Pi turned his attention to Maxifer. "And I won't be rattling this timeline too much to let you in on a little secret, worm-a-pede." Maxifer's eyes focused on Pi and his oral pili froze in place. "I see a rather cute—by Jadderbadian standards anyway—second molt lady in your future as well."

"What about Rudnessipoe—Rudy and Master Veltipoe?" Tadur looked at his distant uncle and teacher in turn. "What will their jobs be? We may need their help. When will I see them again?" Tadur turned to face Ryan. His eyes dropped to look at the slowly turning crystalline image captured in the cabochon hanging around Ryan's neck. "What about Ryan and his mate, Skeets?"

"Don't worry about Ryan, mate," said Pi. "He'll find his Skeets again. When Skeeto returns to your Earth present, she can 'elp introduce everyone to the Menssanans—the Grovian-human hybrids. Everyone will need to work with Gaia and Hydra, you know mates.

Rudy and Master Veltipoe, though—it could be a while before you see them again. Best say your goodbyes for now. Meanwhile, Siyan and Rudnessipoe have a few other details to attend to."

* * * * *

Not long afterwards, Pi's delta-wing saucer re-emerged from the stargate and landed on the beach near them. A door on the side of the craft slid silently open. A boarding ramp emerged like the tongue of a slightly woozy snake, and touched the ground. Phi poked her beetle-esk head out of the door. "'m ready for passengers," she announced.

"Well then," said Pi, "Tadmaxyne has work to do. Time for us to leave." Pi looked at his collection of humans and Jadderbadians, apparently deciding they needed a few more moments alone. "Don't be long, mates. I've got other projects to deal with, you know." With that he scuffled his way across the sand toward his ship, mumbling about the behavioral similarities between superbeings and cats.

"I will miss you, Great Uncle Rudy, although I have not known you long," said Tadur. "I will tell my father of our adventures. He used to tell me stories about you and Grandfather Twill long ago."

"I will miss you too, boy," said Rudy. "A bit of Twill sparkles in your eye now and then. You and Maxifer make a good team. Don't give him a rash when you squirm in that saddle, eh?"

"Master Veltipoe, you were wise to urge Tadur and me to become syncytiotes." Maxifer made a bow toward his teacher, and then straightened to his full second instar height. "My apologies for doubting your guidance."

Master Veltipoe barked through his spiracles with what passed for a Jadderbadian's laugh. "That's what teachers are for, young larva. Go with Tadur and become your own Master."

A few moments later, Ryan, Veltipoe, and Rudy shared an empty beach. Waves lapped the shore. Puffy cumulous clouds rose like white cliffs on the horizon, softened by a humid haze.

Rudy looked at Ryan. "What now, young man? It looks like the crystal trapped in your jewelry there is spinning a bit faster."

"So it is," said Ryan. "Mnemosyne told me you have always

been obsessed with knowing the meaning of it all. I can help with that—using the trans-dimensional gateway here," He tapped the cabochon resting on his chest. "And also the transformative powers that Guardian and Mnemosyne provide when Siyan and Rudnessipoe take charge."

Oh my, Rudy. This will be a test for me. I hope I will be up to the challenge.

Me too, Nessie.

"But first," Ryan continued, "let's see what effect Pi's linkages have had/are having on our timeline."

"How do you propose to do that?" asked Rudy. He even felt Nessie's confusion—an emotional state she rarely experienced.

"Well, we can travel the corridors of space and time, after all." If the Mona Lisa had been the portrait of a male it would have had Ryan's smile. "Let's go visit Gaia in her dotage and see how things turned out."

Rudy recalled two things just before he blinked out of existence in the Cretaceous: As he glanced down at his feet, he identified a very cockroach-looking insect scuttle from the shelter of a rock half buried in the sand to a thicket of nearby ferns. Lifting his gaze to the shoreline, he saw the head of the young dinosauroid regarding him with wide eyes from behind a huge boulder maybe fifty yards away. Apparently, the latter creature suffered from a terminal case of curiosity.

He also remembered Nessie thinking, *No, you can't have a pet or a traveling companion, Rudy—neither a cockroach nor a dinosaur person.*

Data Files:
An image of a Cretaceous seashore

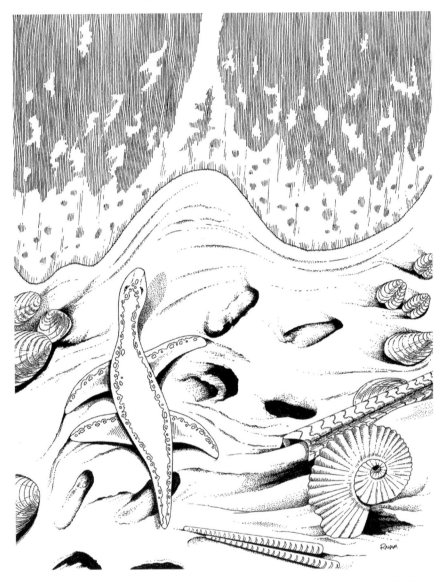

Note clam shells (*Inoceramus* species), a hatchling mosasaur, long *Baculites* shells, and the ammonite shell in the lower right. The incoming tide will soon erase the footprint of a small theropod dinosaur.

59
Making amends with ancient Gaia

Guardian: Mnemosyne, *I believe if we work together as parts of our separate consortia, we can allow our component beings to experience at least a portion of this timespace excursion.* Guardian surveyed the neural engrams of both Siu and Ryan, checking the relevant aspects of their architecture. *I suggest we concentrate on the reticular formation, thalamus, and cortex of both Ryan and Rudy and the corresponding gangliar nodes of Master Veltipoe.*

Mnemosyne: *Of course—although we should anticipate some trauma. I assume whatever they/we experience will have no natural corollary.*

Guardian: *True. But all of our organic components have demonstrated resilience, and a higher than average tendency toward risk-taking behavior in the past.*

Rudy: *And all your organic components are here listening in, you know. Why don't you ask us?*

Siu: *It is hard to fashion a tactful AI, isn't it? I've often wondered if it's an inherent fault of artificial intelligence, or just results from the asocial tendencies and perspectives of people like my Ito, who design them.*

Master Veltipoe: *I've found AIs to be quite annoying in general, but necessary, of course, for many functions.*

Rudy: *I vote for just...* Rudy was going to say, "enjoying the experience," but before that thought could form, it lost its relevance. He had the impression of hurtling through a maze of corridors and branches at tremendous speed. He felt immense forces pushing and pulling at him, as if trying to shred him into strips of quivering beef jerky. He witnessed roiling colors and bursts of light, accompanied by random visions of shifting landscapes and grotesque alien faces. His virtual skin crawled, as if covered by an army of ants taking bites out of him as they wandered here and there—sometimes in the most private of places. Odors assaulted him too, in unlikely combinations—like essence of rose petals competing with noxious plumes of sulfur dioxide.

Finally he completed his initial thought: *...surviving the experience.*

Siu: *I believe we have... arrived. Somewhere.*

Ryan: *And somewhen.*

* * * * *

Rudy found himself standing in the middle of a circle of green perhaps an acre or so in area. He recognized none of the vaguely grass-like plants beneath his feet. *Or are they plants? It almost looks like tiny arms are waving at me.* Twisted shrubs sprouted in scattered clumps, some adorned with red berries. Beyond the green circle, as if fenced in by an invisible barrier, a much more barren landscape of mostly sand dunes stretched to the horizon. *I don't think we're in Kansas anymore, Nessie.*

Nessie took a few nanoseconds longer than usual to respond. *Ah, a reference to the Wizard of Oz. Remember, Rudy, I don't have access to my full database anymore.*

"Do you mind dismounting, Rudy? My saddle hurts." Master Veltipoe fidgeted on his tripod of legs.

"Sorry old worm." Rudy clambered down. He turned to Ryan. "And this place is...?"

"Earth, of course, but one approximately 1.2 billion years in the future of the world you occupied."

"Billion with a 'b' at the front and not an 'm', correct?" Rudy scratched his head.

"Correct: 1.2 billion years—with a b—after your time, and 5.8 billion years after the Earth's formation. At this point in Earth's history, the planet is approaching the end of its most suitable period for advanced life—as you can tell by the austere conditions beyond our green oasis." As he was talking, Ryan scanned the horizon, as if looking for something.

"And this oasis, as you call it is here because…?" Rudy's brow furrowed.

"You might say, we're at the local zoo," said Ryan.

"I don't see any exhibits of flora or fauna, other than the plants we are standing on." Master Veltipoe focused all three primary eyes on the green blades beneath his feet. "Are those plants waving at me?

"We're not here to see exhibits." Ryan fixed his gaze on something within the hemisphere of green. "Ah, there's the interface with Gaia," he said, apparently to himself, as he began walking toward a very bright sun in what must be the eastern sky.

Rudy followed Ryan and finally spotted a globe perched upon a transparent surface affixed to a similarly transparent pedestal. "If we're not here to see exhibits, then what?" Rudy asked.

"Oh, we are the exhibits — as long as we're here, anyway. We're living fossils from an ancient time." Ryan laughed. "The cockroach people always flock to see me when I visit this time and place."

Master Veltipoe pointed two of his upper tier arms to the north. "Ah, those must be the cockroach people of which you speak."

Rudy looked north, and nearly stumbled before coming to a complete stop. An assemblage of roughly humanoid creatures had assembled on the other side of the apparent boundary between desert and greenbelt. They had large, faceted eyes set within faces sporting dangling palps. Their bodies consisted of jointed forelimbs and legs. An apparently vestigial pair of arm/legs about waist high pressed against the barrier. "First dinosauroids, and now cockroach people?"

"Give a planet like Earth a healthy biosphere long enough, and more than one intelligent race will evolve. Maybe some day you'll get to see the ravenoids. You're a biologist, Rudy. It's pretty much a corollary of your Biomic Network Algorithm after all."

Rudy grunted. *He's got you there*, Nessie commented.

"You talked about a Gaia interface, young man. Can we speak with Gaia? Perhaps I can apologize for all the destructive behavior that humans and other so-called intelligent species inflicted on her."

Rudy looked toward the sphere on the pedestal. "Is that a direct link to the Old Girl?"

"It is," confirmed Ryan. "We must speak loudly and clearly though. Gaia's not the young biosphere you knew. In a few hundred million years her metazoans of all kinds will be gone. After all her oceans have completely evaporated, bacteria and viroids will be all the company she has left for her last few billion years. The network of organisms of which she is composed will be a ghost of its former self." Ryan gestured toward the sphere. "The cockroids fashioned this direct interface to Gaia—with a bit of help from Siyan. Just between you and me, Rudy, the cockroids aren't the smartest sentient creatures Gaia ever fashioned, but then she had less to work with this time around. Say hello to the Old Girl. She might remember you."

"Gaia? Are you there, Gaia?" Rudy leaned over the sphere.

"Eh? Someone there? Stand up straight and speak up now!" The sphere pulsed in shades of faded green when Gaia spoke.

Rudy snapped upright reflexively, as if back in Mrs. Whitby's third grade tutorial. "Rudyard Albert Goldstein here," he said loudly. "Rudy—the inventor of the Biomic Network Algorithm."

"Biomythic algotham what? You're not making sense, creature!"

"Ryan Thompson here, Gaia—the human component of Siyan. We've talked before. My friend Rudy has come to visit. You got a bit pissed at humans, Jadderbadians, and Grovians a few eons ago. You vented a super volcano in frustration…"

"Ah, Rusty the human. I remember now. He was part of that nice Mnemosyne being, as I recall. Is she here?"

"Rudy. Rudyard Albert Goldstein. And yes, Nessie is here too. She's telling me if I touch the sphere we might get a better connection."

They did. Master Veltipoe and Ryan touched the sphere too and joined the conversation. With some difficulty, they learned details about the post super-eruption years. The recovery of the Mother Tree forests and the Menssanan population of Grovian-human hybrids who eventually met and merged with Jadamen—after the usual violence and mayhem that results when strangers first meet. Mnemosyne, it seems, along with Siyan and Tadmaxyne, had helped shorten that chaotic interchange of alien biology and culture.

Gaia eventually broke the connection. "Maybe later, boys," she said. "This old lady needs a break. Great to see you again, Rusty."

"So, where did everybody go—when Gaia couldn't support them anymore?" Rudy sat down on the vegetation surrounding the pedestal. Ryan joined him. Veltipoe leaned back on his main support leg.

"In this timeline, which is a pretty good one, after all—they built an amazing structure around old sol that worked quite well for a long time—a kind of Dyson Sphere, you know—to capture as much solar energy as possible for their various solar system explorations and projects. They morphed into all kinds of abominations in the process. Ultimately, they moved to other stars and fooled around there. The universe is big and strange and exciting—because of all the ways you can die in it."

"Do tell." Rudy looked toward the boundary of their zoo. The cockroids seemed to be getting bored with observing living fossils. Many had wandered away. "So why have you shown Master Veltipoe and me this glimpse of a future timeline? What happens now?"

"I'm so glad you asked," said Ryan.

Data Files:
Fact Sheet for Milky Way Galaxy (Pi's synapse)

Form: Barred spiral
Number of stars: Approximately 200 bilion
Diameter: 100,000 light years
Thickness: 1,000 light years
Location of sol (human's sun): 25,000 light years from central black hole (Sagittarius A*)
Total mass: 1.5 trillion times the mass of sol

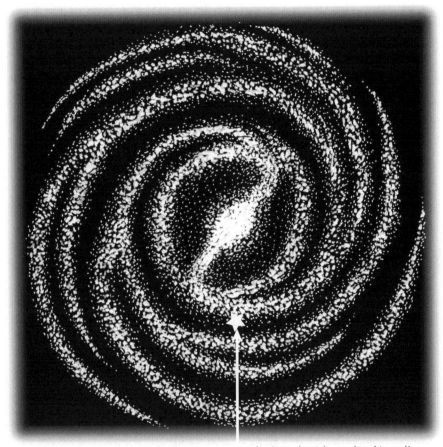

Dinosauroids, humans, cyborgs, ravenoids, & cockroids evolved in sol's solar system. Jadderbadians and Grovians moved here. Gaiia obviously presides over prime galactic real estate. She should have raised the rent.

60
The mysteries of creation

"I'm expecting Pi soon. So, before I get into the details of Rudnessipoe's assignment," said Ryan, "let's eat. You're going to need lots of energy." Ryan touched a control interface Rudy hadn't seen on the pedestal, and a keyboard with various symbols appeared. "The cockroids have an extensive genetic library along with efficient molecular synthesis programs—partly a legacy of Mnemosyne's work at the Citadel, I believe. Let me order something for the two of you. This pedestal doubles as a food service module. Any preferences?"

"I haven't had a chili dog and fries since I can't remember when," said Rudy.

"As a boy on Jadderbad," said Veltipoe, "I so loved puree of Jadschrimp-squid garnished with the larvae of Northern Hemisphere sweet flies."

Ryan's hands flashed around the keypad like a maestro warming up for a concert. "I can do that."

"Add a chocolate malt, if it's not too late." Rudy patted his stomach. "I didn't realize how hungry I was.

"And a draft of Blackworm Port," added Master Veltipoe. His mouth pili fluttered.

Ryan ordered something for himself that resembled stew and dumplings, and what appeared to be white wine served in a long-stemmed glass.

The pedestal expanded into something that reminded Rudy of an archaic microwave machine. It soon disgorged the menu items ordered. They all ate with gusto. The new behavior even induced a few cockroids to wander back to watch primitive creatures actually chew and digest food. Ryan explained how cockroids avoided such crudities. Photosynthetic bacteria layered their outer cuticles and provided all the nourishment they required. Other microbes totally consumed any polysaccharides produced and provided necessary micronutrients. Asshole as a pejorative term most likely didn't exist in cockroid vocabulary, as their bodies possessed no such opening.

By the time they had eaten their fill, the stargate flashed into existence. Pi floated through the archway on something resembling a magic carpet, complete with tassels at the corners. It gave the cockroids something else to squeak about as they pressed their bodies against the invisible surface at the margins of the zoo enclosure.

"Howdy, mates!" Pi said as he landed next to Rudy and Master Veltipoe. "I've got the perfect job for you two academics and your AI facilitator. My galactic brain connections are nearly complete. How do you blokes—in the form of Rudnessipoe, of course—feel about tackling the ultimate challenge: linking all the appropriate 150+ billion galaxies in the universe into one mega, self-aware universal mind?" Pi's eyes grew round, presumably with excitement and anticipation.

"You want us to create the Mind of God?" asked Rudy.

"The mind of the Supreme Female resulting from Final Metamorphosis?" Master Veltipoe's oral chamber grew round, and his colors shifted so blue they became black to Rudy as they moved into the ultraviolet.

"Eh, close enough," said Pi. "I've got a number that defines the whole Mind of God thing, but it never ends."

"Or, you could just call Her Jane. That's the name I used," said Ryan, "when I last saw Her. She's a consummate artist." He removed the cabochon from around his neck. The crystalline jewel inside it rotated slowly, with more shifting shapes and colors than Rudy thought possible. He extended the jewelry toward Rudy. "Here, you're going to need this, eventually. Meanwhile, I've got a date with Skeets at a much different point in this timeline. We've got some catching up to do."

Ryan smiled. Somehow it became contagious—for everyone

except the cockroids.

They just looked perplexed.

* * * * *

It might be time to finally do it, Rudy. The Mnemosyne part of Rudnessipoe made this comment floating above a gas giant planet that reminded Rudy of Jupiter in sol's system of planets. Rudnessipoe was participating in his version of sleeping, allowing his mental component parts the opportunity to muse among themselves in their well-provisioned force field bubble.

Wow. How long has it been since we last saw an image of good old Jupiter? Rudy amused himself by watching the shifting shapes and colors of the atmospheric storms below him.

I think that question qualifies as an oxymoron, Rudy—based on what we know about the nature of time.

And gas giants do look much the same everywhere, added Veltipoe, *with variations, of course, based on just how much gas they contain, and the distance from their home stars.*

Nevertheless, we've made billions of intergalactic connections by now. We've met more things that crawl, ooze, fly, glide, run, walk, amble, breathe, emit, transmit, float, swim, jet propel, flitter, slide, creep, slither, dig, photosynthesize, permineralize, chemosynthesize, vaporize, and hyperventilate than I would ever have thought possible. Rudy sighed. *And at this time and place, there aren't many bright stars left in the sky. Most are cool, red dwarfs. Maybe we are close enough to the end of time now to take a peek at what we have created.*

Perhaps, agreed Mnemosyne.

I have conjured and can activate the trans-dimensional gateway housed in the jewelry Ryan gave us, said Veltipoe. *Rudnessipoe doesn't notice. He still sleeps.*

Then, if we ask…

Jane, are you there? Mnemosyne completed the question.

She will reply…

I'm here. Her voice did sound rather majestic—and not at all like George Burns in the old movie, "Oh, God!" *Come visit me,* she said.

It was definitely more of a command than a request.

* * * * *

They found themselves substantiated in a stark landscape. Rudy stood next to Master Veltipoe's imposing third molt form. Even Nessie stood next to Rudy in the ponytailed avatar he had come to love. The dark sky held russet, unblinking stars. Beneath their feet, a plain as vast as an ancient seabed stretched toward the rounded peaks of distant mountains. A plant began to sprout on the plain. It rose and branched and twisted and rose some more. Rudy thought it looked like a picture he had once seen of a venerable ancient oak, but with pods...

"Ah," said Veltipoe, "a monstrous, Grovian Mother Tree, I believe."

"But with stairways, platforms, and lighted windows," added Rudy. "Everything a primate might enjoy."

"With large spaces to accommodate Jadderbadians, as well," noted Veltipoe. "And that one impressive structure on the lower branch reminds me of my old academy."

A humanoid form came into view before them, apparently topping the crest of a hill between them and the massive tree — or perhaps just appearing out of nowhere. Rudy wasn't sure whether to trust any impressions his senses conveyed to him. The form seemed to flicker into a vaguely disturbing variety of shapes until it stopped a few feet in front of Rudy. Then the form settled into the pleasing shape of a woman with dark skin, Asian eyes, and shoulder-length dark hair. A white sleeveless gown with a shifting pattern of nebulous blue swirls provided elegant contrast to her chocolate skin. If he had made Jane's acquaintance anywhere else, he might have proposed to her.

"Jane, I presume." Rudy found himself performing a slight bow.

"I love your wings," said Master Veltipoe. He began performing a rather subdued dance that reminded Rudy of the mating dance he and his old friend Master Morticue had executed near the end of their life as Rudimort.

"Wings? What wings?" Rudy looked at Veltipoe as if he had just farted in a confessional.

230

"I am witnessing the most beautiful swirl of geometries that I've ever experienced," said Mnemosyne. "I'm breathless, and I'm incapable of experiencing that state—except vicariously through you, Rudy."

"You all are seeing what most appeals to you." Jane smiled fetchingly. "It's one of those quantum uncertainty things, you know, best left to more geekified brains than yours." She gestured toward the monolithic trunk and twisting branches behind her. "Let's go sit on the patio and admire our Creation for a few moments." She turned and led the way. "Don't forget to take off your footwear and leave it at the bottom of the stairway."

Once comfortably seated on the patio, the ambient light dimmed, as if they were about to witness a play. And, in a way, they were—if one could experience all the acts of a play simultaneously.

The crystalline, constantly reshaping form they had come to know as the trans-dimensional gateway appeared, hovering over the plain in front of them, pulsing with seemingly infinite colors as it slowly rotated from one dimension of existence to another—or perhaps pierced one bubble of creation on route to another.

"Here's the universe we've made, fellow artists," said Jane. "What do you think?" And though it was quite dark, and Rudy couldn't actually see Jane anymore, he seemed to be able to smell a heady perfume, and feel Her breath on his neck. "And more importantly," She whispered, "What do you want to try next?"

In case you missed it...

When young paleontologist, Ryan Thompson, finds a new species of mosasaur in Cretaceous seaway sediments, he is thrilled. The discovery should jumpstart his career. Joy quickly turns to fear when he touches an artifact buried among the sea reptile's ribs. Suddenly, he must fight a mental takeover by an alien intelligence committed to transforming the Earth into a refuge for her own race. As Ryan and his girlfriend, Skeets attempt to thwart alien plans to colonize Earth begun in the deep past, even this crisis becomes trivial when the uneasy symbiosis of Ryan and the alien, Siu, generates a new entity with the power to transform the entire universe. **Biostration**, 2011. **$13**. Available on Amazon.com

"Gary Raham, the author of this enthralling book, seems almost to have been there hundreds of millions of years ago when Siu's dim star blinked out and the trees began to die on the planet known as "Grove". This is the magic of good writing, and Raham is no less convincing as he describes the discovery by modern paleontologists on Earth of the jewel-like engram that has carried the genetic imprint of Siu through a galactic gate, out of the void of deep time, and into our lives."
    Kate Gilmore, author of *The Exchange Student* and *Enter Three Witches*

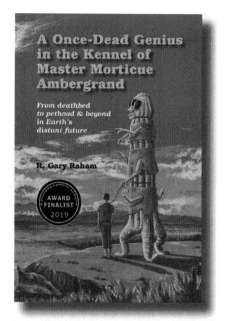

In case you missed it...

W hat happens when you die, but the universe isn't done with you? You might end up as the pet of a giant worm-a-pede alien and...if you survive your evolved descendants and rogue aliens of 1 million A.D...discover you have more in common with intelligent worms than you ever thought possible.

Penstemon Publications, 2018. **$15**. Available on Amazon.

"The arch tone should remind readers of Kurt Vonnegut, although Raham is better grounded in exobiology and science and displays a more upbeat outlook for the human (and nonhuman) condition in this engaging tale... An enjoyable, post-apocalypse mind romp featuring technologically bred demigods, future Stone Age tribes, and supercilious worms."

Kirkus Reviews

Visit the author's website at https://www.rgaryraham.com
Enjoy his writing & his artwork.
Sign up for a free newsletter, and stay in touch!

About the author...

R. Gary Raham writes both science fact and science fiction, and is a firm believer that the latter often excites a new generation of scientists to discover more of the former. Armed with degrees in biology from the University of Michigan, Raham taught high school science before pursuing careers in writing, illustration, and design. Raham has won numerous awards for his books, articles, and artwork. *A Twice-Dead Genius Comporting with Misunderstood Abominations* represents a fusion of his skills capable of making a reader laugh and think simultaneously with no known deleterious effects.

Made in the USA
Columbia, SC
26 September 2020

21645031R00135